WICKED SOUL ASCENSION

The Ascension Trilogy
Book One

C. B. DIXON

Copyright © 2016 by Chianne Benckhuysen
Front and back images Copyright © by Chianne Benckhuysen

Cover illustration by Christine White
Edited by Ann Westlake, Writer's Cramp Editing Consultants

Hidden Words Publishing
Campbell River, BC, Canada

ISBN: 978-0-9958140-0-4

Written in Canada
Printed in the USA

First Edition

To Kimberly Smith
Forever

Contents

Chapter One

Flathill Creek: a grungy town I've called home for eighteen years. The only way people know that it exists is because it's on a major highway. People drive by, wave, and continue up the road to enter Mirror City.

I grumbled and moaned as I pulled into the combined junior and senior high school parking lot on the morning of my twelfth year of school. The entrance to the teenaged prison appeared warm and inviting, welcoming everyone who passed into the grand learning facility it was intended to be. Colorful flower beds and neatly laid pathways made the system seem organized and spirited. The building's red brickwork wrapped stained-glass windows of fields of gold, rich green forests, and majestic mountains. Tread inside and all that merriment and wonder was zapped right out, replaced by faded paint and empty planters.

Every other girl in the school was dressed in fancy, first-day-of-school clothing, but not me. I was the type of girl that dressed in a plain black T-shirt and baggy blue jeans. I stood at the classroom door with my hands clenched to one strap of my backpack that was slung over my shoulder. My chin dropped to my chest. "This again. Why do I have to do this year after year?"

"Don't worry, Blaze," a cheery voice told me. "Just a list of rules, then school policy, then we get our schedules, and then lunch. I know you *love* lunch." Hope emphasized the word love by dragging out the middle.

I peeked over my shoulder with a smirk. I knew her voice as well as I knew my own. "Hope, you're chipper as always. If only I could be like you once in a while."

She bounced on her toes, her thin rosy lips curving up to her vibrant blue eyes. Her tattered zip-up hoodie was a blinding blue. Fitted dark-blue jeans covered her short, thin legs. Comfort, not glamour. She only dressed to impress one person — herself. One of many reasons she held my "best friend" status.

She lifted a blue lily to my nose. "Look! Look! A flower!" She giggled, then took a sniff herself. "Mmm … isn't it pretty?" She slipped the stem into the water bottle pocket of my backpack. "I know your hatred of school makes you gloomy this time of year, so I thought I'd brighten your day with this blue light I found." She patted the stem to make sure it was secure.

I shook my head and grinned. "Oh, Hope, if you only knew the half of my hatred for this place."

But she did know. She knew me to the core of my existence.

My hand gripped the silver doorknob. Hope bounced past me and into the room with a love-filled "good morning" to everyone she saw. She found a seat she liked in the middle of the room and plopped herself into the chair with a bright twinkle in her eye. I claimed the seat next to her and prepped for the lecture of school rules and policies we had to endure year after year.

At lunch, Hope had already found our usual spot, which was in the hallway on the floor against the lockers. The school had hundreds of students, but nowhere for them to eat. She had her face in her lunch bag by the time I took my seat on the floor next to her.

"So, what classes did you get? I got all the ones I wanted. University, here I come!" she bellowed. "Maybe I'll work with bodies discovering how they were killed, or maybe I'll be a surgeon, putting bodies back together … or apart—I'd like that to. Hmm, so many choices … what to choose?"

She pulled out the first thing she wanted to eat from her bag. My stomach flopped. Hope glared at me. "Just because you don't like seafood doesn't mean that I can't eat it." She popped off the top of the container. "It was seafood night last night. Mmm … smell it." She slightly lifted the container to me.

I instantly backed away. *Disgusting.* "You know I can't stand the smell of that stuff. I got a new male teacher," I said as I pulled out my roast beef sandwich. "Yes! I didn't squish it." I tore off the plastic wrap and took in the scent of the sweet meat smothered in mayo and mustard.

"A new guy, eh?" Hope's eyes shifted to a sinister place in her mind as she shovelled in some of her crab salad. After she swallowed, she asked, "Who is he? What does he teach? Is he cute? Married? Lookin' for some love … hmm, Blaze?" She wiggled her eyebrows at me.

I stared wide-eyed at her. "You should see your face. Ha! Me with a teacher. I can't even get a guy my own age. *Sheesh*! What's with men, anyway?"

She shovelled in more food to keep herself from her unloved thoughts. I recognized that lonely gaze and wished there was a way I could help her. Hope was the most caring person I had ever come across, but no one seemed to notice her.

I handed her my schedule as I took another bite of my sandwich. I focused on the melty meat's flavor. She accepted the distraction and examined each class. As I ate, heat began to surge through my skin. The room started to wave and pull. I took another bite as the room spun slowly to the left. Pins and needles bit the tips of my fingers.

"Hmm …" She handed the paper back. "You'll have to tell me how that goes." She examined me while she filled her fork with more of her revolting lunch. Her grin dropped. "Blaze, are you okay? You're pale all of a sudden!"

I ate the last bite and rolled up the paper bag. "I feel a little sick. Maybe I should have gone to bed on time last night," I said with a fake smile.

By the time lunch ended and my next class came, the sickness had dulled somewhat but still made me feel nauseous. Chemistry was one of my favorite classes. I found it easy to combine chemicals and observe the reactions. Experiments thrilled me in a way that I didn't wish to explain to others.

The chemistry room filled rapidly; everyone was thrilled to meet the new teacher, excited to meet anyone new. It was rare in Flathill Creek to have a new teacher. Some of us had the same teachers from back in elementary school. I could understand why they were all on the edge of their seats. A girl in the back fluttered her eyelashes at her friend as they prayed for a hottie. Four guys in the back of the room explained that they had seen the new teacher and that he appeared to be crazed. A true Hollywood mad scientist here to experiment on us.

The door opened, and the room gasped for fresh air. My stomach clenched into a knot. My arms folded around my body as the teacher made his way into the room. A sigh echoed as the girls set their eyes on his boyish figure. His dirty blond haircut made his bangs fall into his icy blue eyes and outline his strong jawline. The girl next to me began to fidget with her fingers as he strolled toward his desk.

"Hello, class," he said with charm. "I am Mr. Robinson, your chemistry teacher," he announced through his thick lips. He placed his bag on the tall desk at the front of the room. "First we need to take attendance. Then we will discuss what you remember from previous years."

He unbuttoned the top button on his designer sweater, and my female classmates sighed. I glanced around at everyone as they gawked. The teens chewed on their bottom lips while the envious squeezed their fists, causing their knuckles to whiten. To me, Mr. Robinson seemed average, just another teacher to give me detentions.

Mr. Robinson opened his binder and placed his finger on the first name. "Please say 'here' when I call your name. Ryan Dillon?" Each word he spoke seemed to stretch and pull the room as the illness straightened, causing bile to sting the back of my tongue.

"Here," Ryan said.

"Annie Fisher?"

"Here," she sighed.

He called on the rest of the class, the students answering in an awed tone. My name was listed last. His eyes stared at it on the attendance form, frozen for a heartbeat before he glanced up. He cleared his throat and regained his composure. "Blaze Nemasa?"

"Here," I said, my voice weakened by nausea. I wondered if I should ask to be excused from class.

His eyes turned cold, blinked, and grinned at the other students. "Okay, everyone! What do you know about chemistry?"

Class seemed to tick by. Each second felt as if a lifetime had passed. Mr. Robinson called on me many times, but I couldn't answer — my mind was distracted with feverish chills and a revolving room. He didn't seem to be too impressed with my absentminded behavior.

Art class was next on my schedule. Mrs. Hritz's extreme expressions and the wacky ways she taught drew me into her lectures, even art history. It was hard not to pay attention.

"Okay," the short, round woman slammed her binder to her table, "in front of you is a single white sheet of paper. In the middle of your tables are different types of shading utensils. Today we will be experimenting with mixed media." Her arms flung through the air as if she were painting an extravagant world before her. "Markers and pencils and charcoal. Oh, my! Markers and pencils and charcoal. Oh, my!" she sang.

I glanced down at the table to the eight by eleven sheet of paper as she lowered her song to a light hum. Up in the corner of the shared table were cups full of pencils, crayons, charcoals, pastels, and markers.

"What I would like you to do is draw me exactly what's on your mind. Use any tools you see or ask for things that you can think of to enhance your work. You have all class to work on it. Use the time well." She smiled. "Ready? Begin."

At first, I stared at the white sheet and thought, *Draw what's on my mind.* Well, I could've drawn the slight sway the room had or the knot in my stomach or Mr. Robinson as he had clawed his way into my head. *Hell no.* The distance from him seemed to loosen the knot, and remove a few of the pins from my fingers.

"Blaze?" My teacher rested her hand on my desk. "It's not going to draw itself, you know. Feel. Imagine. Put the tool to the sheet and let it flow from you to the page. It may even surprise you when you're finished." Her hand gripped an invisible pencil and floated through the air as it drew an imaginary masterpiece.

"Feel?" I asked and picked up a dark graphite pencil and a sharpener.

"Emotions make the best type of art. Let your body and heart guide you." She turned to the next student, who had already mixed and smudged pastels into a vibrant blurred rainbow.

I placed the sharpened pencil to the page. It glided across with sharp bends and turns. Soon it was transformed into a heavily-clothed male body. *Mr. Robinson? I really hope not,* I thought.

The room had steadied and the knot untied. The picture transformed into multiple shades of gray to create a stone-work backdrop behind a cloaked man. My gaze connected with the man's wicked glare. An energy trembled under my skin as I stared at the sketch. Angry, narrow eyes were half-covered by a thick gray hood. A sharp grin bared razor-sharp fangs. The hood was attached to a dark robe that draped over his shoulders and collected on the dirt ground.

The more I added, the more my skin trembled. I didn't know him. I'd never seen him before. His soul-snatching eyes bunched every nerve in my body. He wore an all-knowing smirk that told he knew something I didn't.

"Okay, class, it's five to. Pencils and other materials down. Please clean up your areas and put away anything that you have taken out. There is a purple basket on my desk. Please put all your projects in it. Those that need to dry, please put them on the rack over there."

I put away all my pencils and held up my project, but I couldn't look into the man's eyes. I had drawn the picture, and I couldn't even look at it. With a heavy frown, I walked to the purple basket with my picture facedown so that no one would have to see what a fucked up person I was.

But Mrs. Hritz noticed, and picked up the sheet of smudged gray. "Let's see what you're hiding," she said as she flipped it over to view my monster. "Well, Blaze," her lips twitched up at the corners, "look at all the shades you used, and the sharp line work. You must have really been into this project. Your sizing of a few parts is a little off, but look at the deep emotion behind it. Tell me, Blaze, when you look at this piece, how do you feel?"

"Terrified."

"You drew this with fear," she said, not meaning for it to be a question. She could see it as she studied it. "I really like it, one of your best works, if I may say." She turned her brown eyes to me. "I'm giving you an A. You put a lot of yourself into this work. I hope to see more. Even if it's scary."

I liked it, too. The narrow jawline that peeked out from under the thick hood was nothing like Mr. Robinson's rounder one. The thicker lips that revealed only a slight glimpse of his teeth seemed angrier than he could pull off. The way the hood shadowed the face made it hard to tell who I had drawn, or if it was a figure that I had created due to my nightmares. Pleased with that thought, I smiled and waved good-bye to Mrs. Hritz.

Hope twirled by my car and lipped whatever song was on her mind at that moment. Her hands shot out as she silently hit the long finishing note, the book in her hand her microphone. Nothing seemed to ever dampen her spirits. Her long last note ended and she spun around with her flashy finish. She caught me in her sight and bowed.

"Blaze," she yelled, her arms swung wildly through the air. "I just learned a very fun song in choir. We all danced and sang. Oh! It was so much fun. Before that I had math. We did skill testing, and I almost came out on top. It was close. I got an easy question wrong and lost points, but then I gained, and just before I took the lead, the bell rang." She stuck out her lip. "Stupid bell. One of these days I'll melt it down and make a toilet out of it." She made a fist and shook it at the school. "You hear me bell? I will. Don't think I won't."

"You do know it's not actually a physical bell, right?" I smirked.

"Smart ass."

I unlocked my car doors and threw my lunch bag, backpack, and text books into the back. What was left of my lunch was squashed by my oversized binder. Hope's purse and school supplies toppled onto the clutter. Her aimless hurl of her backpack and binders jumbled it up more. She plopped into her seat and slammed the door shut.

"What should we listen to?" Hope questioned as she played with the buttons on the radio, switching it to the auxiliary port to hook up her iPod. "Hmm, something happy and bouncy. Yep. Yep." After she found a song she liked on her iPod, "Shake Tramp" by Marianas Trench, she plugged the auxiliary cord in and turned the music up, rolled down her window, and stuck her head out. The air moved fast around her face and caused her long bangs to dance. She didn't seem to mind as they tickled her face.

"How was the first day? Fall asleep in any classes?" Her eyes were closed as she enjoyed the light touch of the wind. When the chorus came on, she danced as if she were in a music video.

"I got an A already in art. That was really awesome." I turned the wheel to drive on to Main Street.

"That's fantastic. Let's celebrate and get slurpees," she said cheerfully, pointing at the 2GoFast gas station on the right across from the hospital. "I'll buy." She nudged.

"I think that's a great idea. Hmm, tough choice, though. They have so many flavors. I never know which one to try."

I pulled my car into the parking spot beside the building. Hope jumped out before I turned the car off and ran off to the door. I was quick to follow. I walked past her as she held the door open.

The man behind the counter greeted us with a smile. "Hello, ladies! May I offer something new?"

Hope pressed her eyebrows together. "Is it free?"

He nodded and pushed a tray of samples to the edge of the counter. "Before we buy a soft serve ice cream machine, we want to know if people will actually drink these."

"Ice cream mixed with slurpee. We'll give it a try." Hope picked up the blue one, and I picked up the pink one. I sucked up the interesting combination and loved it. Best thing in the world. We both bought one with a huge "thank you" to the man.

"So," Hope began, as she slurped up some of her sugary goodness, "you haven't mentioned the new teacher." Her eyes shot a cold glare my way and then a twisted smirk grew as she opened the car door. "Did you get into trouble? I could see that. You testing out the new guy, pushing his boundaries. That's a common thing for most students to do to a new teacher. I haven't seen him yet. Word in the halls is he's charming, handsome, and best of all, young." She wiggled her eyebrows.

I slipped into the car and started the engine. "I didn't really look at him. That's something you'll have to judge anyway."

"Yeah, you're brain dead when it comes to scoping out a hottie."

I shot her a look of disbelief, even though she was absolutely right. She was always on the look out for "the one," her Prince Charming. I never saw the point. I watched people get together and break up all in one day or within a month. To me, it seemed like a waste of time. Fall in love just to have them leave you.

"Earth to Blaze." Hope waved her hand passed my face. "So you get in trouble or what?"

"No, and yes. I couldn't shake the feeling I had at lunch, and it actually got worse in his class. Then after class, I went to art and it got better. By the time, I made it to my car it was gone." I bit my tongue. I wanted to tell her I thought it was him but didn't want to sound insane.

Her face lightened. "Blaze, you know what this means?" I shook my head as I turned the car into her single car driveway.

"You could have a connection with him." Her eyes were wide and believing. "You hear it all the time in stories. Handsome man comes in and sweeps you off your feet. He's young enough."

I narrowed my eyes. "Not cool. Totally not cool."

"What if he's going to try to kill us?" she gasped, holding her neck. "He could try to slit our throats and drink our blood. He could be a daywalker, you know."

"I have to warn your mom not to let you watch any more horror movies or read anymore scary novels. That's it! You've gone off the deep end. Get out! Bye, Hope. See you tomorrow, you loon." I flashed her a goofy grin to show her I didn't mean it to be harsh. She rolled her eyes and leaped out of my car. I watched her skip into her house.

I drank the rest of my super sweet drink before I reached my house, chugged it fast enough to ice my brain. The driveway was empty and the house lights were all off, just the way I liked it. Amy, my younger sister, could have been home if she had gotten a ride from a friend, but the bus didn't drop her off that early. Another hour or so and she would be in.

I collected the few things that I had brought home with me. My body hunched over from the day, I entered my dark house. The thick maroon curtains that covered the windows snuffed out any outside light. An electronic clock lit the room with a blue electronic glow. I closed the door behind me and slipped off my shoes. To the left of me was the upper floor staircase, and at the top, I could see into Amy's dark room. No one was home but me. Statues of elephants observed me as I made my way through the house. Black shelves that held Mom's tiny treasures accented the cream walls. Family photos in wooden frames stood on the small, cube coffee tables that sandwiched the couches and arm chair. "Homey" was what my mother told me her style was when I asked her why she cluttered the house with useless things.

I didn't know what to do first — eat or have a shower. As I thought about it, I walked over to the basement staircase which was only a few more steps to the left. I slid down the stairs into the cool basement. There was even less light down there. The blacked-out windows gave the room a movie theater atmosphere.

My room was in the back corner, below the kitchen. It was unfinished, just bare concrete on two of the walls and a skeleton ceiling. My definition of "homey." I loved my room and the little bit that I had in it. A bed with a table beside it. In the far corner, a tall dresser blocked a hole that I had once kicked into the drywall. A carpeted floor lingered somewhere under piles of clothes. No pictures or posters. No fancy lights or plants. Just two gray concrete walls and two white painted ones.

"Erg." I flopped onto my duvet. "So comfy."

I tried hard to see anything in the black room that I stood in. I blinked a few times to make sure my eyes were open. They were. I raised my hands close to my eyes, only able to see the shadow of my hand. I could do nothing to brighten the space around me. I stepped forward, my foot fell through the ground. Yet, I didn't fall. I floated, suspended in the air by an absence of gravity.

A cool hard metal glided against my neck for a sprit second. I whipped around; my eyes failed me. A deep, quiet laugh echoed.

Stopped. Cool metal brushed my arm and the laughter started again, louder and louder.

A sound of meat being ripped apart filled the air, along with a scream from a woman in severe pain. The voice laughed louder as the tearing turned to the snapping of bone.

For minutes I stood in the dark, alone. The sounds replayed in my mind. A thick droplet of liquid splashed onto my cheek, then proceeded to coat my face. The twisted laughter made my skin crawl. My hands pressed against my ears, but it echoed in my head. I screamed, trying to drown out the laughter. It didn't work. I brought my knees to my chest, buried my liquid-covered face into them, and waited for it all to stop.

"Blaze, did you hear me?" My mom shook me awake. "It's not healthy to sleep in clothes. Get up and get ready for bed."

I lifted my head out of my duvet, surprised to see where I was. "How long have I been sleeping?"

"Well, it's one, so you tell me." She gave me a disapproving mom raise of her eyebrow. "You look pale, honey. Are you getting sick?"

"No, Mom. Just tired. Long day." *And a nightmare.* "I will be fine. Did you happen to save me some supper? I'm starving."

* * *

The next day, Hope tapped the tip of her shoe onto the curb as she waited for me to pick her up for school. An open book held tight in her hand, her eyes twitched over each word.

A huge grin grew, then was slapped away by a turn of the page. The book's emotions played on her face. She noticed me without a peek up from the tale. She snapped her book closed and waved.

She opened the door, and then jumped in with her usual cheerful grin. "Mornin'. You didn't sleep well, I'm guessing." Her eyes examined my face, then dropped down to my plain black attire. With one hand, she draped the seat belt over her shoulder. Her blue hoodie scrunched around the waist, showing off her Zelda belt buckle.

"How'd you know?" I asked as I drove away from the curb.

"Those dark rings ... you being late ... those sort of hints are a few giveaways. And did you even try to pick your clothes? Don't you know that all black is out?" Her fingers turned up the radio. "What happened? Did the new teacher come and suck your blood or sacrifice your whole family? Or ... hold on ... I made a list." She rummaged through her bag and pulled out her notebook. There must have been thirty or forty items written down.

"I see you kept busy with the important things." I reached over and pulled the list from her hand and read number twenty-eight. "New teacher turns into an alien and covers the world in orange slime, demanding all things that have the color pink. And burns anything with purple." As I read, my eyes bounced between the sheet and the road. "Hope, you're really strange."

"I don't mind if he takes away the pink and purple things, as long as he leaves blue alone." She took the page back and giggled at a few inside jokes. Then she stuffed it back into her bag. "So why couldn't you sleep last night?"

The speed bump in the school parking lot surprised us both.

"Um, well … I had a nightmare."

"A nightmare? That's strange. You haven't had one of those in a long time."

"Yeah. This one was different. It felt real. Like I was really there, listening, feeling. Mom woke me up just before I gave in. Then I got to eat yummy potatoes and cream corn and pork chops. Mmm, pork chops. I wish the school had a microwave, so I could have brought them for lunch … oh, well." I turned the car off, pulled the key out, and popped open my door. "Well, another day."

"Oh, don't be so glum." She wiggled out and locked the door as she closed it. "Mom got me a new book," she said. She then rounded the car and headed for the building. "It's really neat. You can borrow it if you want. I'll be done this morning. You can take it for your spare."

"I think I can go without."

"Reading is good for you. Try it some time. Or are you too afraid your brain might explode?" She pushed her back onto the door to block me from getting in. "Blaze, what was the nightmare about? You seem absent and not yourself."

I smiled weakly at her. "Tired, just tired."

Hope turned and pulled the heavy door open. "Maybe you're coming down with something." She felt my forehead.

"You still haven't answered my question. What was it about? The fire?"

"No, I haven't thought about the fire in a long time."

We entered into the school and a warm gust of air greeted us.

"Sorry. Did I upset you?" she asked. "I know we agreed never to talk about it again, since we turned up empty handed in our search."

The hustle of school life made it easy to distract myself by watching happy teens strut around in their perfect lives with their minor bumps and upsets. Sixteen years later, and I was still the biggest news story to hit the town. I knew I wasn't the only one to lose something along the path of living, and to be honest, I was happy that it had happened when I was young. I lost my parents, both, in a freak fire accident. Only I made it out safely. I had nothing to hold on to, other than the singed clothing I wore.

Hope leaned into the locker beside mine and waited till I unlocked it, even though she knew the combination. "Your new mom and dad are so nice. You're lucky you didn't have to leave town … Oh, my God … if you had left, we wouldn't know each other. How would you've survived without knowing me? I hold you together. Come on. You know I do." Her brows wiggled.

I unlocked my locker with a genuine smile. "You do. If it wasn't for you, I'd be locked up in a white padded room, alone with my nightmares."

"And don't you forget it." She raised her finger and tapped it on her lower lip. "Though, I most likely make things worse by playing along with some of them. I love quests and your little brain has the best adventures." Her eyes widened, hinting that she wanted juicier details.

"It was black. No lights —"

Ring. The bell saved me. I didn't want to remember the heart-wrenching scream and the wicked laughter.

"Aw! Until lunchtime then. And you won't be able to escape my curiosity," she said as her eyes burrowed into mine, making sure I caught her hint. She wasn't going to let this one slide.

"You making a list of my dreams now, too?" I raised an eyebrow as I walked past her to English class.

"Maybe," she whispered and headed in the opposite direction.

The students in my English class gossiped as I quietly set up my binder and slid my bag under my chair. I had no interest in their petty lives, not that I thought mine was better. I just didn't need to hear about Jane from Sue, and Lin from Jane.

As I pulled out my text book, Mrs. Callahan entered the room, her plump structure draped with a floral fitted dress. Her hair was tightly wound and pinned into a bun at the back of her head. Her hands were filled with books. "Good morning, good morning, class."

The class fell silent and the day began. We each wrote about our summer and read it to the class. I wrote about Hope and me watching night after night of horror films, then day after day of watching anime. Okay, I wanted to write the last part, but decided to save myself from being bullied that afternoon.

Just before the bell rang, Mr. Robinson entered the room. He didn't glance once at the class, but I watched him intently. Mrs.

Callahan peeked at me once, then whispered to him. He nodded and left. She smiled at the class and told us to pack our things because we were finished for the day.

"Blaze," she said, as I made my way through the rows of desks, "I need to speak with you a moment. I have a message for you from Mr. Robinson."

"Ooo," teased one of the students as he walked out. "Blaze, the pet, has a message."

I stepped up to her and readjusted my backpack over my shoulder. "What does he want now?" My voice was laced with an unknown anger. "Sorry," I breathed, and then calmer asked, "What message did he leave?"

Concerned, she smiled. "He wants to speak with you before lunch. Something to do with your behavior in yesterday's class. You've been nice to the new teacher, right?"

She had known me since elementary. I had had her for grade four, and I had been quite spirited. Then I had her for every year in junior high and high school. I was never the worst of the worst, but never the best, or even close to the best.

"I got sick." I lowered my head. "I know, lame excuse, but it's the absolute truth. Even call Mom. I passed out as soon as I got in."

"Blaze, you sleep all the time. I don't think I've had a week of your full awake attention."

I laughed. "Yeah, all right. It's the truth, though. Anyway I have to go. Yippee, social studies class with Mr. Glen —"

"He's not that bad."

"He's boring to the extreme."

Social studies came and went faster than I could have
hoped. I'd rather have a lifetime enduring monotone Mr. Glen
than be alone in a room talking to the creepy new teacher.

Students flooded the halls as I made my way to the other
end of the small school. I bumped shoulders with the crowd,
and accidentally got pushed into a small grade seven student
and tossed her books all over the floor. I bent down, collected
them for her, and apologized. I took it as an omen that
talking to Mr. Robinson would destroy my peaceful, worthless
existence, so I spun on my heels to make a getaway and crashed
right into him.

"Hi. Sorry. I was running late." His charmed grin gave me
shivers.

"Uh, yeah. No problem." I turned back toward the
chemistry room, and he kept pace behind me.

"Come." He gestured to the door. "I have something
important and," he lowered his lips to my ear and said,
"*Private.*"

We entered the room, and he closed the door. My mouth
dried. I wasn't dizzy or nauseous, nothing like yesterday.
My palms were sweaty because his close proximity made me
uncomfortable, but not in a sexual way. There was this skin
crawling effect I got whenever he was around.

He sat down in his chair behind his desk and eyed me.
"How are you feeling?"

"Fine," I answered dryly.

His grin grew and his face got a twisted smile. He sat there.
Waited.

The room took on a life of its own, spinning out of control. A headache grew into a hammering pain. I wrapped my arms around myself, wished it would cause the room to still. I glanced in his direction but only saw a blur of spiraled color. Then it stopped. The room stilled. My eyes locked with his. I was fine.

"You can go." He waved to the door, picked up a stack of papers, a red pen, and ignored me.

Stunned by what had happened, I left without question.

Chapter Two

Hope had already eaten her entire lunch while she waited for me. She spotted me down the hallway, pulled in her lower lip and bit, her bright eyes hidden behind slits. Her nostrils flared. When I reached her, she was about to pack up and leave. A solid glare watched me slide down the lockers into my spot and open my paper lunch bag.

She cleared her throat, then let me in on her morning, all frustrated spirits lost. Hope's hands waved through the air as if her story was guiding an orchestra through an intense piece. Her eyes shined as she embraced all school could offer her.

I listened with a smile and began to eat my chicken wrap. *Lunch and a show,* I thought with a chuckle.

When my wrap was finished, so was Hope. She vibrated with questions. That was the first time in lunch-time history I had ever been late. Even when I had detentions, I'd pop by for a quick laugh and then off I went.

Hope took hold of my arm and yanked me close, squinted her eyes and asked, "Where were you, hmm?"

Times like those, I couldn't lie. She had her scope on and would be able to tell if I hid pieces or strolled off topic. I told her where I was, and what happened.

"There is something wrong with that teacher." She let go of my arm and relaxed back into her comfy position. She rested her elbow on her knee and her chin on her fist. She gazed off into the distance. "This proves it. He's from another planet and has come to …" She turned her sickening grin my way, "Experiment on you."

"You're wrong in the head, you know that? Wrong, wrong, wrong."

"Aw! A teacher's finally giving little Miss Blaze's attention, but for all the wrong reasons."

"You're just jealous."

"And why would that be?"

"It's a Hope thing, mysterious and strange happenings. A possibility of being abducted by aliens. Or a wicked secret revealed in the darkest of ways."

Her eyes narrowed to a frightening glare. "I'm happy being the observer. At least, I will survive in the end." She wiggled her eyebrows, then jumped up to her feet. "A walk. Then it's back to class for us."

"I'm not excited for my next class." I moaned.

She offered her hand in front of my face to help me up. "Come on. He's a creep show, yes. But you still need to pass his class to get out of here." I placed my hand in hers and hoisted myself up. "Plus, it will make this year interesting. Every other year has been the same this, same that. Now we need to keep on our toes and guess his next move."

I sighed. "Oh, yeah, real live action." I tried to sound optimistic as I wondered, *Why me though?*

"Blaze!" a girl hollered from behind me. "Blaze!"

I turned to see who called out my name. It was one of the popular girls, makeup caked on, clothes over the top expensive, and long, curled, blond hair.

"What's the deal? I heard that you were asked to go to Mr. R's room before lunch." Her high-pitched voiced twisted with envy.

"Yeah, so what? He had to ask me something."

"You stay away from my man, or I will make this year *Hell* for you. I swear it."

Hope pushed me to the side a little and took the stage. "If he calls for her, she will come. There's nothing you can do about it. Looks like 'your man' has eyes for a real woman. Not some fake-faced bitch."

The girl's face scrunched. *Oh, how dare Hope speak to the queen that way.* A taunting smile grew, and I let it shine. Hope winked then nudged me to the door. The girl moved her mouth to say something snappy, but the bell blocked it out, if she said anything at all.

"Great! I'm off to Doomsville. See ya later, Hope."

Mr. Robinson had entered the ten-minute mark of being late — five more, then we would have been home free. Just as my spirits lifted and I thought I could make a clean break —

"Good morning, class," he sauntered in with his twisted smile plastered on. His iced eyes fixed to mine. "Today we start our actual lessons. I hope you pay attention." His eyes sifted through the class from behind his desk. "Let's see who is here."

He took attendance, then asked us to flip open our text books. Class went by normally, well, other than the fact that only time he acknowledged I existed was when he first entered. After that, he called on everyone else for answers to his questions, explained what we read in full detail, handed out a work sheet and gave us twenty minutes to complete the assignment. I picked up my pencil and began.

The bell rang. I packed up and headed for the door. I listened to hear if he was going to hold me back for another one of his strange talks, but he didn't. He concentrated on his papers and nothing else.

My double spare came after lunch. Usually I loved them. I'd go to the library and lay out on the table and have a nice snooze. Or go into the common area and gorge on salt and vinegar chips. But today, I needed to get as far away from the school as possible. Hope had last block spare, so I planned to swing in and grab her after a nice, long, quiet drive. Sounded nice.

I threw all my unnecessary binders and textbooks into my locker and grabbed my car keys and sweater. I jumped when I closed the door, and my art teacher was standing right beside me.

"Sorry. Didn't mean to scare you," she said. "I was marking last night, and I pulled out your class's projects. When I reached yours ..." She flipped up a piece of paper so the backside of my artwork faced me. "I don't know how this is possible, but ..." She turned the page toward me. "You're drawing is ... well ... he's missing."

The jagged sharp stone background filled the page, where I had drawn the wicked and sinister man — white. Plain. Like it hadn't been touched by my pencil. I took the sheet and held it closer. There was no indication that he had been there before. She couldn't have erased it that well.

"It's like he's up and left," I said and passed the sheet back to her.

She took the page and stared wearily at the stone work. "Blaze, I don't know what to say. I'm not joking if that is what you're thinking. I know how you young people think, but this is no prank."

"I still get an A, right?" I attempted to joke.

"He's gone, Blaze." Her arms shook, causing the paper to rattled.

I placed my hand on her shoulder in hope that it would help calm her. "It will be okay. Maybe someone is just trying to scare you."

"Normally I wouldn't say this to a student, but this isn't normal. I had just shown my husband your work before I settled down with some of the grade seven pieces. When I came to your class ... he was gone."

"That's freaky. Would your hus —"

"No, he's a practical man. He tells jokes and likes to be funny on the rare occasion, but he's never, in all our thirty-seven years, tried to scare me." Her shaky eyes pooled with fearful tears.

"Is your room empty right now?"

"Yes. Why?"

"Let's go to your classroom before someone thinks I'm making you cry and I get a detention. There's a few teachers here who love to hand them out as if they are candy."

She followed me to the art room. I wasn't a bit scared. My art had run off on its own legs, and I didn't care in the slightest. I peeked over my shoulder. Fear wrapped Mrs. Hritz like a blanket.

She pushed the key in and unlocked the door. When the door opened, the room took in a huge cold breath. "It's freezing in here." She tightened her purple sweater, pulling it closer to her body.

I followed her in, and every time I breathed out, a white cloud exhaled from my lips. "Yikes." I rubbed my arms. "It's normally chiller in your room, but this is colder than outside."

We both jumped as the phone's loud ring took over the silence. She rushed over to it and answered it. After a few nods and yeses, she smiled and hung up.

"They are having trouble getting heat to this room and the drama room." Relieved she relaxed her tense shoulders. "Blaze, maybe I'm just being silly. Let's just forget about it and get out of this ice box."

My fingers numb and body vibrating from the chill, I
agreed to follow her out. "See you tomorrow then. Hopefully
they fix the problem and heat returns to your room."

"Yes, I hope so, too," she said with a brighter smile and
walked down the hall to the office. "See you tomorrow."

A brick planter took up the center of the portable. There
were no living plants in it, just plastic ones plus rocks and wood
chips. The frame was made out of the same brick work and had
a lip that stuck out to create a bench that wrapped around.

I stepped up on to the bench and sat on the rim of the
planter and buried my face in my hands. The fear I first felt
when I had completed the artwork bubbled up into my once
calm mind. Even the way I had drawn the man in the picture
made my skin crawl. For some reason, even though I had never
seen him before, I was scared. Now there was a possibility he
was loose in the school.

I lifted my head out of my hands. My eyes were shocked by
the bright blue sweater in front of me. "Hi, Blaze. What you
doin'?"

"What am I doing? What are you doing? Aren't you
supposed to be in class?"

Hope twirled around on one foot. "Nope. Class got
canceled. It's freezing in the drama room. So we got let out."

"Well, then, let's go home." I hopped down from my seat.
"I have to tell you something once we get in the car. You're not
going to believe this."

Hope bounced with anticipation beside me as we
approached the car. Its dirty gray body peeked out from behind

a short green Jeep. With all that had happened in the sum of two days, I was ready for the year to end, though it had just begun. This year I planned to work at every class, so there was no way for them to hold me back, so I could get on with a real life. Find a job doing something I enjoyed, although I never knew what I enjoyed. Normally I followed Hope wherever she went. I knew I would be on my own once she went off to university. I never thought much about life after school. The idea terrified me over anything else.

On the way, I explained what happened to my art project, my teacher's face, and the freezing of the art room. Hope's mouth opened to give her input, then closed to let me finish.

"Blaze," the horrible, yet pleasing voice of Mr. Robinson called from behind me.

Hope's eyes widened as she peeked behind her, but I kept walking as if he hadn't called out to me. Hope's eyes darted to mine. "Blaze, he knows you heard him," she whispered. "He's just standing there, waiting for you to turn around and answer him."

"I don't care," I whispered back.

She turned just as we reached the car. I pulled my keys out of my pocket and focused on finding the right one.

"Look," Mr. Robinson said as he leaned against my driver's side door.

How the hell did he — he was just — I looked back to where I left him standing, a good nine feet away.

"I don't have time for games," he said in a cold tone. "Here." He handed me a large orange envelope.

I took it with both hands. It was heavy and thick. I ran my fingers over the seal, a sudden strong pulse to rip the thing open overwhelmed me. I never even got that impulse on Christmas.

I glanced up, and he was already gone.

Hope tapped me on the shoulder. "How long are you going to stand there and stare at that?" I looked at her confused. "Let's go already."

"Sure." I unlocked the car and hopped inside.

I started the car and peeked at the clock. There was no way. "Hope, how long was I standing there?"

"At least, two minutes. I thought I would give you the time to process your new gift. Although I could be exaggerating slightly, you were making me nervous. I have never seen you so zoned in to one thing before."

I held up the envelope. "No. That's not possible. Two minutes has to be an exaggeration. He just handed it to me. Then you tapped me on the shoulder. It was only seconds apart." I peeked at the clock again. It was ten minutes after one. She could have been right, for all I knew.

"Chick, you've lost your mind. Art running off on its own, staring off into space." She reached over to grab the envelope, but I defensively pulled it away and glared at her, angered that she'd even tried.

"What's wrong?" she asked, recoiling.

I vibrated. I couldn't figure out why there was a sudden burst of rage. *Breathe, breathe.* "I don't know ..." I reached

31

back and placed it onto the backseat. "I'm really tired. I'm going to go home and straight to bed."

"Strange, though. After all you've been through, he gives you something. We should open it." She lifted her elbow, then lowered it again. Her smile dulled. "You got really mad at me, really mad."

I drove down the streets toward Hope's house in silence, not really thinking about anything. She was right; I had gotten mad at her. I felt the anger heat my body the moment she reached over to touch what Mr. Robinson had given me.

We had almost reached her house when I broke the silence. "I'm sorry, Hope. I don't know why I did that."

"You sleep extra long tonight. No more fiery Blaze. You big grump." She stuck out her lower lip and made her eyes as big and sad as she could. She reached to the radio to click it on. The sound of heavy electric guitars and drums filled the car. I, somehow, cracked a smile. "There you go. Maybe being back at school is getting to you. And it doesn't help that, even though we are almost full adults, most of the people around us act like they're still in grade two ... *erg.*"

"I really couldn't care less about anyone in that school. If they all died tomorrow, I wouldn't be affected one way or the other."

Hope's long white house came into view with her mother's green car parked in the driveway and her brother's old rusted truck sitting across the street. A few birch trees decorated the townhouse yards. Each had its own little garden, but most were left unattended and had become overgrown during the summer months.

"Home at last," Hope sighed. "Are you sure you don't want to come in?" She eyed the envelope. "We could open it together."

"I really should go to bed. Sorry, but I'm going to go home. I can't shake this anger that I'm feeling. I'm going to try to sleep it off."

She rolled her eyes, then leapt out of the car. "You're going to open it without me, aren't you?" she asked, disappointed.

"I don't know. First sleep; then I will decide. If I haven't by tomorrow, then we will open it together. Sound good?"

She sighed, then nodded. "Okay." She breathed. "Have a very, *very*, restful sleep. Then I will see you tomorrow. Bring whatever is in there, got it?"

I saluted. "Yes, ma'am."

The drive home eased my mind. I turned off the radio and listened to the quiet hum of the engine, the rush of the few cars that passed, and the silence of no one around. I enjoyed solitude; any minute I got of it was bliss. I love to sit in the cool basement, TV off, no one home but the cats, and the only light up in the kitchen, beaming down the stairwell with a dim yellow. I found comfort in the darkness.

Our greenish-blue, two-story house came into view. Three wide spruces wrapped the yard and separated it from the neighbors. Needles from the trees turned the grass red and brown, and small surviving green patches awaited their poison or the cold winter blanket. Mom's van was parked crooked on her spot in the driveway.

Sigh. *Looks like I won't get the house to myself a second time,* I thought as I turned into my spot.

I collected the envelope and lunch, then strolled up to the house. No light peeked from the cracks in the curtains. I turned the cold metal doorknob without needing a key to step into the dark building. I glanced at the shoe rack as I removed mine. Mom had hundreds of different types, so it was hard to keep track if a pair was missing.

"Mom?" No answer. "Mom, you home?"

With no reply and no sounds coming from any end of the house, I realized that I was alone. I walked into the kitchen and turned on the lights located under the cupboards. They gave the room a little bit of light but not enough to overpower the space. I tossed my lunch onto the counter and tried to ignore the orange envelope that was tucked under my arm. Yet it tempted me, begged me to open it and reveal what was within the orange paper.

I wanted to go down and flop onto my bed till morning. The envelope ... no, more like what lingered between the thin orange paper, drew me to obsession. I needed to know. A powerful sensation washed over me. I took it in both of my hands. I needed to know. Had to. I ran my finger over the seal; my mouth went dry and my breath staled in my lungs.

Chapter Three

With overpowering curiosity and drive, I guided my hand to open the mysterious package. Mr. Robinson hadn't said much when he had given it to me. He hadn't really said anything at all. My fingers touched the rough paper. My heart seemed to stop. The world stopped. My finger slipped under the loose edge and began to rip open the seam. I had to know.

A door closing snapped me out my trance. I took a breath in, my lungs hurt as if I hadn't used them in a while. My eyelids felt like sandpaper as they slid down my eyes. My tensed body relaxed and ached. *What had happened to me?*

"Blaze, darling," my mom called from the doorway. "What do you have on for dinner? I'm starving."

Dinner? I glanced at the clock. *Already nine.* "Um, I was busy with homework. I lost track of time." I tucked the envelope under my arm and met her in the entrance with a forced smile. "What do you think of ordering pizza? Where's Amy?" I asked, hoping she didn't hear my fear.

"Pizza sounds great," she said, heading up the stairs. "Amy is sleeping over at a friend's. It will just be us. I want meat lovers. Oh! And get pop." She dragged herself up the stairs and turned toward her room. "After you order, let me know how much and I'll pay."

I called the pizza parlour down the street and ordered a large meat lovers, a pepperoni, and a six pack of Coke. The envelope still tucked safely under my arm. I went upstairs to Mom's door and yelled though the thin wood, "Mom?"

"Yes?" she called. Her voice echoed out of her attached bathroom.

"It came to thirty-seven fifty."

I heard the toilet flush and the tap turn on. Moments later, her bank card slid under the door. "Thanks. Come get me when it's here. I'm going to have a shower now."

I took the red card and jolted down the stairs faster than normal. My full attention shifted to the package under my arm. I plopped down on the black leather couch. With Amy away and Mom in the shower, I had all the privacy I wanted.

This time, I didn't hesitate to tear open the top. The paper ripped smooth and straight. My greedy fingers reached in. I bit my tongue. Soft fabric surprised my fingertips. I gasped it and pulled out a crimson velvet cloth wrapped around a large, thick rectangle. A braided leather kept the velvet in place. The loose ends of the braid were tied to a metal ring positioned in the center of the object. The ring seemed to have some sort of runes or ancient alphabet carved into it. I couldn't tear my eyes away. My lungs screamed for me to breathe. I bit down harder on my tongue to prove I wasn't sleeping.

Knock. Knock. Knock.

I breathed in. *The pizza already? No way.* I placed the object down on the coffee table. A strong pull told me to pick it up again; it begged not to be left. A spell was cast over me, drawn by an invisible force. I almost listened but I couldn't. With all my willpower, I needed to answer the door empty-handed. I would klutz out and drop the pizza. As much as it pained me, I left the tempting crimson package on the table.

With Mom's bank card in hand, I opened the front door. My mind was so fixated on what I had left a few feet away that I didn't even notice who delivered my supper.

"That will be thirty-seven fifty," the delivery man said.

I handed him the bank card. "Here." My eyes strained to see the dark-red fabric through the door.

"Thanks, Blaze."

Stunned, I looked at the delivery man. It was him. Mr. Robinson. "After school job, really?"

"Yep." He handed me the debit machine. I took it and punched in the pin and then handed it back. "What? Only a five-dollar tip?" His eyebrow raised. "And after that wonderful gift I gave you?"

"Gift?" I then thought back to the velvet-wrapped carving on my coffee table.

"Guess it's not technically a gift. You gave it to me long ago for safe keeping. I wasn't sure how long you wanted me to keep it. I'm sure that it's time for you to have it back. Your reaction to it in school was a sign." He handed me the pizzas and pop. "Look, I've got to go back to work. Talk to me tomorrow at lunch, after you've opened it. You'll have more questions then."

I rested the hot pizzas on my hand and blinked a few times. "How do you know I didn't open it?"

"I'll know when you do." His lips curled into a charming smile. "We are a team, you and I. I'm like a ... a bodyguard, here to protect you anyway you see fit. Right now, what you need more than anything is to fully understand what I gave you, but to do that, you need to unwrap it and see it for yourself." He leaned in closer, as if someone else may be listening, and said, "Don't let anyone know about it. If the wrong person finds out then ... well ... when that time comes, I'll be right here at your side." He turned away and waved. "See you tomorrow."

"One last thing ..." I stepped outside of the house. "I drew something in art, and my teacher is freaking out ..."

"Oh, that." He laughed. "We can't let anyone know your memory is returning, so I took it in hopes that you would still get full marks." He paused and then asked, "She saw what you drew before I made that necessary change, huh?" His cold eyes froze me to the spot. I nodded a silent yes. "Hmm ..." He turned back to his truck and left without another word.

Unsure if I should have said anything at all about the art, I went back into the house. The hot pizzas burned at my palm as the door closed. I stuck my head in the stairwell. "Pizza is here!" I yelled.

"Okay," Mom replied through her closed door.

I placed the boxes down on the counter and hurried back to the living room. The crimson-wrapped mystery waited for me, longing to be discovered.

"Did you hear me?" Mom made me jump as her hand rested on my shoulder.

"No, sorry. What?" I turned my attention away from the table and rested my eyes on her tired face. Bags lined her strained eyes.

"Let's eat dinner together tonight." Her warm motherly grin filled her face.

"I'd love that. I'm starving. Let's eat."

She wrapped her arm around my waist and pulled me toward the kitchen. Her body paused as her eyes caught a glimpse of what I left on the table. "What is that?"

I didn't dare look. "A prop for art. I'm going to draw it, then use pastel and maybe glue and some tissue paper."

"Oh, well, in that case, it's nice," she lied.

Supper tasted great. Even if it was delivered by some whack job teacher.

Later, I hid myself in my room with my nightlight on its lowest setting. The soft fabric teased my fingers. My eyes were drawn to the metal ring that the leather rope seemed to wrap around. I reached out and touched the metal. "Hot!" My finger shot to my mouth as if that would cool it down.

The rune lit up in a vibrant baby blue color. *Snap.* It broke into four and dropped on to my lap. The velvet unfolded at my fingertips and revealed an aged, brown-leather book.

I let the fabric fall into my lap to view the fullness of
the book. Engravings coated the cover. Each mark was more
different than the last. They circled a large, white, and milky
stone, the white wisps in the stone appeared to flow. I flipped
the book over and imbedded in the back was a large black stone
with liquid crimson spots. I ran my finger over the uneven
cover, and stopped at a thick leather strap that bound the book
closed. A familiar warmth danced through me as I touched the
rough leather and the smooth warm stones. My eyelids became
heavy, and my body drooped onto the fluffy duvet. I tried hard
to keep my eyes open, tried hard but failed.

*At first, I heard a far-off girlish giggle. My body felt numb and
empty. The laugh didn't bother me. It was off in the distance and
added sound to the void that surrounded me.*

*I then became aware that my eyes were closed. As I opened
them the giggle faded away, replaced by birds as they sang their
last notes in the trees. The dark orange sun lit the sky with its final
touch of light.*

*The red-bricked school stood a few foot steps away. The front
door was wedged open with a tattered binder. The wind pushed
me, and I slowly stepped forward. I placed my hand on the latch
and pulled the door wide. Inside, the halls were quiet. The glow
from the setting sun seeped in from the long, narrow sunroof. I
made my way through the entrance and into the common area.*

*Students, still and silent, filled the halls and the room, hanging
from the ceiling with rusted meat hooks through their backs, necks
or skulls. Unaffected, I pressed forward. Blood dripped, making no*

sound as it contacted the puddles below. Bullies, friends, teachers. All present and accounted for. All but Hope.

I wandered the gloomy halls. Every door was shut tight and locked. Even the lockless lockers wouldn't open. I passed my art teacher, her hook perturbed out of her mouth as if it were her tongue. Her eyes were open and downcast. I turned from her and continued down the hall, passed my locker and entered the art, drama, and chemistry portable. As I entered, I noticed one of the lockers was opened, no more than a hair. I approached it. Hope's locker. I curled my fingers under the handle and peered inside.

A lush hunter green forest lay within. The smell of fresh air filled my nose and washed away the stale smell of blood. A voice echoed through the enchantment of trees and shrubs. I peeked around the school halls at the corpses that hung around me. Not a sound. Not even my own breath or heartbeat could be heard. My eyes found a small assortment of flowers lingering under a tiny bush. I reached in to see if I could pick one. As my arm met with the crisp air of the forest, my body was pulled in too.

The cool air gave me goosebumps as the wind brushed my thin arms. I glanced at my small, childlike hands. A smile crept up and surprised me as the wind rustled the leaves. The birds perched in the treetops and sang their merry song. I hummed to their tune. It brought back a hidden memory, a lullaby I had long forgotten.

Deep within the forest, I heard a woman call out my name. Her voice echoed through the trees and caught my full attention. The soft moss wrapped my bare toes as I ran. She called again, and I picked up my pace. The cheerfulness I once felt was replaced with panic and fear.

41

Blotches of blood splashed onto the greenery from the clear sky above that peeked through the tall dark spruce and broad leafed trees. The closer I got, the denser and darker the forest became. Blood poured from above. My legs became longer, aged with every footfall. And yet the woman called to me with joy.

The crimson rain pooled on the ground and coated the leaves, bark, and stones around me. The trees died and shed their once healthy leaves and needles. Shadows shifted across the grim world. The forest faded. Just before it vanished, I slipped and fell forward. I braced myself for the hard hit to the ground. My body toppled through the mulch and stone, deeper and deeper into the dark void below.

Sinister growls welcomed me. Crimson eyes stalked me. I watched the shadows of monsters shift throughout the void.

I caught the tune of the lullaby as my eyes scanned behind the beasts. A faceless child stood in the distance, humming the mystical tune. She reached up with her tiny hand. The silver claws of the nearest creature caught my eye, just before it wrapped its boney talons around my neck.

I gasped for breath. The child giggled. I swiped with my hands but went right through the monster's silhouette. The other creatures howled and gnashed their fangs.

I shot up from the duvet and fought for breath. Sweat poured from my face. My lungs ached and my neck throbbed. With huge, deep gasps, I steadied myself. I peeked at the wicked book that lay beside me. My fingers touched the white cool stone. A sinister force pulled me. I loved it and hated it.

Wanted it and didn't. No matter how I felt about the book, I needed to touch it, feel it, be with it always.

A shiver ran up my spine as the images of the nightmare returned. Twisted thoughts of death and cruelty. Void of all emotion. Wrapped in a blanket of evil.

Chapter Four

Hope already had unrealistic ideas about my past. It was like a jigsaw puzzle with many missing pieces that she loved to try, over and over again, to put together. I'd discover more pieces for her to play with, and she'd be ecstatic.

Packed and ready for school, I snuck back down to my room with my backpack in hand. I lifted the pillow from my bed. Underneath slept the wicked book. My eyes studied the marks again. A particular indentation caught my eye. A thin man wielding a broad sword stood on the white stone. I sat down on the side of my bed and ran my finger over it. A blue light filled the indentation then leaked out in a crescent shape behind the man. When the light faded, a new image had formed. It was larger than the man, a black outline of a crescent moon.

"Blaze, you're going to be late!" my mom yelled down from the top of the stairs.

I snapped out of the trance, slipped the book into my bag, and bolted upstairs and outside to my car. I had to find a way to control the connection I had with the book.

I drove to Hope's under a beautiful sky of blended pinks, purples, and oranges. The light fall breeze caused trees to dance and flowers to sway. I rounded the corner and saw Hope dressed in bright fall colors. She impatiently bounced on her toes as her fingers twirled her hair, and her eyes searched the street. Once her eyes spotted my car, she smiled and waved. Her smile filled her face, lit by the bright light of the morning sun. I pulled up to the curb. She popped open the passenger door, tossed her backpack, binder, and a few textbooks over her seat and plopped in.

"Morning," I said with a yawn.

"Tired, are we?" she asked with her eyes fixed to the side of my face as I drove us to school.

A slight grin grew as I thought back to the book. "Yes, had a rough sleep."

"Oh, that's fascinating. So …" She bit her lip and let her eyes search around for the orange envelope I never called her about.

"So … it was exhausting," I growled.

"That's nice." She put her hand on my bag to bring it forward.

"Don't!" I snapped, hitting my steering wheel with the heel of my hand. She dropped it and clasped her hands together. Never before had I yelled at Hope. I swallowed the festering rage. "Um, wow! Sorry." I ran my fingers through my hair. "Guess I'm more tired than I thought."

Oddly, she sat quietly in her seat, rubbing her thumbs together. I must have really scared her because she turned her head from me and gazed out the window.

"I had another nightmare last night," I said, filling her in. "A bad one, too. Everyone was dead. Everyone." I went on and told her in detail about what I saw and felt.

"Emotionless, eh?" Her smile returned. "Like when we first met?"

"Yeah, just like that."

"You didn't talk, didn't smile. You did absolutely nothing." She giggled. "Remember how we met? I didn't remember the full details of it, but Mom reminded me last night."

We arrived at school, and I parked the car. She pushed the release on her seat belt as I turned the car off. "Please tell me what your mom said at lunch, I don't remember. Things from those days are hazy."

"I will," she said, beaming.

The first bell rang. I closed my locker door and made my way to English class. Students, full of energy and spirit, rushed passed, like a busy colony of ants. The people around me marched to their assigned places. I sighed. My chin was low; my backpack seemed heavy. The mystery of my past weighed it down as if I had captured a mountain within the fabric and zipper.

In the classroom, students chatted around me, happily sharing stories of the summer and everything else on their minds. "Hey!" A boy nudged my shoulder. "Blaze."

I turned around and glared. "What?"

"Rumor has it that Mr. R dumped you. That true?"

I rolled my eyes and reached down to my bag to pull out our novel study.

"It's true then." He turned and hollered to his buddy on the other side of the room. "Yo! It's true. Totally dumped."

"Noah, take your seat," Mrs. Callahan said as she entered the room. Noah smiled and did as he was told. "Now, class, I have some tragic news. Everyone is being informed today." Her eyes watered, and she moistened her lips nervously with her tongue. "Please listen closely to what I have to say. If anyone needs to talk during or after class, that will be all all right, and I will be all ears."

The class grew silent.

She blinked and a few tears escaped. Inhaling, she calmed herself. "Class …" She teared. "Mrs. Hritz … she …" Mrs. Callahan closed her eyes. "She passed away last night …"

The class gasped and whispered to each other.

"No way!" one of the guys whispered.

"Oh, my God! How?" a girl asked.

"Isn't she the art teacher?" another asked a friend. "That's so horrible."

Mrs. Callahan raised her hand for silence, and the class respectfully obeyed. "Now I know this is a shock to you all."

It was more than a shock to me. *What happened to her? Why? Did Mr. Robinson do something? Did … did I kill her because I told him?* I couldn't fight the vibrations that streamed out from my core.

"Let's take a moment to remember her and all the joy she brought to our lives."

I abruptly stood and slammed my hands on my desk. *He did something. I know it,* I thought. I scooped up my things and left the room. I stopped in front of the closed chemistry door, raised my hand to knock, but froze. *What if he didn't? Fuck it.* I knocked. The door swung open and he appeared. Those in his class saw me and whispered. He must have just told them. Showing up after made the whole thing look worse than it was.

"We need to talk," I whispered.

He exited the room and closed the door without a word to his students, his icy gaze fixed to me. "Yes. What is this about?"

"Mrs. Hritz. What did you do?" I accused, my body hot with rage.

"Me? Well … I did nothing." A sly grin grew on his face.

"Then who did?"

"And what makes you think I know?"

My lips pressed tight.

He placed his hand on my shoulder and lowered his head. "You best get back to class. Come see me at lunch, and we can talk about the book and get your mind off the loss of your teacher. I have a class to teach. Excuse me."

"Aren't you supposed to be helping me?" I questioned, trying to get some sort of answer on why he entered my nice, quiet life.

He stopped with his hand on the door knob. "I am." He turned and his twisted smile was replaced by a charming, sympathetic one. Then he opened the door and was gone.

I backed up into the lockers across the hall and closed my eyes. I took in a deep breath. He did something, or told someone who did something. I knew it. I felt it.

When I reopened my eyes, Noah stood within arm's reach.

"I knew there was something between you two," he teased. "Ah, man, that's fucked. He's so old, and you're … well, you're so you."

"Fuck you."

"Aw! He did break up with you. Blaze, the teacher fucker. Ha!"

"Noah, I'm warning you. Stop." Heat warmed my skin. I bit my lip to contain a sudden attack on him. *Breathe.* Hands clenched. *Breathe.* I tried to regain the control I had lost. *She was my favorite teacher, and that fuck killed her.*

Noah pushed his lips out and wiggled them. "You missing his handsome lips?"

I clenched my fist harder and drove it into his face. His body dropped to the floor. I cocked my hand back, ready for another enraged swing —

"Blaze!" Mr. Robinson caught my fist before it snagged Noah. "Calm down."

I didn't want to. I turned and swung at him with my free hand, but he caught it with ease.

"You killed her!" I screamed. "What did you do?"

He pivoted and swung me into the lockers, both hands pinning my wrists down. He freed one of my hands and cupped my mouth. "I didn't do anything. I told you to keep everything a secret. The others must have found out. Your past is a secret for a reason. Even hidden from you. Now stop this." He released me, and I remained against the lockers, but I let my hands drop to my sides.

I breathed heavily through my nose. "Will you tell me everything I want to know?"

"Everything." He stared down at Noah. "You knocked him out cold. Was the next one to —" He glanced at me and whispered through a grin, "to kill him?"

I turned from Mr. Robinson and headed back to class.

"Sorry, Blaze. I'm still a teacher here and have to do my job. He's out cold. I have to follow protocol."

I stopped and glared at him. "Fine. I will be suspended or expelled, so then there would be no point for you to be a teacher here," I said as I continued to make my way to class, and he didn't stop me.

Moments after I found my seat back in class, Noah strolled in with a skip in his step. The swollen cheek I had given him was gone, as if I'd never hit him. My knuckles still stung, so I didn't imagine hitting him. He found his seat and class resumed.

What would happen to Hope if I told her? Would "the others" kill her, too? I gasped. There was a slight chance that they would. I couldn't tell her, as much as it pained to keep a secret from Hope; I had to.

Just before lunch, there was an announcement over the intercom. A few students had put together a memorial in the gym, and everyone was welcome to come in and participate. I had to go. It was the least I could do for her, since I drew the picture that murdered her.

Hope stood by the lockers and waited for me. Her eyes were wet from tears that remained suppressed. Her arms were wrapped around her torso, her back pressed into the front of my locker. She heard the announcement and wanted to go, too.

"The Celebration of Life." I am positive that's what they called it over the intercom. My body still felt hot as if my blood was sucked out and replaced by lava from the anger toward whomever had wronged Mrs. Hritz. I was glad that Hope wanted to go with me. I needed someone there. We placed our things in my locker and walked to the gym together.

The packed gymnasium made it difficult to see the colorful, artsy decorations that hung over the cream walls. A small table held white roses and a large black book opened to a page filled with signatures, stories, and hand-drawn pictures. I signed the guestbook, with a happy memory for her family to see.

"Here you are," Mr. Robinson said as he reached down and took the pen from me. "Hmm …" He tapped the pen on his bottom lip, then signed his name and dropped the pen. "Now that's done. Come with me." He headed for the exit. Hope and I followed. "Hope, I need to speak to Blaze about private matters. You're not invited."

Hope grabbed my sleeve and whispered in my ear, "Is he for real? I'm coming, too."

"Sorry, Hope." I patted her hand. She released my sleeve and watched as I walked away. I glanced back, my heart broken. I left her behind. This hurt her in the worst way possible. My eyes fell to a picture of Mrs. Hritz inside a sculpted clay frame. I couldn't have Hope killed, too.

Hidden and alone in the chemistry room, Mr. Robinson sat in his chair with his arms crossed over his chest. I sat on one of the tabletops nearby. Questions buzzed in my head and I didn't know which to choose. I bit my cheek as an avalanche of possibilities swept through my mind. *What does he want?* I knew nothing about myself: where I came from, what my family was like, nothing. A huge black hole tormented my mind.

"Where would you like to start?" he asked. "Oh, question — have you told the girl about anything that has happened so far?"

My mouth went dry. "No, nothing. She saw you give me the envelope but knows nothing beyond that." The truth, but I doubted he'd believe me. "She's asked and I haven't even hinted. We really haven't had a chance to talk."

"Good." His eyes iced over. "Did you bring it with you?"

I pulled the wrapped book out of my bag without hesitation and cradled it tight. "What connection do I have with this book?"

He reached out his hand. "Here. Hand it to me." I hesitated. The idea of it being in another person's hands sickened my stomach, acid stung the back of my tongue. "I'm here to guide you," he said warmly. "Let me show you." He rose and placed both hands on my shoulders. His eyes warmed as if he told the truth.

I sighed and handed the book over to him, every ounce of me screamed not to.

He ran his fingers over the moon while he sat back in his chair. His eyes darted up to me. "It was time. I'm glad I gave this to you when I did. This new mark that you added connects you fully to the magic within its pages."

His finger slid over the bound book. My heart stopped as his finger slid through the leather strap. I bit my tongue. I wanted to rip the book away from his wicked fingers and run straight to the safety of Hope. *If I did, would he kill her?* I wasn't willing to find out. So I let it be.

"Have you opened it?" he asked as his fingers glided over the cover. They slid smooth over the indentations and stone.

"No, I haven't. I've been too afraid to," I lied.

"Hmm." His lower eyelid twitched once; the rest of him stayed composed.

He then held out the book and gave it back. I wrapped myself around it. A surge of electricity pulsed over me that caused my whole body to relax. I touched the rough leather, traced the man and his broad sword. The spirit that dwelled within rejoiced as we reconnected.

"You feel it, don't you?"

"Feel what?"

"The bond that you have with the book. You lit up as soon as you touched it. Your soul is bound to the book in a way that only your mother would have been able to tell you about. Your family is gone now." His voice shifted from matter-of-fact to a low mumble. "All but one —"

The school bell rang, blocking out the rest of what he said.

"Wait! They told me I had no family left after the fire." My eyes widened, my heart raced. I had family, blood-related family? "Where? Who? Please, you have to tell me."

"Your brother sent me to collect you after your memories started to awaken. He's waiting for you. He misses you a lot, and now that you're old enough to handle what will awaken, you can come home. Back to him. He loves you and misses you, Blaze. The book is a gift —" He lifted his head toward the door. Noisy students collected at the door, waiting to go into class.

"Let's talk about this later." He eyed the chemistry storage room door. "Go in there and leave through the back door into the hall when the second bell rings. We don't need any more of those nasty rumors." He grinned. I hid the book in my backpack and slipped out of the room.

I skipped chemistry that day. My mind tried to wrap around the idea that I had a brother. And he wanted to meet me. *But why wait all these years to contact me?* I pushed through the side doors and followed the outside trail to the parking lot. *He could have, at least, let me know he was alive … a brother. I have a brother.* I lifted my head and gazed at the white clouds as they drifted by. I wondered, *What's he like? Maybe he's just as messed up as I am.*

I peeked at my car. Hope was leaning up against the hood. Her eyes were cast down; the corners of her lips met the bottom of her jawline.

"Hey, Hope," I said once I was close enough for her to hear me.

She stared at me for a moment before her eyes narrowed and darted away. She stomped her foot as she moved to her side of the car. Silent.

"I'm sorry. There's loads of things that I would like to say, but I can't. I wish I could, but I can't."

"What happened to the art teacher?"

I looked around to make sure no one listened. My gaze dug into hers as I tried to tell her, *Not here, not now.* "That was really tragic." I tried to sound like I knew something but couldn't say at that moment.

"Yes. Hey! Can we drive and listen to some music? I need to clear my mind." Her eyes started to water. I nodded, then unlocked the car. "She was a really great teacher. She was in the library all the time looking at all types of religious books."

I opened the car and hopped in, tossing my bag into the back. We buckled up and cranked up the tunes. I turned to the open road and drove away from our little town of Flathill Creek.

There was no car or person in sight, just us and the road. I kept to the speed limit since I had nowhere to be. Hope cracked the window open and pressed her face into the breeze. I reached back to pull my bag up front and then withdrew my hand. *What if they killed Hope, too? No, she needed to know. There was one person in the whole world I trusted, and it was her. No matter how deep my troubles, she always willingly helped. Plus, she'd be pissed if she ever found out.*

I drove down several random, back-country roads before I pulled over beside an empty canola field and turned off the car. I filled her in with all I knew. Mr. Robinson. The art teacher. The book. How I had a living brother. My eyes darted around the empty fields as I spoke. I expected some freak to take Hope away.

"A brother?" Hope gasped. "All this time? You've had a brother this whole time?"

"I don't know, really. I have this gut feeling not to trust him. He hasn't done anything to harm me yet, but what if he needs me alive?"

"Don't be silly." Hope waved her hand. "Family is family. Family looks out for one another. Mr. Robinson did say you needed to be old enough to handle whatever it is you need to do, right?"

I sighed.

"Can I see it?" She peered into the backseat.

I looked away as I nodded. The zip of the bag made me shutter. I could almost hear the pounding of Hope's heart as her curious eyes gobbled up her first sight of the strange book.

"Wow, Blaze! This is really awesome!"

I glanced over. I wanted to rip it from her hands and hide. Instead I bit my tongue hard and watched her feel the smooth cover and stroke the rugged pages. Her finger slid through the strap.

"Hope," I whispered, "tell me exactly what you see."

"Huh? I see a book."

"What's on the book. Tell me in full detail."

"It's brown. Yellowish pages. Very aged and rough. Dirty, too." Her finger touched the mark I'd made. "This crescent moon." She turned it over a few times. "Yeah, that's it."

"You don't see this?" I pointed to the man wielding the sword.

"Brown leather. A black outline of a crescent moon."

I shook my head. "What about the strap?"

"Nope." She placed her hands on the front and back. She readied her thumbs to peel it open. I kept quiet, not sure what to expect. Her face scrunched. "Are they glued?" She pulled harder.

Violent blue light beamed from the pages. The book refused her entry. I wanted to yell "stop," but the words stuck in my throat. I reached over and pulled the book from her hands.

"Are you okay?" She placed her hand on my shoulder as I fought to breathe.

"I don't think that's how we will open it." I rested my head on the steering wheel and turned my head to her. My hair fell over my shoulder and bared the right side of my neck.

"Blaze?" She poked my neck, then withdrew her finger to her lip. "It's hot."

"What's hot?"

"The tattoo on your neck. It's like the one on the book."

I lifted my hand and placed it where she poked me. *Hot, burning hot.* I adjusted my rearview mirror. Behind my ear, a crescent moon was tattooed in black. *My mark.*

"My mom's going to freak." I laughed. My eyes drifted to the book. My finger traced the outer rim of the strap. "It needs a key … right here. Oval hole the size of a fingernail."

My stomach growled. I had forgotten to eat lunch, and it wasn't pleased. I placed the book back into my bag and turned on the car. "I didn't say anything to you. You know nothing." Hope nodded, her mind racing with possibilities.

As we drove, Hope watched the scenery blur by. When we entered town, she broke the silence. "Can I stay over at your place tonight? We can watch some happy movies and eat ice cream." She eyed the school go by, and then glanced at me. "Where we going?"

"Call your mom. Tell her what happened and that you'll be at my place."

* * *

After Hope and I ate supper and helped my mom with dishes, we slunk down into the basement for some quiet movie time. Hope picked out a funny chick flick and set up the system.

Once the sound filled the room, she peeked around in search of something that might be out of place. "Looks like I'm okay so far," she whispered joyfully. "While you did dishes, I wrote everything down in this book. And now to hide it." She walked over to the old wooden table that was used for folding laundry. She bent to the floor and rolled onto her back. "We will hide it in here," she said and opened the compartment we had found years ago. A loose board, when pushed, popped right up. We hid toys we didn't want Amy to find or notes from boys. It was our secret spot that no one knew about. Hope rested the coiled notebook inside. "No one will ever know about it." She hopped to her feet and jumped back into her spot on the couch. "Now while I watch the movie, you think about your key." Her eyes drifted to the television and watched the movie.

I propped my head on the arm of the couch and curled into a comfy ball. The cheery instrumental soundtrack of the movie distracted me, the flash of images kept my eyes busy. I closed them to concentrate. *Key. A key from my past.*

The world went black. I recalled the tune from the nightmare, the lullaby. At first I struggled to put all the pieces together in the right order, then it became whole ...

Snug and warm under a thick, fuzzy blanket. Pink ballerinas danced around the top of purple painted walls. Outside the door, I could hear the lullaby being hummed down the hall. The voice sounded young and exuberant. Bare feet tapped against the hardwood in rhythm to the song.

"Come play with me," the girl child called, then continued the hum.

I peeled off the blanket. "Who are you?" I asked in a childish tone.

She continued to hum. Her feet hit the floor as if she were dancing. "Let's play hide and seek. I count. One. Two." A silhouette peered in through the open crack. "If you just sit there, the game won't be much fun." She vanished, but her counting continued as she made her way down the stairs. "Three. Four."

I jumped out of the bed and placed my hand on the door knob. My hand appeared tiny, childlike, or the door too large. I peered into the hall. To the right, there was another door, cracked open. I could hear the low rumbles of a man's snore. My body seemed to act out on its own, or it seemed driven by a powerful curiosity. I tried not to wake him and tiptoed down the stairs.

"Five. Six. Seven."

I turned to the right and looked straight ahead. A couch, love seat, and large, comfy, armchair surrounded a low glass table. Black empty frames hung neatly on the walls. The rest of the details were fuzzy and clouded.

The girl's voice came from around the corner. "Eight. Nine."

I darted between the window and back of the couch. Just in time.

"Ten. Ready or not, here I come."

The temperature in the room skyrocketed. I peeked out from behind the couch. Fire! The picture frames, the china cabinet with an old tea set in the adjoining room, lamps, carpet, walls — all in flames.

I scurried out from behind the couch and into the hall. I looked toward where the girl counted. A white sundress clothed a faceless girl of flames. She floated above the charred hardwood floor. She raised her finger and shook it at me. "That's not fair. You didn't let me find you," she said and laughed. Her hands cupped together, and she pulled them tight to her chest. A silver heart-shaped locket dangled at her waist. She continued her hum as the world around me was devoured by flames.

My body shook, and a voice repeated my name in my head …

I peeled open my eyes as Hope stood there, shaking me. "Blaze, wake up!"

"I'm up. I'm up." I swatted at her with my hand.

"Good! It's almost time to leave for school." She twirled and danced into my room.

"School?" I yawned.

"Yep. You slept away the movie, through the whole night, even the conversation with your mom and I talking about if we would attend classes today, and even slept through the answer. 'Blaze, if you want to go to school, stay quiet ...' No reply. Wow! Blaze actually wants to go to school! I think we better then." She laughed and came out of the room with a brush in her hand. "Best part? I'm still alive. Yay!"

"We could have taken another day off, you know." I rubbed my face in my hands. Even though I had just slept the entire night away, I was exhausted. I rubbed my eyes. The fiery picture of the little faceless girl flashed into my mind. Her skin of flames. Her white frilled sundress that shimmered in the red fiery glow. What she had around her neck ... I bolted off my seat and into my bedroom, pulled away my dresser and revealed the foot hole I left when my sister pissed me off. I reached in and curled my fingers around the forgotten treasure. A wooden handcrafted box with a hidden secret.

Hope gawked over my shoulder. "What's that?"

"Dad made it for me. It's special for what is hidden inside. He made it so I would never lose this treasure or break it. The chain was too long and slipped right over my shoulders as a child." I cracked open the lid and dumped out the little worthless trinkets I had collected as a child: rocks, coins, elastics, photos. "See? It's under here." I knocked against one side and caused the other to raise. I pulled off the tiny plank, and there in the hidden compartment, the sliver heart-shaped locket the child wore in my dream.

"Do you think that's the key?"

"I hope so."

Chapter Five

Hope and I were unable to test out the locket with the book. Late, we rushed out of the house. On the drive to school, I rubbed the locket between my thumb and index finger. It dangled past my chest. The thin chain felt sturdy and strong, though I still feared that I may snap it if I pulled too hard.

Hope said nothing while her mind buzzed with ideas. A few she giggled at, others she gasped. A few of the gasps startled me and I swerved. She reached up to the handle above her head and glared at me. Then her eyes wondered and caught a glimpse of the locket grasped tight within my fingers. Her creative mind would again distract her. She turned to the window and grinned.

I parked at the school just in time for the bell. Quick, but not running, we rushed off to our first class. The locket bounced against my skin. *If I opened the book ... what would I find? What if it isn't the key?* I gasped, "What will happen?" My feet stopped in the empty hall. Fast footsteps echoed from around the corner. My heart skipped. The tear in my chest throbbed as if Hope tried to rip open the book again.

Hope noticed my sudden halt. "What's wrong?"

"If it doesn't work and it rejects the locket … what will happen to us?" I whispered as if the air were going to betray me and tell the others.

Hope stepped closer. "It will be okay." She placed her hand on my shoulder. "I'm here for you, no matter what. I'll venture into Hell, if I must."

"I know. And I might, one day, need you to. After all that has happened to me over my lifetime, I might be riddled with sin."

"Come on, you emo." She pushed me ahead of her. "Get to class before you get into trouble and we have to stay another year."

English class sounded great. "Everyone pull out your novel-study and read." For the full forty-five minutes, we were to read the next three chapters. After that, we could finish our other homework that she knew no one had done the night before.

Twenty minutes into class, Mrs. Callahan got called out. Seconds after she left the room, the class was a buzz about yesterday's news. My foot bounced, knocking against my bag a few times, but I hadn't noticed. Noah peered over my shoulder. He pounced and snatched the book out of my bag and stood before the class with a full-toothed grin.

"Well, well. What do we have here? Blaze Nemasa's diary, I presume?" His eyebrow raised along with my fiery rage. The other students lost interest once they heard my name.

His finger slid along the cover and under. The leather cover lifted from the pages and revealed the first page. I opened my mouth to ask for it back, then closed it. My body leaned forward, breath stilled in my lungs as his eyes twitched from word to word. His brows pushed together and the corners of his cocky smile dropped, showing concern and confusion. *What did he see?* I bit my lip and swallowed. The book sapped shut on its own and dropped to the floor. Noah stood frozen. Fear. I licked my lips. I could almost taste the sweetness of it. His stunned gaze met me, and I flashed him a crooked smile.

"Noah, take your seat," Mrs. Callahan strolled into the room and scooped up the book.

I raised my hand. "Mrs. Callahan, he took that out of my bag. Please, can I have it back?"

She handed it back and continued settling the class. I glanced at Noah; his eyes were fixed on me. I waved. Served him right. His eyes — there was something off about them. They seemed glazed and red. I tilted my head. *Swollen?*

Over the extent of the class, Noah's conditions got worse and worse. I then felt guilty. The book had done something. I just knew it.

"Mrs. Callahan, I need to talk to Noah, explain to him the importance of what he just did. Could you excuse us for a moment? He seems upset about it, and I'm done with my chapters and my homework. Please?"

Confused by the request, she glanced over at Noah. To her, he looked like just another high school stoner. She sighed and nodded, "You have five minutes."

I could think of only one person who could help Noah. The thought pained me, but I had to take him to Mr. Robinson. A shiver crawled up my spine as I collected my books and backpack. When all my things were away, I dragged Noah up by his arm. He let me tow him from class as he rubbed his painful eyes.

Out in the hall, Noah leaned on the wall opposite from me. He covered his eyes with his hand as moans and whimpers escaped his lips. I grabbed his arm again to pull him down the hall. He tossed his hand and refused to move. His eyelids twitched to blink, the lids suctioned in place. A vein burst, and blood seeped into the whites of his eyes.

"You have to come! Quick!"

"No way in hell I'm going anywhere with you!" Noah hollered.

I shrugged and placed my hand on the class door. "Fine, not like they're my eyes. If you don't want help, then I'm going back to class."

"Wait!" he said. "Fine. I'll go with you."

I guided him to the chemistry room. *If anyone could help him, it would be him. He brought me the book, so he should be able to reverse what was done,* I hoped. Noah's eyes bulged and swelled. The sight of them made my eyes ache.

"We're at the chemistry room, aren't we?" he snapped. "No way I'm letting that quack of a teacher see me. This part of a sick joke?"

I shook my head and knocked. Mr. Robinson opened the door. His eyes widened at the sight of Noah, and he swallowed a laugh. He turned to the class and instructed them to read ahead.

With a cruel quiet laugh, he exited the classroom and closed the door.

"My, my, you've been busy." He took a few steps to the adjoining lab. "Come on. This room won't be used this morning. He'll be safe in here." He unlocked the door, opened it, and then waved us in with his wicked grin.

Once inside the room, Mr. Robinson rushed over to the desk, ripped out a piece of paper from a coiled book and scribbled a few spiraled syllables I could not recognize, then taped it to the door. "Now that we have some privacy —"

"You have to help him," I demanded.

His eyes narrowed. "Why? He's mean and nasty. Let your book devour his eyes. It will give it more power." His grin widened at the pleasurable thought. "You're powerful. This will make you more so."

"What have you done to me, Blaze? What the fuck is that book?" Noah whimpered. He reached to rub his eyes.

"I wouldn't do that," Mr. Robinson warned. "It will make the magic work faster. The heat from the friction amplifies the affect. Never mind. Forget I said anything. You should try it."

I stomped my right foot forward. "If you don't help him, I will walk away from this. I won't go see this brother of mine if he isn't willing to help others. You cure him now, and I will go with you when you tell me that I am ready."

"Your brother *help* others?" He tried to hide the humor he found in those words. "Once you regain your memories, you're going to wish you had devoured this worthless chunk of meat's eyes."

I reached into my bag and pulled out the book. "Here." I handed it to him. Mr. Robinson's whole body recoiled as if I'd passed him poison. "Take it. If you're not willing to help him, then I'm out. You'll just have to explain to my brother that I refuse him."

"All right. All right. Fine." He sighed and strolled over to Noah. Mr. Robinson's fingers wrapped around Noah's throat. Noah gasped for air. "I'll help this human. But only once. The book isn't for prying eyes. Oh, and ..." his twisted grin found its way back. " ... this is really going to hurt."

He bit the tip of his finger and hissed a few quiet words into the droplet of blood on his fingertip. He raised his finger above Noah's eye, and he tipped the drop downward. Noah tried to flinch away, but the tight grip around his neck made it impossible. The drip connected with his swollen eye. Noah screamed in agony mixed with gags. My eyes drifted from Noah to Mr. Robinson. He seemed to enjoy the pain that radiated from Noah.

Mr. Robinson's hand went up again. I watched as the crimson droplet collided with the other eye. Noah cried out, the pain he felt filled the air, and rang in my ears. My tongue tingled, my heart throbbed. I tried to look away, but my eyes were fixed to his. Noah tried to blink, but the lids of his eyes refused to close. The scream echoed throughout the room. My head spun. My body tensed. Still I watched, amazed by the sight, sound, and emotions that rang throughout my body. The book in my hand seemed to vibrate with excitement as Noah went limp.

The room fell silent. Noah dropped to the floor with a thud. His eyes twitched closed as the spell the book had placed on him was lifted. He relaxed and fell into a peaceful sleep. Thin amounts of blood teared from each eye.

"Well, now that that's done —"

"You will stop the others from harming him," I stated.

Puzzled, he glared at me. "What makes you think I can?"

I crossed my arms and glared back. "A hunch, and normally they're right. If anything happens to anyone else, I will disappear and you won't be able to find me."

"I will. I have my ways. And you should hope that it's me on the hunt for you and not your brother. He won't be as kind as I am."

"So my brother ... he's a cruel man?" I asked, unsure of whether or not I wanted to meet him.

Mr. Robinson's face loosened and relaxed, his eyes brightened and lips formed a pleased grin. "It's hard to say, really. He has a lot that he needs to do, creatures to govern over, and he needs to have a hard-as-stone reputation. He is powerful and respected by many. If his followers heard he had a soft side ... well, they might take advantage of it." His eyes drifted to me as he spoke of my brother. I could see he admired my brother and would do anything my brother asked without question. "He has you, though. You're the only family he has left. And now you're at an age that you can fully grasp why he had to give you up and let another family raise you."

I slouched forward and let my elbows drop onto my knees. I thought long and hard about what he was asking me to do.

"If I do go, I have one request. Take into consideration that, if you say no, my brother will have to be the one to come and collect me." I let my gaze drift from him to the empty tables and chairs. *Leave? I could do that.* "I want Hope to come with me. And there has to be a way she can get home whenever she wants."

Mr. Robinson's face scrunched as if he smelled something foul. He nodded. "If that is what will make you come with me, then she can come. The return will have to be taken up with your brother."

"We will give her the option to go with us and meet my brother or to stay here and wait for my return. These 'others' you speak of must not harm her."

Mr. Robinson left the room to go retrieve Hope. I stayed with Noah in case he woke up, and if he did, I had no idea what I would tell him. As I thought, Noah started to groan. I rushed over and placed my hand on his side. His face gained color as his eyes moved under his closed lids.

"Noah," I asked in a panic, "are you okay?"

Groggy, he placed his hand over his eyes. "What happened?" His eyes opened. They appeared normal white, brown, and black, as if it had never happened. The blood seemed to have absorbed into his skin, not a trace left. "Blaze? Why are we in the lab?"

"I walked by and saw you passed out on the floor," I lied. "While I was coming over, you woke up. How do you feel? Should I get a teacher?"

"No, I'll be okay." He sat up and peered around the room. "I should get to class. Don't tell anyone what happened, 'kay? I don't want to be known as the fainter."

"Sure thing."

He stumbled to his feet and disappeared out of the room without hesitation. My eyes followed him until he vanished into the hall. Once I shut the door, everything set in. *I have a brother, a brother who kept a secret from me all these years. What is so important that he had to keep me with another family?* I fell into the computer chair at the teacher's desk, the book firm in my hand.

I held it up. My eyes caught the man wielding the sword. I wanted to know him. I traced the indentation with my finger. The moon behind added to his enchantment.

Hope barrelled through the door. "Blaze!" she yelled into the room. "Where are —" She spotted me in the corner. "He said you needed to see me. That it was urgent. Are you okay? What happened?"

I placed the book in my lap with a smile. "Nothing really happened. Um …" I glanced at Mr. Robinson as he strolled in behind her. "You explain."

He shut the door, then explained what I needed to do in vague detail. Hope nodded at each word. His monotone description and rotation of his wrist made his explanation dull, and yet she absorbed everything. He ended by asking if she would like to tag along. Her blue eyes blinked, her hands balled as she pivoted on her heels and wrapped me up in her arms.

"And one other thing," he turned to speak to me, "the others will be joining us soon. They will not like this one bit."

The others, the ones that killed an innocent person because I drew a picture. Wicked beasts. "They will be traveling with us? I really don't want to meet them."

"They follow orders."

"My brother's orders?"

"Yes. It had to be done to keep the realm unknowing. All will be explained when we arrive. Don't judge them for obeying their superior."

"I won't judge them. I'll judge their superior."

He laughed and ran his fingers through his hair. Heat flooded my face. Whatever they knew and whatever they had to offer me, I didn't want any part of it. Nothing at all.

The lab door opened, and a woman walked in dressed in a form-fitted black dress, followed by a shaggy-haired man a few years older then me. They both nodded at Mr. Robinson, then closed the door. The woman's fiery eyes met mine, as a chill creeped up my spine.

"Robin." Her tempered voice ignited the room. "We should have left days ago with her. Even if she is unable to open the book, the master is waiting." Her eyes shifted to Mr. Robinson.

"Robin?" Hope asked what I thought.

"Right." He turned to Hope. "My name is Robin. Mr. Robinson was a name created to get myself into the school as a teacher." He glanced at me and raised his hand to the others.

"This woman here is Krista. She is scary most of the time, though she means well."

Krista stepped closer to me. Her eyes scanned me, then did the same to Hope. Her rose-colored lips pressed into a firm line, her eyebrows bunched in the middle. "What is the *girl* doing here? We are only to bring Nemasa. Not some —" She bit her tongue. "You made a deal that you couldn't keep, didn't you?"

"She refused to come otherwise. And if she is anything like her brother, stubbornness is in the blood. She will refuse us with every ounce of energy she has. A deal's a deal. I can't back out now."

The two argued on. I ignored them by turning my attention to Hope. My mind was made up. If she couldn't come, then I wouldn't go. If Hope didn't want to go, I'd stay. Hope held on to her answer as she observed the actions of everyone in the room. Her eyes were on the man that hid in Krista's shadow. He took no notice of her, and stared at me.

Hope scooted onto the desk behind her and raised her hand. "Um," she said, even though no one seemed to notice her. "I haven't even given my answer," she announced.

The two argued on.

I cared, even if they didn't. "What's your answer, Hope? It's up to you. I don't care what answer you give. My family is here now, and I don't like the way these people treat those around me. If you say we stay, we stay. I won't argue."

The room fell quiet again. All eyes shifted to us.

C. B. Dixon

"Well," she began, "I don't like them either. It would be nice to get some insight on your past, though. And I think an adventure is what everyone needs once in a while." I knew her answer; it was written on her face. I could see the sparkle in her eye. "I choose to go."

Robin grinned and Krista grunted. The hidden man stood with a face of stone. His eyes locked onto mine. I didn't know what to think of him. I reached up to fidget with my locket. Krista strolled across the room to Robin, the clicks from her stilettos echoed off the concrete walls. She raised her hand to cover her lips and whispered into his ear. He nodded and whispered back.

Krista exhaled heavily through her nose. "Fine! Have it your way. Remember I played no part in bringing that *thing*. The law is on your shoulders, you —"

"I know the law well and have a full understanding of the cost. The master will hear from me later. Right now, we need to go."

"Has she found a way into the book?" Her eyes narrowed and searched me for an answer. The chill from my spine spread over my body, crawled, itched.

The locket tapped against my skin as I shuttered. "I think, *think*, I know how to open the book."

I lifted the locket over my head. I carried it and the book over to Hope. Her goofy smile reached her sky blue eyes. "Ready?" I asked.

She placed her hand on my shoulder. "*Duh.* Although there is one other question I have to ask." She eyes found the third member of their party. "Who's he?"

"We had hoped that, if he was here, Blaze's memories would come back to her." His eyes shifted between the two of us. "Do you recognize him?" I shook my head, confused. The man stepped into the light. His dark, untidy hair lay about the top of his head. His eyes remained in a relaxed squint that hid the color. I shook my head again. "Maybe his name may help. This is Quade."

Quade ... the name struck a note. *I've heard that name before,* I thought. I stepped toward him, but nothing about that man seemed familiar. I didn't know him. I did, however, know the name.

"Come on, Blaze!" Hope tugged my sleeve. "Open it."

I grabbed hold of the silver, heart-shaped locket. I took a huge breath in as I guided the locket to the keyhole. Hope bit her lip, and her grip on my sleeve tightened. It took no pressure at all to sink the locket into the slot.

I turned the silver key.

Chapter Six

The floor beneath our feet cracked. *Snap!* Hope and I plummeted down into blackness with large chunks of the school's flooring. She clung to my sleeve with both hands; her eyes strained to see into the darkness that swallowed us. Our bodies were then illuminated with a dim pulse of white light. Encased around us was the nightmarish void I had visited before but only in my dreams. Empty and cold. This time, no monsters reached for me. My ears twitched, the now familiar lullaby hummed. Hope remained unaffected by the sound. Her head pivoted left and right, unable to see anything.

Closer and closer the singer came, lit like a star. She danced to the slow, calm tempo, her face without feature. Her dress twirled at her knees as she spun and bent and skipped.

"Why are you afraid?" the child asked as she twirled.

"I'm not afraid," I answered, mesmerized.

Her feet stilled and her body twisted to me. "You are. You're very scared. Terrified even."

Large droplets of blood seeped down from above. The void heated. The child floated up to meet me face-to-face. Her blank face showed no emotion, though I could feel her anger vibrate through the air around us, as if the void were a part of her.

"Play with me. Come. I will show you." She raised her palm up to me. "Come dance in madness with me."

"Blaze!" Hope called out.

I looked to my arm. Hope was no longer there. I hadn't felt it when she had let go.

"Come," the girl coaxed, her voice giggled once.

"Blaze," Hope yelled from behind me.

I spun around, ignoring the child's request. "Where are you?"

* * *

My lungs burned with each gasp of hot air. My eyes sprung open. A blinding orange light caused me to blink several times. Once adjusted, my eyes caught the movement of the fiery sky. Orange, red, and yellow swirled together, clashed, and erupted. Blasts of flame rained down partway, then barrelled back up.

"You're finally awake," Hope shoved at my shoulder, her face beaded with sweat.

I wiped away the few droplets of sweat I had with my sleeve. The pain in my lungs lessened with every breath; the once-scorching heat cooled to an almost chill. I peered at Hope. Beads of sweat dripped down her face, hair clung to her temple. I reached up to wipe my face again, but it was dry.

"Where are we?" I let my eyes fall from the lava sky to the dead trees that towered over the land. No bird or leaf clung to the barren, twisted branches. No moss or lichen climbed the rough black bark. I pressed my hand into the sand to prop myself up. The book, opened, slid to my lap.

"I don't know. The floor vanished. Then, *zap!* I woke up here. You've been out for a while." She sat back and pressed her hands into the golden sand.

"The others?" I asked, staring at the man on the cover. *Who is he?* I curled my arms around the book. *I must meet him. I have to.* My finger slid down the smooth spine. "Find me," I whispered to the image, loud enough that only I could hear.

"Here," a voice answered from behind a tree. Quade then moved into view dressed in a dark brown cloak. The hood hung over his face covering his eyes. His stride toward us seemed careful, as if any sudden movement might cause us to bolt the other way. I sprung to my feet and eyed him cautiously. My body itched to run the other way. "Come, Robin and Krista went to alert your brother of our arrival. We will be granted safe passage through the Keep and into the castle. We need to go now." He walked forward with his hand held out to me. "Please, we should hurry. The woods are not safe."

Hope rose to her feet, and dusted the sand off. "Okay, okay. Well, we best go. Who knows what could be lurking around in a place like this? Monsters of multiple shapes and sizes?" She smiled at me.

I nodded. *We did choose to do this with them, so best follow their lead and not get lost in this desolate wasteland.* I sighed and stepped toward Quade; the book pulsed in my hand. My eyes darted down. *A warning? Or —*

"Come." He quickened his feet to us. "Hope is right. There are things that creep and won't hesitate to have us for a midday snack. We are in danger here. The safest place is in the castle. He waits for you there."

I lifted my foot to move forward, and the book pulsed again. I lifted the book, flipping it over and over in my hands. There had to be something wrong with it. My mouth opened to ask — a hooded figure dropped down from the trees and ran in between Quade and me. The stranger turned its back to me and growled at Quade. My mouth dried. A broad sword peeked out from underneath his long dark gray cloak.

Quade drew his sword. "I knew you'd come, traitor." He sprinted forward and swung at the newcomer. The stranger blocked and countered with a knee to Quade's side. Quade let out a grunt and swung again. The clash of steel vibrated in my ears. The stranger hurled his sword through the air, but Quade rolled to the side just in time to escape the blade.

Hope grabbed my sleeve and pulled me down to her. "I think we should make a run for it." She nudged her head to the trees behind us.

My eyes were fixated on the stranger. The book pulsed again. Tingled. A soft electrical current ticked my nerves. I tightened my fingers around the spine. Quade raised his thick blade and swung at his opponent. The stranger stepped to the left while his eyes remained on me as the sword dug into the sand next to his boots. Before I registered his movements, the stranger sprinted toward us, slid his fingers into the book and flung it open. He flashed a full-fanged smile back at Quade, pressed his hand onto the first page and whispered a word I could not hear.

The world blurred and shifted. The trees stretched into solid stone walls. The sky darkened to gray-black, and the hot air cooled, giving me shivers. Once fine sand turned to ridged solid rock. A crack of fire filled the silent air.

The stranger released the book and whipped around, stomping off with a grunt. Crates and pails filled the tiny space he entered. We were in a cave with arched walls of stone and a floor that matched. To the far left of me, a pile of furs had been laid out to form a bed. A ladle hung from a barrel filled with water. To the right, a wooden couch and chair covered in a blanket of brown fur encircled a small fire. I glanced to the ceiling. Smoke from the fire rose straight up and disappeared through a ring of orange light embedded into the stone above.

I pulled Hope to the fire and found a seat. My eyes caught the stranger. He cursed as he busied himself in the kitchen area.

Hope leaned in and whispered, "Who do you think that is?"

I shook my head. Then I remembered the book was unlocked. My eyes dropped down. The flap hung and the chain gathered on my leg. I flipped to the first page, half-expecting the world around me to vanish and end up back in the lab at school.

The page showed no symbols or pictures, no inscriptions, markings, nothing — it was blank. I flipped and flipped, each page as blank as the last.

I didn't notice that the stranger stood inches away, hunched over, observing me. "Give me that." His annoyed voice startled me. "You'll break it." He went to snatch it from my hands, so I drew it to my chest.

"I will not," I barked. "I just figured out how to open it. I'm figuring it out fine. Back off."

"No, you're not," he said in an annoyed yet playful tone. "Give it here." He yanked it from my hands, and thumbed through the pages, his eyes twitching as if they read passages. I didn't feel the desire to take the book from him, or the pain that festered deep inside my chest when it wasn't in my grasp. I had questions, but the words wouldn't, couldn't be said.

I glanced onto the page he could apparently read, and there on the page were black symbols in neat, diagonal, tiny rows. I couldn't make them out, but he could. He glanced at me with a smirk.

"You can read that?"

The stranger snapped the book closed. "You're hopeless." He rolled his eyes.

"No, she's not," Hope snickered from the chair behind him. "Uh, hello? Hope is right here …" She raised her hand, palm up, a little higher than her shoulder.

"I don't know why I let you come. I have never let a human into my home before." The hood from his cloak cast a shadow that hid the color of his eyes.

He tucked the book into his cloak. The distance between me and the book seemed to have no effect on me. I watched the flames lick the logs and wondered why that was. When the stranger returned, he carried two pots, one large, one small. He hooked them each to a cast iron hook and swung them over the fire. He then sat down on the couch beside me and crossed his arms.

We all sat mesmerized by the flicker of the fire. My eyes grew heavy. *No. I can't sleep here.* Through slit eyes, I glanced at the stranger. His hard-pressed eyes were fixated to the flames. I wanted to reach over and uncover his face. Something about him seemed natural, like he was always there, even though I'd never met him before.

He peeked over. "What?"

I let my eyes return to the fire. I wanted to ask if I had met him before but couldn't find my voice. I spotted Hope, her eyes shifting between the stranger and me. Her teeth gnawed on her lower lip as she created possibilities of what was unfolding before her.

"Who are you?" I asked curiously. "You didn't give us a name."

He rose to his feet and stormed back into the kitchen. He grabbed a large spoon then returned to the fire. He stirred the pots without a glance up as steam lifting into the air with a wonderful smell of meaty stew. Hope shot a worried look my way. I answered with a shrug.

"Food is almost ready. Until then, don't talk," he demanded.

I should have felt trapped because that man had kidnapped us, and yet I felt safe. Hope played with her fingers. I doubted she shared in my sense of security. After a few minutes of silence, the stranger lifted the lid from the large pot. The seasoned smell filled the room. He scooped out two bowls, jabbed a fork into the bowl, and handed it to me. He rested the other bowl down by his legs and closed the pot. The small pot had a bland smell, if any, and a thin soup of light brown liquid.

"This is all I have that you are able to eat. I'll have to go out later and get more things for you," he said as he handed the bowl to Hope.

She moistened her lips with a dry tongue. She nodded her thanks and sunk into her seat. Hope's finger pinched the spoon, giving the thin brown gravy a stir.

The stranger rose with his meal and returned to his spot on the couch. "Have you tried it?" He gestured to my bowl with his hand.

I shook my head. The meal, a rich blend of spices, tingled my tongue. I could taste the sweetness without raising the fork. There were chunks of meat coated in a juicy gravy. "It looks really good." Saliva filled my mouth. I stabbed a chunk and took a nervous bite. The taste sent my head into a spin — *delicious*. I had never tasted anything so flavorful. The tender meat melted in my mouth, so I hardly had to chew. The sweet and smoky sauce brought out the spices that had been rubbed into the meat. Tender meat. No carrots, onion, or potato. My taste buds danced on my tongue.

Hope didn't look as pleased with her meal. Her tongue swished around to try and find any taste. "What is this? Are you sure it's edible?" She slopped the liquid around with her fork. "He's trying to kill us. I know it. This is poison."

"It's not poison. If I wanted to kill you, I wouldn't waste food."

"Foods in this realm isn't meant for your kind. If I gave you this, you'd puke, maybe even become deathly ill." He thought for a moment, pushing his bowl forward. "Want to try? I don't actually know the details. We can experiment." Hope pulled herself back, disgusted.

I had eaten my serving before they were finished their conversation. "That was really, really, good." I put the bowl down on my lap.

"I'm glad that you enjoyed it. Wasn't my best cooking, but it seems to have done the trick. Would you like another?"

"Please," I said and handed my bowl to him. He kept his eyes cast down as he reached for the bowl. I move forward to sneak a peek at his face. He noticed and hid further into the hood.

"How come she can eat it?" Hope questioned as she tolerated her last bite.

His fingertips touched the bowl, and his head twitched to the side. He spun and stood, sword drawn, ready to attack at any moment. The bare wall rippled. A woman emerged from the stone. Her steps were taken with care and grace. She stood tall and straight, hands folded together at her hips. Long black hair tickled the back of her knees.

"The Keep is in chaos. I know you have something to do with it." Her enraged words flowed from her lips. "What have you done now to upset the king? The castle has been emptied into the streets. Shacks ripped apart. They are looking for someone, and my instincts tell me you know why."

He sheathed his blade and rushed to the wall. "Were you followed?" He ran his fingertips over the stone. "It was stupid of you to come. You could wreck everything," the stranger barked at the sturdy woman.

"I would not be foolish enough to let myself be followed. You, on the other hand, have unregistered humans in your home." The woman turned to study Hope and me. "How will you explain being caught with them?"

"I don't plan on being caught."

Her skin seemed alive in the fire's light. The teal dress she wore fit her perfectly. The color enhanced her dark blue eyes. Above her eyes … *horns*. My jaw dropped as my eyes took a second look. Her horns perturbed out of her head and twisted up to her hair line.

The stranger went to her and whispered in her pointed ear. I leaned forward to hear but was unable to understand what they were saying. The woman nodded; her eyes pierced mine. My stomach jumped. Shivers vibrated up my spine. Her eyes told me she knew me.

"I wonder who she is?" Hope asked, her eyes mesmerized by the woman's beauty. "A girlfriend maybe?"

My jaw clenched. My glare fixed itself to the fire.

The woman stepped toward me and bowed her head. "My name is Sati, milady, and I will help you in whichever way you please."

My eyes shifted to the stranger. He read the puzzled expression on my face and placed his hand on Sati's back. "Her memories are still out of reach. She has no idea who she was."

She lifted her head and straightened her back. "Have you not made her remember?"

"And why would I do that?" the stranger barked. "Those memories are locked for a reason. If she does't want to remember, why should I force her?" He crossed his arms tightly around his chest. The loose robe wrinkled as he turned his back to her.

"My memories? What have you been keeping from me? You both know something. What am I doing here?" I had risen to my feet as I yelled, my hands flying through the air. "First Robin goes on about a brother that wants to see me when, in fact, I have no living family. Then he gives me that book. It transports us here." My face is heated; my fists are balled. "Now you both whisper and speak of my memories like Robin and Krista did before we left." I took a breath and glared at the stranger's hidden eyes. "And you, you're the only one able to open that book you've hidden from me. Robin stepped away from it like he would be harmed. You seem to know all its secrets. Why? Who are you?"

"You haven't told her?" Sati turned from me to him. "Why?"

The stranger's lips tightened. He wanted to tell me, and, in the same way, wanted to let me figure out things for myself. His heel pressed hard into the stone ground, his body twisted to the wall. He lifted his foot up and disappeared into the stone.

"Don't mind him," Sati said in a kind tone. "It is just as hard for him right now as it is for you."

"Oh?"

Sati glided over the ground and folded her hands loosely in her lap. "Milady, it has been many years since you were sent to the Earthly Realm for protection. In the days that led up to your leaving, horrible things happened. Many creatures were killed, and ..." Her eyes grew dark and distant.

Tiny reflective scales covered her skin. Her stone face seemed unaffected by the topic, but her ocean blue eyes swirled with pain. "You have time to remember all that was before your rebirth. It is okay to remain innocent to the past, I cannot blame you for not wanting to remember."

"I don't even know where I am. How can I remember a place I know I've never been to? Nothing about this seems familiar. You have the wrong person." I leaned my head back, and closed my eyes.

"There was a third with Robin and Krista, hiding behind them most of the time. Then Hope questioned who he was. They told me I should have recognized him ... I didn't know who he was, had no clue." I opened my eyes and looked into hers. "They told me his name was Quade. That name. I know I haven't heard it before, and then — I know it, don't I?"

"This place has been sealed from you. That book holds all the answers you seek. I am not capable of teaching you how to use it. I am sorry, milady. If you wish to know more about the secrets of that journal, you will need to ask him." The light of the flames flickered on her face. "I see why he didn't tell you. You have a cheery innocence that lingers in your soul. What is it like where you live?" she asked with a smile.

"Dull."

"Blaze!" Hope snapped.

"Well it is, and you know it." I breathed. "Okay, it wasn't so bad. Hope made my life there bearable after I lost my family." A smile grew on my lips. "She always toyed with the part of me that didn't fit in. I seemed to have no connection to anyone around me until she forced herself into my life. Ever since, I haven't been able to go anywhere too far without her."

Hope slid to the edge of her seat. "There was one vacation I missed, and her family had to come home early. Such trouble you were. Like a little fireball burning everything it could reach."

Interested, Sati leaned forward. "You were an outcast?" Her small smile grew, the fangs under her rose-colored lips peeked out. "Even though you were reborn to their realm, you still kept the essence of your being. The ritual that you went through had never been performed. It's a band magic only my bloodline can perform."

"And what made you use this *band* magic?"

"Milady, you will have to remember within your own time. There is one other way that you can unlock what has been sealed." She turned to the wall the stranger exited out of. "You would have to ask him how."

* * *

91

Hours passed. Hope slept soundlessly, sprawled out on the couch. Her hand hung over the edge, and the tips of her fingers teased the stone floor. I pretended to be asleep, curled under the fir across the room from the fire. Sati sat still as a statue on the wooden, fur-covered chair. The fire remained its original size, not a log had been laid on it since we arrived. *Magic, a world filled with magic.*

I worried about the stranger. He hadn't come in, not even once. Then I was confused why I thought about him in the first place. I petted the furs with my hand. *I wouldn't have chosen to sleep here.* I knew that it was the stranger's bed, but Sati insisted and Hope backed her up. *Would he be mad that I took his bed from him?*

Quiet footfalls made their way from the wall to the fire. Sati jumped to her feet and rushed over to him. In a panic, she whispered loud enough for me to hear, "… injured? How? What did you do, you foolish boy?"

He just grunted, and then a muffled wimpier of pain struck my ear. I raised my head and stared. He was hunched over, his arms pressed tight over his stomach. Blooded footprints glistened in a trail behind him. Sati's lips moved, but I could no longer hear them.

She shook her head and placed her hand over his left ribs. Hope's voice filled my head as I recalled what she said: "A girlfriend?"

A blue light lit at Sati's fingertips, then seeped into him. Quade bit his lip to keep from making any noise. His eyes closed and his head dropped on to her shoulder. My jaw clenched. The light went out and Sati stepped into him, letting him fall toward her. Her lips parted, and a whisper told him something that made him smile.

I lowered myself back down to the furs and covered my face. I couldn't watch. I closed my eyes and let my body relax. Let the room fall silent.

"Awe, baby," the girl taunted. *"Your mind is like an ocean storm. Which way will you be thrown?"* She tiptoed closer, each step hitting an invisible floor. I heard her inhale deeply. *"Smell that? Know what it is?"*

I sniffed the air. *"I don't smell anything."*

"It's envy. Can you taste it?" Her arms lifted and swooshed through the air; her sundress bounced at her knees. *"It's warmer here. Summer's coming."*

"It's not even December yet."

"I don't live by those seasons. I live in whatever your mind creates. Right now, it's spring, the new beginning. The liquid showers. The air's becoming warmer." Her head tilted back as if to catch the warmth of the sun in the darkness of the void. *"She's coming."*

I rolled onto my back, the air smelling of crisp bacon and steak. The pop and crackle of the fire scared away the idea that I may have fallen out of bed and whacked my head on my nightstand. I wasn't home. I was living out one of my nightmares.

Near the fire I could hear quiet voices chattering. I soon uncovered myself from my warm blanket and joined them. Sati and Hope faced each other, unaware of me being a few feet away. The stranger was asleep on the chair, his clothes changed. I peeked over to the place where I had seen him and Sati, and the footprints were washed away.

"You're awake," Sati's calm voice welcomed me. "When he wakes, we will be leaving. The king has set out countless search parties to find you. It won't be long till he finds you here. There is a bowl. Have something to eat," she said and pointed to the base of the fire where a small stone bowl with a stone plate on top sat nearby to keep warm.

I stepped closer to the fire and sat down on the ground. "Thank you," I nodded and reached for the bowl. "How are we to get out undetected?"

"This place has a back door. It may lead us into more trouble than going out the front, but the creatures that linger there hold a grudge toward the king and may grant us safe passage. A risk we will have to take." Sati bowed her head. "If that is the path you choose we take, milady."

"Why do you call me — never mind." I raised the fork. "I'll find out on my own." I didn't feel hungry until I had my first bite. The melty textures, the sweet juices, I gobbled it fast, ready for more.

The food seemed to make me hungrier and hungrier. The more I ate, the more I craved. I chewed a meaty chunk, savoring the juices. My fork dropped into the bowl. *More, I wanted more.*

"Blaze, are you okay?" Hope slid from the couch and put her hand on my back.

Okay? "I don't know … there's something that doesn't feel right." I slouched, defeated by uncertainty.

"Did you sleep okay? You look really tired."

I placed the bowl on the floor and licked the flavor from my lips. The taste seemed to be amplified, each spice made my tongue beg for more.

I looked up at the man asleep in the chair. His face still remained a mystery, and then he moved. The hood slipped back; his white horns turned a fiery red, his dark hair framed his pale face. I knew him. I'd seen him before. A familiar overwhelming urge surged through me.

Shocked, I turned to Sati. "His name is Quade," I whispered. "Isn't it?" He resembled the man I'd met earlier, could've been his twin. She nodded with a faint smile. When I turned back to him, his vibrant violet eyes were fixed to me. He had heard me. As much as I wanted to remember more, I couldn't.

The real Quade leaned forward to place his chin against his knuckles. "They didn't make a very good imitation of me, did they?" I raised an eyebrow at him, not sure what he meant. "There is a creature who lives in the castle named Wilder. He can shift into any creature's form as long as he's tasted the blood of the one he wishes to be."

Hope scooted her forward on her chair. "The one that looked like you was a shifter?"

"Shifter?" Quade lifted his head from his fist. "Is that what they are called in your realm?" Hope remained silent. "Wilder pretended to be me, but you knew different." His eyes locked with mine the same way Wilder had tried to do in the lab at school. Quade's gaze caught mine and held it where Wilder had failed. "Tell me, how is it that you knew he wasn't really who he said he was?"

My mouth went dry. I thought about the moment he had followed Krista into the class room. I felt angry and disgusted at the sight of him. "When Hope and I woke in the Sinful Realm and he appeared, I wanted to run away from him as fast as I could, but then, the book, the book pulsed."

"It did what?" Quade asked, shifting his weight forward.

My eyes dropped to the book that hid beneath his robe. "This Wilder told us that we should leave and coxed us to go to the castle. The book pulsed as I stepped toward him. I didn't know if it was because I was making the wrong choice, or if it was right. Then you appeared. As you fought with him Hope suggested we leave, then it did it again. Before I knew it, we were here." I lifted my gaze back up to meet Quade's. "What is the connection between me and the book? Why does it like you?"

He straightened in his chair. "You can tell that it likes me?"

"Well, yeah. When Hope held the book, it was fine, but I felt pain when she tried to open it. When Robin held the book, it made me sick, really sick, and that was just from him touching it. Then you come along and make it transport us here, and read it, and have had it on you since I've arrived." I paused to breathe. *I could feel the book's emotions, but that was impossible.* "The book has felt safe with you. Why?"

Quade ignored the question. "I have to start packing."

* * *

96

Everyone had a backpack filled with survival supplies: food, water for Hope, a pot, furs to sleep in, and a few extras. Portions were split between each bag, just in case we got separated.

"Hope," Sati said as she raised her hand. "I am going to use a spell to hide your scent. Creatures become more hostile in the lower levels."

"You're a walking treat, is what she's trying to say."

"Quade!" Sati scolded.

"What? Sugarcoating the facts won't help her cope with what's down there."

Sati's hand gripped Hope's shoulders. "We better be on the safe side. Close your eyes. It will feel warm and tingle. Should last a week." Both their eyes closed. Blue light formed over Sati's skin and absorbed into Hope. Hope's lips pulled up at the corners. She inhaled through her nose, taking in the sensation of the magic.

I tightened the shoulder straps of my bag. Quade came up behind me as he finished tightening the belt that held his sword and placed his hand on my shoulder. "Here …" He held out the book with his other hand. "Keep it on you. Make sure no one sees it. Never open it. If a creature gets it while it's unlocked, they could collapse the entire realm, maybe all of existence."

I turned to him and took the book. Strangely, I got the same safe sensation from the book as I did from him. "What is this book? Can you, at least, tell me a little bit before we go?"

"This book contains all the memories from all the rulers of the Sinful Realm, this realm. By reading it you gain the knowledge of the kings' ancestors and, for a brief time, borrow their abilities. Each creature in this world is given a soul element — one of the four elementals. Depending on the temperament of the soul, it is then given an animal or insect form. The reader of the book can borrow from one of many souls in the book and combine it with their own." His eyes narrowed. "Don't let anyone get it."

Sati walked over with a small leather side bag. "This should be just big enough for it to fit. Keep it on you at all times, and you won't have to worry."

A vision of them the night before tore through my mind. I faked a smile and took the bag. "Thanks," I said, and then slipped the book inside. Envy burned at my heart, her beauty and grace stung worse than a misstep into a hornet's nest.

Bags packed and double-checked, we faced the wall at the head of the fur bed. Quade raised his hand and pressed it into the stone. The solid wall ripped and faded into a six-foot arched opening. The light from Quade's small cave reached down a few steps, then an eery black swallowed the light.

Sati took the first move forward, and the rest of us followed. The door way behind us sealed closed, leaving us in absolute darkness. I raised my hand. I could barely see it, or thought I could.

Over here, the child called.

I shook my head and pinched my arm — *awake. She's coming to me when I'm awake.*

Come ... lower ... dance in the madness with me. Come play. Her laughter echoed from below. *Come. She is waiting.*

A bright orange ball formed in Quade's hand, then divided into four. Two floated to the rear and two up front. My eyes searched for the tempting child, but her voice vanished with the light. Her power still called, tempted me to disappear into the blackness, abandon all that I've known.

"Are you okay?" Quade asked with a tremble in his voice.

"Yeah," I said, unsure of what to tell him. "I've never seen anyone use magic before."

"Never seen magic, *huh?*" He rolled his eyes and waved us forward. "The way back will be blocked as we move forward, like it never existed. We won't have to worry about something coming up behind us as we make our way down."

"I'm glad it's down and not up. I don't do well going up." Hope smiled with a skip forward.

Chapter Seven

Hours passed, and then more. The uneven stairs seemed to grab at my tired, worn feet. Hope used the sharp wall for support. Her hands were roughed up by the stone. Mine were sore, each trip causing my hand to slap the wall to keep my balance. Quade and Sati showed no signs of fatigue. She walked tall, straight, poised. Her long hair swished with each declining step. He would stroll down the stairs, then would stop and wait for us when he ventured too far.

I'm sure I heard Quade laugh at a few of my stumbles. My knees felt as if they'd buckle at any second. The thought of asking to stop made me feel weak. I straightened up and pressed on.

Hope pushed her body to keep moving. Her mouth hung open to gasp in larger breaths of air. Her body began to rely more and more on the wall for support.

Hope stumbled again, but Sati caught her before she toppled down into the black mass ahead of us. "We will rest here. Your human bodies won't be able to take much more."

"Milady, Hope, please sit. Rest." She gestured to the ground with a palm up wave of her hand.

Quade plopped down with a groan, comfortable on the stone steps. Hope then collapsed to the ground beside him. My pride didn't allow me to sit even though my body begged for it. The lullaby's tune hummed in my head, not the child's sweet girlish voice, but mine. I stared down into the endless darkness. The deeper and deeper I descended, the more intense my emotions swirled. Sati and Quade's touches and whispers burned my skin. My weak and tired *human* body pissed me off, and I was hungry, painfully hungry.

"Blaze!" Hope snapped me out of the spiral of thoughts. "What do you think is down there?"

I looked up from the shady stairs. Hope sat beside me, her arms wrapped around her legs, pressed deep into her chest. Her eyes held the spark of adventure, one she could keep within her memories for when she rotted away, years from now, at the nursing home. The elderly women around her would chatter about their old careers, flings, family, and their eye-candied physic. Hope would remember the time she visited a different realm, a wicked realm, where monsters crept in the dark. Hope's future — how come I could see her there, alone? Why didn't I envision me there at her side, a memory shared between lifetime friends?

"I've got a better question. Where are we?" I whispered as I sat down beside her. My body ached the moment I let it relax. "They mention the Earthly Realm and Sinful Realm. Sinful Realm?"

"Oh, no! My mind's going to be disappointed. It's on a creative rampage. I've been putting the pieces together as we've been walking. I've come up with a theory, actually two. First one, don't bother asking them. They won't tell us anything, no matter what the question. The second is that we are in a world filled with monsters." She lowered her voice and leaned in. "Look at their horns. Sati is nice, and I know we can trust her. Then there's him ..." Her eyes shot Quade a glare, then bounced back to me. "He's trouble. How do we know this isn't a scheme to bring us to the king? If I were the king of Sin, where would I live? In the scariest place. And down there looks scary to me."

I leaned in close to Hope and whispered, "Have you seen anything? I mean, other than them? Since we first made the jump here? Have you seen anything, heard anything weird?"

She shook her head. "Nope, you're just crazy."

"Remember when we were little, I'd dream up ..." I turned to make sure the others weren't listening; they were rummaging through their bags. I hoped they'd find food. "Anyway, it's happening again."

"Really?" Her head got closer. "What about the ..." She rubbed her arms to hint to the way I felt. A spiral of wicked emotions caused me to be aggressive. I nodded. "Hmm, that's a problem. Last time we had to go camping for a week."

I nodded again.

The incident she referred to was during the grim days of my past. A few children from my class had bullied me to the point where I snapped. I slammed one of them into a wall and knocked him out, punched another and broke his nose. They had gone off about me being the cause of my parents' deaths.

I had been in grade six, and had routinely seen the counselor about the fire that had swallowed our home and my family. Most children that age don't hospitalize other children. I did, every one of them. They were about to label me as a threat to other children when Margaret, Hope's mom, had suggested quiet time in the woods with Hope. A perfect idea.

Hope and I got a quiet spot by a nameless lake. It wasn't a registered camp site, but Margaret had lead us into a patch of woods and set up camp. She stayed close, but let Hope and me do our own thing. I explained to Hope how I felt when I tossed that boy into the brick wall, and when I broke the other's nose. Rage flowed throughout my body and took control of my mind, my body. The worst part was the after-effect … I enjoyed his pain, his body dropping like a doll to the ground, and the way he stilled.

"That's not good." Hope pressed her hand against my forehead. "I can't tell if you're warm in this heat. It should be cooler as we get lower, right? Oh …" She turned around at the wall that kept on our heels. "We're always at the top. It's like we've made no progress at all."

"Heat?" To me it felt cool, almost cold.

A chunk of dried meat appeared in front of my face. I reached up and took it; my stomach growled with anticipation. I turned my head just as Quade crouched behind me. "You are hungry, aren't you?"

I nodded and took a bite of the salty, sweet, delicious, and chewy meat. "Yes." My eyes locked into his. They seemed deep, almost endless. "Can you tell us more about this world?"

He fell back onto the step behind him and ran his hand through his hair. "Nah, I'm not a great storyteller. Sati, you tell them." She overheard the conversation and lowered herself down a few steps to stand at eye level. Hope curled her knees into her body the way she did when we were kids. Her smile at Sati was filled with mischief. Her eyes shook with excitement.

"This realm, the realm of sin, is filled with creatures of tainted souls. Therefore, it has the name Sinful, for all the sinners' souls that it collects. Souls travel through three realms; Sinful, Earthly, and Enlightened. The realm the soul is born into depends on the choices that the soul has made in the time it is given a physical body. Souls that have made wicked choices come here to learn from their sins or expand their sins. All depends on the soul's choices. View the realms as a tree. The roots represent the Sinful Realm: thick, twisted, dirty limbs that remain unseen. The trunk symbolizes the Earthly Realm: sturdy and strong in between the roots and canopy. And lastly, the Enlightened Realm is represented by the canopy, the part of the tree that sees the most light and has the most vibrant colors.

"The combination of the realms makes a whole existence. Without one, you can't have the others. Within each realm, the souls are given a choice. Every soul is unique. No two are the same. The path the soul chooses leads to the realm best suited for its physical life."

Hope leaned in. "Many people and cultures in our realm have come up with theories about life after death," she said and took a drink from her water pouch, then continued, "a place where a pure soul is given peace after a life of hard work and pure intentions. And a place where the damned go to dwell in their evildoings."

Quade shifted then stood. I finished the last bite of my snack while he slung his bag onto his back. "That's enough stories for now. We're almost there. We should get moving. I want to make it to the bottom of these nasty things before we set up camp."

* * *

I took my last step down and let my body collapse on to the ground, fatigue winning the inner battle with pride. We had made it to our destination. The air was thick with the smell of brimstone. The orange orbs' glow lit the area; a low ceiling curved to form the walls. The staircase vanished, leaving no trace that it ever existed. My legs vibrated and feet ached. I struggled to catch my breath.

"We'll camp here tonight," Quade stated as he tossed his bag down. "Come with me." He walked passed me and away from Sati and Hope. Two of the orbs followed behind.

I tried to stand, but my legs wouldn't budge. He noticed and slowed his pace. I forced myself upward and hobbled behind. When the others seemed to be a distant orange glow, he stopped and dropped, cross-legged, on the ground.

"Come." He waved me over, and then patted the ground beside him.

I sat down, stretched my gelled legs out and gave them a wiggle. With both hands, I gave them a good rub. Quade watched fascinated. He reached over and grabbed the small bag that was slung over my neck.

I pulled the bag back and held it tight. "You said not to take it out."

"Yes, unless I'm around. You do want to learn how to use it, to be able to read it properly, right?" His calm and patient voice stunned me. "It will be fine. I promise."

I retrieved the book from the bag, removed the locket from my neck, and then handed both to him slowly. He slid the heart shape down, then down once more. The back, middle, and front created a chain of hearts, forming a key. He slipped the key into the lock and opened the book.

He nodded with a smile. "You really are unsure of me, aren't you?" He seemed cheerier than the previous times we talked, a hint of humor lit his face and eyes. "You don't have to worry. I'm not going to harm you. Maybe if I was more formal, you'd be more trusting. Do you want me to start saying, 'milady,' like Sati?" he teased. "Though it would be hard, I never was good at formalities. Got myself into loads of trouble because of it."

I leaned my head closer to see the pages — blank. He turned his body and rested the book in the middle of his lap.

"Why does she call me that?"

He ignored the question. "Here, give me your hand," he said and reached over with his free hand. I placed my hand in his warm, rough fingers, which wrapped around mine. He turned my palm down to the page and pressed it firmly to the paper. "Now close your eyes."

I entered into the void. My frantic and strained eyes searched for the wicked child and found nothing. A dim glow emanated from my body, the only light visible in the void. The still, cool air chilled my heated body. Goosebumps formed on my arms as a single shiver ran over them.

"Odd spot," Quade said from behind.

I whipped around. What was he doing in the void?

He lit with his own dim white glow, like the child and Hope. I swallowed a dry lump and begged the child to stay hidden.

"I was hoping that you'd show me a bit of what the Earthly Realm has to offer." His face lit with a grin. "Though this makes sense." His eyes traced around the blank space as if things caught their attention for brief moments. "Can you see the doors?"

"Doors?" My eyes scanned the empty space.

"I didn't think so." He closed the distance between us. "You've locked everyone, even the ability to see the gateways." His hand raised and brushed my cheek. "The one I know doesn't want to be found, or be let out."

"So I do know you … I knew it."

He dropped his hand and his eyes examined the space around us. "I can't help you with this. I'm sorry. There is nothing I can offer you. No spell that I can use to help you unlock the things you've sealed."

"Why would I want to seal my mind?"

"Because of what you have seen. I was hoping that some of it was sealed to keep you safe while you lived in the other realm, but you did it all on your own."

A distant childish hum began to fill the air. I lifted my hand from the book to sever the connection.

Quade glared at me. "What did you do that for?"

"Um, I want to take a nap."

"Really? Doesn't have anything to do with the sound we heard?" His eyebrow raised.

He heard it. Crap. "Food, then sleep. I think that's a great idea." I attempted to stand and failed.

Quade locked the book and shoved it back into the bag. He grabbed my hand and helped me up with a sharp tug. We headed back to camp in silence. He grumbled and kept his head turned away from me. *If he wasn't going to answer all of my questions, then why would I answer his?*

"Wow! You both look grumpy." Hope laughed as she stirred a large pot that sat in a pile of red embers. "Something happen?"

As I sat down beside her, the steam from the pot made my mouth water. Anything was better than having another chunk of dried meat. I needed flavorful greatness.

Hope noticed my appetite. "If you keep this up, you'll eat all the food before we even know what to do next."

"I don't eat that much," I barked.

I glanced at Quade seated across the fire. His eyes were cast away, his lips in a hard pressed line and head rested on his knuckles, his gaze lost in thought.

"You know," Hope leaned over to me and whispered, "every time I look to see what you're doing, you're looking at him." I bit my tongue and scowled. She laughed a quiet, secretive laugh. Her hands rested back on the gray stone behind her. "Why so mad?" she asked. "Is there something I'm missing?" Her eyebrows wiggled.

I shook my head and crossed my arms. The fire popped and the lids on the pots vibrated as the steam made its escape.

"I don't know why you're so mad. When I check to see what he's up to …" A playful smile grew on her thin lips. "He's watching you." She observed my hidden, shocked expression. "Hmm, well, well, you like that idea."

Sati peered into the pot. "Done. We eat."

* * *

Later, my mind spun as I laid wrapped in my fur blanket by the dwindling fire. I could hear Hope breathe a quiet snore as she slept by my head. Sati and Quade left to scout the area. They told us they didn't sense anything around but wanted to make sure. I recoiled at the thought of them alone.

My eyes closed, yet I lay wide awake. I turned on to my back and stared up at the jagged rock above. The uneven ground was uncomfortable and a flood of questions buzzed: *Why am I here? Why do I feel possessive over a stranger? Why am I hungry again? Who … who is my brother? What does he want with me?*

Sati and Quade returned from their journey; my eyes snapped shut and my ears listened to them move around the camp. Sati's movements were silent, and Quade's footfalls made little sound. They each found their pre-made beds and settled in for the night. Soon only the sounds of the fire could be heard.

After an hour or so, Quade slipped out of his bed and walked over to mine. "Can't sleep?" he asked as he took a seat at the head of my bed. I didn't reply. "Still not going to tell me, are you?"

"No."

"Why not? I can help you." He crossed his arms. "You're being stubborn. I know more about that book than anyone, and I know the effect it has on you. If there's something that the book is creating that's bothering you, I could help."

"I don't think it's the book that creates what I see." I rolled over and gazed up at him. "You wouldn't tell me your name, wouldn't tell me anything I ask. Why should I tell you everything just because you say you can help?" My cheeks were heated from my rage.

"I keep things from you that you're keeping from yourself," he said. "I promise you, when you remember, you'll understand. Until then, you have to be open with me."

"Really?" I kept my eyes on him as I sat up. "How do you know Sati?" I slipped. The question weighed on my mind, but I never meant to ask it.

"Sati?" He glanced over to her asleep upright, soundless, close to Hope. "We lived within the castle together. My mother was a friend of the queen's and hers was the high sorceress, the adviser to the queen. When the queen was murdered, we fled the castle together and hid. She was the only one who knew I was still alive.

"Recent events have now shown that I am very much alive and the king is not pleased. As soon as she saw that the Keep was being turned over, she knew that he was searching for me." He smiled. "She didn't expect to see you there with me." Amused, he relaxed his arms onto his legs and rested his elbows on them and his chin on his knuckles. "You being here has rekindled hope within her. She has regained the will to fight on."

"Childhood friends?"

"Yes. What did you think she was?" he asked, concerned.

"I — I don't know …" My eyes dropped.

"She's a close, loyal friend to both me and you." He lifted my chin and whispered, "Please remember me soon …" He parted from me, and went to his bed.

I laid back down once he stopped moving. He seemed heartbroken. I was wrong about him and Sati. Friends, just childhood friends. I closed my eyes. My mind finally at ease, sleep graced me.

Emptiness of the void soothed every nerve. The child stood before me, her face blank and yet filled with glee. Her blood-stained dress flowed as if there were a breeze. Her intertwined fingers pressed tight to her chest.

"Ready?"

"Ready for what?" I asked.

"I will give you the key to all that you've locked away. Like me. Your mind is filled with the nasty little secrets you don't wish to share."

"Can you show me what I ask?"

"Yes."

"Who are you?"

"I am what you made me to be. I am all that you wish to be and all you wish not to be. I am your darkness, and I am your light. You have created me in the only image you remember from both your childhoods. The one where you were Nemasa and the one where you were Blaze. Both times, you lost your parents because you were too afraid and weak. Alone."

"You're me?"

"Yes."

"Where is your face?"

"Do you wish to see it? It's beautifully tormented."

Her face morphed and twisted. Her jaw was ripped from lip to ear, and stretched down to her collarbone. Slits in place of a nose, the skin over her eyes was sunk in and empty. Blood seeped from the fresh wounds. Her cheeks lifted to the empty sockets, the torn jaw giggled as she smiled cruelly.

"Why?" I took a step back to keep the shudder of horror at bay. Her shredded face bled down her tiny neck and added to the blood that decorated her dress. "What happened to you?"

"Your memories made me this way."

"Why?"

The void cried crimson tears for her. Dripped from the vast spaces above. I took a breath in. I wanted to weep for her. I did this to her. This cruelty is my doing. Why? Why did it happen?

"Nemasa, you will remember in time. Now come. Come with me and play with the madness."

My eyes opened. A tear escaped and rolled down the side of my face into the fur that wrapped me. I wiped the trail away with my hand and sat up. Sati tended the fire with Hope beside her. Questions shot out from Hope's lips and received little to no reply. Quade wasn't anywhere to be seen. Frantic, I looked over the dark space of the cave, but still couldn't see him.

"Morning," I said with a yawn.

"Morning, sleepy head," she chirped.

I sent her a grunt. My body ached from the downward climb, my back pained from the jagged rocks under the thin layer of fur I had to sleep on.

"Here." Hope handed me a steaming cup. "Sati told me to give it to you the moment you woke up."

I took the cup in both hands and grimaced. The bitter smell left a bad taste in my mouth. "What is it?"

"It will help," Hope said with a full-toothed smile. "I already drank mine down, didn't taste good, but it worked wonders. Just drink it quickly, the aftertaste is … well, you'll find out."

I pressed the stone cup to my lips, and then shot back several gulps of the warm liquid. The horrible taste twisted my stomach. After it was all down a bit came back up, but I forced it back into my stomach. Warmth traveled from my center outward. Within seconds, my sore limbs and tired mind relaxed and settled. The aftertaste wasn't as bad as I expected, like tangy, uncooked egg.

"Feel better, milady?" Sati asked as she took the empty cup from my hands.

"Much. Thank you."

She bowed her head. "I am very happy to hear that it worked." She removed herself and went back to attend the pot she left by the fire.

Quade startled me when he materialized by my side. "After we eat, I have something I would like to teach you. This world is filled with many dangers, and you will need to know how to defend yourself. As much as I want to, I won't be there every time you need me."

After we ate, Quade led me away from the camp, through a tunnel that hid it from my eyes. The two loyal orange orbs lit our way as he came to a stop at the tunnel's dead end. The space bubbled out of the ceiling and reached a few feet higher than the path that led in. Near the back wall, a seven-foot black crack separated the floor from the stone wall. When I peered over, I couldn't see the bottom, even with the orb's glow above.

"Come," Quade commanded, cross-legged in the middle of the cave floor.

I took my seat in front of him and crossed my legs. His shoulders rolled back, and he rested the backs of his hands on his knees. He breathed in deeply through his nose and exhaled from his mouth. I copied. His eyes closed, so did mine.

"Keep like that," he whispered.

The lullaby filled my mind. The child danced to the tempo. Her blank face glistened with her light. Her bare feet bounced off the imaginary floor. The white dress twirled while she spun, bounced and wiggled. I could almost hum the tune with her.

"Our lullaby," she sung as the tune played in the background. "This is ours, from her."

"You can open your eyes now," Quade said softly. My eyes opened and took a few seconds to readjust to the bright light from the orbs. "We will start training by clearing our minds. Tomorrow, try to keep your mind blank. Ignore the thoughts and questions your mind thinks up. Relax and clear your mind."

"What makes you think my mind isn't clear already?"

He laughed. "No one can clear their mind perfectly the first time." He offered for me to take his hand. "Let's see how well you can use your feet."

I placed my hand into his strong grasp. With little effort, he lifted me to my feet. He guided my other hand to his shoulder and placed his on my waist. He then held out our cupped hands. His feet moved back and pulled me along.

Dancing? Horror struck me. *No. Don't make me dance.* I fumbled with each little step, pulled him into my awkward movements.

"Do women lead in your other realm?"

"No ..." My face heated. "I'm just a terrible dancer."

He pulled and pushed my body, keeping to a tune in his mind. "This is a great way to learn how to use your feet and trust your instincts. Keep your eyes up and let your body tell you where to go."

I stumbled and struggled to keep up with him. He'd bit his lip to hold in his laughter. Then he'd fought the corners of his lips down to force the humored grin from them. I'd flick my eyes down to watch my feet; he'd painfully squeeze my hand. I slammed down on his toe; he'd bite his tongue.

"Relax," he insisted, "follow my lead."

"I've never been good at following other's leads." I tried to step back as he pushed, step to the side as he pulled. My feet moved as if made of lead. I tried to stop, but he pushed me to go on. "I'm no good at this. Your toes must be hurting by now..."

"I'm fine. Try to concentrate." His eyes stared into mine. They reminded me of deep amethyst.

He slowed to a stop. "We'll have to practice that more. Your coordination and grace ... well, I won't comment just yet." He laughed. I agreed.

Quade took several steps back, and then raised both his hands to his mouth, whispered words into his palms. Two green orbs formed and grew to the size of baseballs. He tossed them to my feet, and just before they hit the ground, they each transformed into a wooden sword. He then repeated the process once more, creating one more that stayed in his hand. He gestured for me to pick up the two wooden sticks at my feet. Once I grasped the two sticks, he started to pace a circle around me.

"Two?" I asked, unsure if I should hold one at a time.

"Yes, two." He sounded pleased. He watched as I slashed them down through the air. "You used to practice the twin-bladed art. Never before had I beat you. I'm interested in seeing how well your body will remember that which it has never done before. Will you draw from the sealed memories or leave them locked behind those doors?" He paced around me, accessing me. "Now, attack. Don't worry about harming me. I doubt that you'll even get a chance to touch me in that human body of yours," he taunted.

I raised the right sword high and kept the left low. I rushed to him and swung heavy with the right. The force of his defence sent violent vibrations throughout the wood that caused my hand to release and skid across the ground.

"Pick it up. Again," he demanded.

Again I attacked him, this time striking first with the left. He blocked and sent my wooden sword through the air. Both hands throbbed. He hid power behind his cloak. I reached for my wooden sword. Bits of it splintered from the pressure he defended with.

"Keep a grip on your blades. Next time I will strike you. Prepare yourself."

I struck with my right, he defended and smashed my sword to the ground. I held up the left and blocked his second strike, and to my surprise, I kept a strong hold.

"Well done," he praised. "Again."

Again and again. My hands pulsed. Blisters formed. My arms could no longer swing the wooden sword through the air.

Getting them up from the ground became a task all on its own. My hands burned as if they had caught fire.

Quade reached down and lifted the grounded sword, and took the other from my hand. Blood stained the hilts, and the splintered blades looked as if they couldn't take another blow.

"We are done for the day," he said in a humored voice. He dropped the three practice swords to the ground. They bounced once and exploded into a flash of dim green light. "Your mortal body did better than I expected, though I think it was more your drive that helped you do so well. Your dance needs work, but your swordsmanship has increased over that short time. I better watch myself tomorrow, you might actually land a strike."

Chapter Eight

Everyday for a week, Quade took me to the distant cave to train. And everyday we did the same thing: clear the mind, step on his feet, and then lose over and over in sword fighting. My slow progress irritated me, and yet he kept trying and trying to help me succeed. He never became frustrated with my lack of ability with dance. And he enjoyed taunting me as I failed to land any strikes.

"Keep a clear mind, don't attack with your anger, attack with your wits. Emotions will cloud your judgement," he said as I struck at his left shoulder with my right. He easily blocked, and countered, hit me hard on my right leg. I cringed and swung up from the left.

Left. Right. Over and over. The vibrations from wood against wood became easier to withstand. The blisters turned to small calluses, and Sati's potion helped with all the bruises and cuts from days of hard training. I enjoyed the time I spent with the swords. Each day I felt as if I had become better, stronger, faster. Quade had suppressed his skill, and with each day that passed, he released a little more; every day was more of a challenge than the last.

"I'm trying to keep a clear mind," I retorted.

"Try harder." His right shoulder lifted, I raised my left sword and blocked his upper right strike, and then struck hard with my left — a gasp of pain from him made me freeze.

I got him.

A sly grin filled Quade's lips. His hand rubbed his ribs where I had hit him. "Nicely done, but I doubt you can do it again." He let out a small laugh as he watched me stand in front of him, dumbfounded. He raised his sword. "Attack!"

I barrelled in, left then right, then right, left. Each one blocked. Determination fueled my movements. The orange glow from the orbs of light faded to a dark shade of red. He blocked my left-handed strike, while my right responded by reflex and jabbed, the tip embedded into his shoulder. He painfully breathed out.

"Quade — I'm ..." A small amount of blood dripped down the wood. I swallowed hard. What had I done?

There was no pain in his eyes. They sparkled with pride.

"Perfect." He reached up and tore the wood from his flesh. "Don't you dare be sorry. I told you not to worry about injuring me." The blood-soaked sword dropped to the ground alongside his. He lifted my face lightly with both hands. "If only you could see through my eyes. If only you could see what I see."

The red glow of the room returned to orange as my body calmed. "Are you okay?" I mumbled. My entire body shook, knees almost giving out beneath my weight.

"I've had worse," he said. "Don't worry. It will heal in a few hours. I think that's enough for the day. Did you remember to bring the book with you?"

My body stilled. *Yes.* I rushed to our things stored by the entrance. "Yes, right here." I lifted the bag and brought it to him. The wound leaked down his side, and he held his breath as he moved his arm.

Quade lowered to the ground and retrieved the book from the bag. I handed him the locket, opened and ready to use. After he took it, I sat by his side. A guilty expression refused to remove itself from my face.

"Don't worry. The bleeding has already stopped. And you missed the joint. I'm still able to move it." He lifted his elbow a bit. "When I place my hand on this page, you place your hand on this one," he told me, pointing to the pages. "This time we will go into my mind, like we did with yours. I will show you the control you can have over the space you create. Sound good?"

I bobbed my head, excited to see what he would show me. I watched as he closed his eyes, then placed his hand on the left page. My eyes closed and I placed my hand on the smooth paper.

A gentle breeze brushed my cheeks and rustled the black-green leaves of the trees that surrounded me. The thick, black-brown bark of the trees shielded the underbrush from the scorching heat. The breeze cooled my skin. The fiery glow from the liquid sky lit the forest with a red-orange glow.

"This is what the surface used to look like. The trees used to grow strong and proud. The small shrubs moved from place to place, devouring anything dead they found. The creatures from the Keep used to live here in the open space. The original dwellers of the underground were kept separated. There are many levels to Sin and with each lower level the more sinister the creatures become. The surface dwellers used to consist of minor sinners and those who wished to ascend to the Earthly Realm. Since the new king came to power, he forced those who had little sin into slavery along with the human-breed slaves."

"Humans here are slaves?"

"Yes, they were born to this world without the power of their soul animal and were, therefore, kept as slaves, underlings to the power of the creatures around them." Quade laughed.

"Is that why you have a hard time with Hope?"

"Yes. Still do, to be honest. Though Sati says that she has spiritual powers that are dormant. In a way, your human has become an interest to the High Sorceress's daughter, her plaything."

"Hmm ..." I stepped forward and admired the gigantic trees. A low shadow shifted in the distance. I thought to respond, then thought that it might have been a fallen twig. "There was something I wanted to ask you." He followed behind as I walked toward the movement. "What does Nemasa mean?"

His movement behind me stopped, so I turned to face him. His crystal eyes shimmered. "How do you know of that name?"

"When I was adopted into my new family they kept my original sir name. When Robin and I first met, he was stunned when he read it. I was just wondering if that name carried over from this realm?"

"You're Nemasa. As was your mother before you. It's a name and a title." He stepped forward and began to walk again, closing the distance between us. There was pain in his eyes as he spoke. A longing that I couldn't quite figure out. "In time, you will learn the meaning."

I sighed. Another question left unanswered.

The air stilled and cooled as he broke the connection. His hand hoovered above the page as he thought. He wanted to tell me everything he knew, I could see it on his wounded face. Hope and I were close childhood friends. If she one day couldn't remember all that we had been through together, I'm sure I would have felt the same way.

"How's your shoulder?" I peeked at the wound but couldn't see past his clothes.

He locked up the book and passed it to me. "It's fine. I'm hungry. What about you?"

Sati and Hope had dinner on the fire when we returned to camp. Hope got the bowls out when we arrived. I thought about what Quade said about Hope being Sati's plaything. She did seem tired and worn out at nights. She smiled weakly at me, then proceeded to dish out the meal. I didn't know what Sati and Hope did while I was out training with Quade. His new information left me guessing.

"Quade!" Sati said, alarmed. "You're injured? Did something happen?"

"Yeah. She stabbed me," he said with a grin. The others didn't seem as amused. "Didn't expect her to learn so quickly. I'll have to be on better guard next time."

Sati rushed to his side to examine the wound. She pulled down on his robe and revealed the blood on his shoulder. My fists balled as her eyes searched his bare skin. She raised her hand and touched his skin with the same blue glow I had seen the first night. She pressed them to the wound, and the ripped flesh healed until there was no trace that I had struck him.

"It was almost better. You didn't need to waste your energy." He rotated his shoulder and fixed his clothing. I released my hands but began to chew on my lower lip.

Hope handed Quade a bowl of stew. "Here."

He accepted it and grunted at her. "Thank you, human."

Human. That's all that he ever called her. Never once had he used her name. Sati had scolded him countless times, reminding him that she had a name and that she wasn't like the humans in this world. They needed to respect that she was from another realm. *Respect.* He cringed at the idea of respecting a human. A lower life form. He could kill her where she stood and there would be no way she could stop him. She was a quick meal, an animal created to serve or be eaten.

Hope handed me my bowl without the same cheery spark she once did. I felt sorry for her. The world had absorbed all the positivity out of her. I didn't even know that was possible till I saw that the blue in her eyes had dulled, almost gray.

"Thank you." I took the meal with a smile. "How was your day?"

She smirked, then glanced at Sati.

"She has been doing well with her studies," Sati praised, then shot a cold glare at Quade. He snickered and wolfed down a few bites. "You will come to find that Hope will be a useful ally, Quade."

"Humans are only useful in a few ways, and you already know my ideas on that." He shovelled in another bite.

"Don't make me force you to like her," I warned.

He sloughed, pulling his bowl closer.

"Well, looks like you two are getting along," Hope announced. She and Sati exchanged glances before they both giggled together. "My day was hard and —"

Stones fell from one of the tunnels. Sati and Quade jumped to their feet. Quade rushed forward to investigate but stopped just outside of camp. The figure came closer into the light, a tall, lean silhouette.

"Who goes?" Quade asked the creature. The shadow shifted closer, floated over the ground toward us. "Sati," Quade whispered, "it's him. Guard her."

Sati moved to Hope, grabbed hold of her arm and pulled her away from the creature. Two figures emerged from the shadows, blocking their exit.

I put the bowl of food down and stood. The figure entered the light, dressed in a long black robe that dragged behind. The two creatures to the left remained in the shadows.

Quade placed his hand on his hilt. "You must let us remain. We hide something of value. The human is not for you or any of this realm."

The figure reached up with his long, boney fingers and slid the hood off and rested it on his shoulders. The creature's chalky white, narrow face was skin and bone. His sharp cheekbones seemed as if they'd rip the skin at the slightest pressure.

"What would I care if she was of another realm? All that I prey on are from her realm. I must not let one slip past my grasp," the elderly man stated. His pale thin skin stuck to the bone as if he had no muscles underneath. The white horns above his eyes reflected the orange orb's light.

Sati turned to the man and bowed. "Extractor of Souls, I am the High Sorceress's daughter, Sati." Her hair slipped over her shoulders as she bowed her head. "Understand we come here for the safe keeping …" Unsure if she should continue, the pause caused an ominous silence.

"I see." His empty gaze met with me. "You are Nemasa, are you not?"

"I am," I answered. Sati and Quade tightened. "And you, who are you?"

The elderly man floated to me with great speed. Once he was within reach, he brushed my cheek with his icy fingers. "You are." He turned to the two that lingered in the shadow. "Soleil, Lune, bring them to me. Allow them to pack their things. Help with what you can." He raised his hood and vanished back into the blackness of the cavern.

Soleil and Lune slinked over, unsure of their master's command. Identical twins appeared in the fire light, dressed in a loose combination of dark leather and cotton. Short, shaggy hair, tall, firm muscular bodies with a cold glare.

Sati's eyes widened. She knew them. Her graceful footfalls made her flow to them. She wrapped her arms around them both. They stood stunned then returned her embrace.

They released and joined us by the fire. One of the twins scanned the camp and then his eyes met with Hope's, then went back to Sati. "We must hurry. Spiders and snakes have been on the prowl. You're what they are looking for."

The six of us started down the tunnel that the eery man had first appeared from. The twins led the way and the rest of us followed closely. We stayed to the wall, one orb lit beside us. Quade kept close to me, his hand firm on the hilt of his sheathed blade.

One of the twins turned around with his finger pressed to his lips. We all stood still. I heard a slip of a few pebbles ahead. My heart skipped.

The twin that had turned to us stuck out his arm and wiggled his fingers. An orb of silvery light formed, stretched, and gained physical shape — a long seven-foot pole — at the ends two mirrored crescents receded down, almost to his hand.

"We've been found." He crouched his body, ready to pounce at any moment.

From the darkness, four monstrous arachnids crawled out along the ceiling, their bodies weaved together then apart. Old webs stuck to their enormous black furry bodies. The one on the far right was missing a back leg. The largest seemed to be the leader. It stopped and the others followed.

"Mother will be pleased," whispered the largest. Its two back right legs kicked out, and the spider to its right retreated backward.

The pole-armed twin rushed to stop its escape. The spider to the left of the largest dropped and released a silky bullet, missing his body by a hair. The twin twisted his body and slashed upward to the creature — it spat again, this time catching his forearm. He let out a yelp of pain. The web coated his arm, burned and sizzled.

"Foolish boy," whispered the largest. "We cannot have you doing that. Mother will not be pleased if she is delayed on being informed." Its black beady eyes found me, its fangs twitched with pleasure. "There's the one we need. Eat the rest."

Quade drew out his broad blade, ready for their attack. I searched everything on me. I had nothing ... no weapon to defend with. The other twin had summoned his weapon: a red-hot bladed scythe. He rushed to his brother's aid, slashing up at the spiders.

"Lune?" he called to his brother who scratched at the web. Each touch singed his fingers. Soleil grabbed his bother's unharmed arm and rushed him back to the safety of the group. "Stay here. I'll kill these filthy insects."

I looked back at the creatures. *Two? Where did the other go?* My eyes shifted around the darkness, seeing no sign of movement.

"Here," said Hope as she pushed past me and grabbed Lune's hand, careful not to touch the web. "Sati, poison right?"

Quade turned to her, interested, then his eyes shifted up behind us. He found the missing arachnid. He moved away from the group, toward the beast.

"If it's a poison, I'd have to use the incantation, plus the symbols," Hope continued.

Quade dashed forward. The spider spat rapid darts of web. Quade dodged low, then jumped. His sword connected with the beast's head. The arachnid twitched as its feet lost control of its footholds. The massive body crashed to the floor with a screech. It stumbled to its feet, wobbled, then lunged, fangs out. Quade raised his sword, shifted, severing the head from the hairy torso. The cheer of his win was lost as he turned and rushed to Soleil's aid.

The two creatures struggled against the double attacks. The largest attacked with webbed poison darts, the other with a constant change in position. A trail of draped poison threads fastened in his wake.

"Almost there," Hope's voice brought me back to the injured Lune. "It will burn, a lot, but then you'll feel fine … I think …"

With her index finger, she drew an invisible symbol over Lune's webbed arm. Her face then lowered to the invisible symbol and her lips whispered soft words. The symbol lit white then sunk down onto Lune's forearm. He bit his tongue as it fused with his arm.

The web slipped from the arm and melted into the stone. The wound underneath sizzled then healed. Lune looked at his arm, then back to Hope, a human, one that healed him with little effort. His eyes narrowed and darkened with each thought that passed. How could he be weak enough that a human had to heal him? Then they lightened, reopened to a new idea that his whole life he had thought humans were nothing more than cattle ready for the harvest.

Lune scooped up his weapon and rushed to the other's aid. Both Soleil and Quade seemed amazed that he was up and ready to battle.

"You'll pay for that," Lune hollered to the missing-legged creature. He ducked down and navigated through the treads that hung a little lower than his head. Spits of web tried to force him into the trap, but he was not fooled.

His staff came up and the creature tried to retreat. The blade came down, sliced the beast in two. "Who's next?" he yelled out in anger. His irises burned crimson.

The larger spider began to back from the group. Quade judged its movements, stepped to the predicted spot and swung at the creature. It stepped backward, into Soleil's strike. The scythe ripped thought the beast's thick shell. The creature dropped to the ground, screeched in pain, and one final blow stabbed through its head, leaving it still.

"We better quicken our pace or else there will be more," Sati urged.

We followed the passage to the faint glow at the end. The group emerged out near a gelled river. The thick water pulsed with dim white light. I leaned over the stone embankment and gazed into the faces within. Men and women who were struggling to keep from drowning still remained in their space, unable to reach the surface. Their frantic arms reached for the air above, their scared faces screamed soundlessly. My heart throbbed for them.

"It is their punishment for the sins they committed," Lune said to me as he joined me at the edge. "Each soul shares in the fear of water or drowning. Trapped in their fear to ripen."

"Ripen?"

"Yes. Each soul will be a sinful creature once its sentence is fulfilled and its soul is twisted, ripe."

Millions, upon millions, of souls made up the river. It carried on around the bend on both sides, out of sight. The river lit the cavern in a feeble white light.

"Human!" barked Lune as he grasped Hope's arm tight. "Tell me how you possess such magics." Hope remained quiet. "Answer me, slave."

"She is no slave," Sati stated, placing her hand over his. He calmed from her touch, loosening his grip on Hope. "Creature from the Walls, you must not harm Nemasa's human. I fear she will be quite unpleased."

Lune's glare chilled me. "Your human?" I nodded. He released her and backed away. "Forgive me," apologized Lune with a bow of his head. "I didn't know."

Sati patted Hope's arm where he had grabbed her. "Hope, be sure not to look into the eyes of the river, for it

133

will draw out your living soul and you will be lost." Her sweet, soothing tone lit Hope's face.

"Okay." She grinned. "Did I do good?"

"Very well. You have learned much in the short time of my teachings. You will, one day, be powerful among your kind."

"Thank you, Sati."

"You speak to the human as an equal," Soleil whispered to Quade.

Quade grunted. He didn't, but they didn't needed to know that. Quade then eyed me and sighed. "Leave her be. She helped your brother. Be grateful."

"Lady Sati could have done the same."

"Yes, but she didn't. It was by the *human's* hand that he was healed."

Quade unbuckled his belt; the sheath and broad sword were removed along with it. "You will need a way to defend yourself. Take this." He wrapped the belt around my waist and buckled it. "In case we are separated or I am unable to aid you, use this."

"How will you—"

"I have other methods of battle; you do not."

I rested my hand on the hilt and grinned. "Just one?" I asked with a raise of my eyebrows.

"Don't get cocky." His playful smile revealed his fangs. "We must move. I fear more are on their way."

Soleil and Lune led us along the River of Souls to an iron door built into the rock wall, lit by a single torch. The door creaked opened as we drew nearer. They watched the cloaked eery man exit.

I remembered Sati had a name for him, but I couldn't recall the words she used. *The extractor of what?* I asked myself as I stood in awe of the ghastly creature. The door slammed shut behind him.

The twins stopped a few feet away from him and knelt in respect to their master. The Extractor raised his hand and the twins rose.

"Go to your duties," he said in a ghostly voice and then floated closer to me. "Dear child, for a long time, I have waited to look upon your face." My mouth went dry as his onyx eyes locked into mine. "Come! You are a guest in my house. There is much we need to discuss." He turned and glided back to the iron door. The torch to its right flickered ominous shadowed claws at the rock that surrounded it.

I stepped forward and the others copied.

"I only invited one," his voice warned.

I turned to Quade, sure he knew if I should proceed.

"Well, well, look what I found." Robin's charmed voice called from behind. "Master will be most pleased."

Our eyes gazed at the man behind us. He was dressed in a rich green robe, embroidered with twisted images of snakes creeping up from the hem. Hundreds of serpents slithered around and over his boots. Some thick and long, others thin and short, the colors varied in every shade. Their bodies flattened on the side closest to us. They all seemed to press into an unseen wall.

"Robin." My voice cracked.

"Yes, I've come to rescue you from the traitor." His eyes shifted to Quade.

"You lie. You don't want to rescue me!" I hollered.

His happy demeanour perished, and his face filled with a fake sorrow. "I traveled far to keep you safe. I even healed that rotten friend of yours. I am your friend, not your foe. Have they used some sort of spell to create a friendly image? Can you not see them for the monsters they are? They wear masks to keep you from the truth. I have all the answers you seek. I will share them with you. Have you asked them, asked them why you were sent to the Earthly Realm? Did they answer you?" He paused. When I didn't reply, he continued, "They didn't, did they? Come to me. I will share."

I was tempted to take his offer. I wished for all the answers to my questions. I wanted to know why the child wore a tormented face, and why I was sent away.

The snakes twisted around Robin and each other. I thought about all I knew. It was enough to step back. "No, I will not go with you. You're right. I do seek what you offer, but I will do it my way, and that means I stay as far away from you as possible. I do not trust you, or the others."

"Very well." His charmed voice deepened. "I have a letter for the Extractor of Souls from the king." A red envelope poked from under the robe. "I suggest you take it."

The Extractor drifted past at an alarming speed. He stuck out his boney hand and retrieved the letter. There was a brief pause before he finally slid his finger over the wax seal and cracked it.

His eyes scanned the information. "They are not my prisoners; therefore I need not take action, so you will have to capture them yourself. Since they are, in fact, intruders, you will be momentarily allowed through the barrier as per our agreement." He swiveled around and began a slow float back. "Now, child, you are a guest as I have mentioned earlier. Come into my home."

"I get all the intruders!" Robin hollered. "Including that one!"

"She was invited to my house before you arrived. The others were not. You know the laws of the chamber."

The iron door opened without aid. A waft of hot air escaped, as the sound of hammers and chains filled the tunnel. He waited at the door. With a slow wave of his hand, he welcomed me in.

Quade shoved my shoulder toward the doorway. I glanced over at Hope. I couldn't leave her. His eyes shifted to her, and then back to me. He gave me an understanding nod and moved his body closer. He would protect her. I had to leave.

Chapter Nine

I stepped toward the chamber, nervous to leave my friends behind. A loud pounding of hammers thudded, the rattling of chains, and constant shrieking awaited me. The Extractor beckoned me with a wave of his hand. I pressed forward into the heat of the room.

Smoke from the roaring fire made up the ceiling of the red rock cave. The iron door slammed shut when we entered the great room. Torture tables, hooks, chains, mallets, and horrified bodies were laid out before my eyes, filling the vast chamber. Bodies were attached to wooden and iron machines. Thin, frail men and women cried out from the pain of their beds.

"My work," he said as he rounded me. "I am known as the Extractor of Souls. The name was given to me because of the work that I do within my chamber. I remove the souls from the physical bodies of the dead. With the seeds I collect, I plant them within my garden around the tunnels and river. I quite enjoy my work. Nothing in existence could make me happier. This is where I belong."

My eyes watched as hammers struck spikes into a man's flesh. Another was being stretched to the point of ripping apart.

"I induce pain to the body and mind, and once their souls can no longer withstand the pain, they reject their bodies. The process creates a seed which I harvest, then plant. Each seed needs the right placing for the best fruit to ripen."

The chains clanged and cinched tight. Other's chains slacked and rattled from the vibrations caused by the pounding of mallets. The painful screeching made my heart throb. Though I wish I could have looked away, my eyes scanned each machine. Gears twisted. Metal links tightened. A metal bull over a fire bellowed, steam screaming from its nostrils.

"Child, there are things we must discuss."

I turned my head to him, but my eyes stayed fixed to the sight before me.

"Fascinated, are you?" His ghostly voice noted his pleasure. "Have you noticed your foot yet? You tap to the beat of the music I create."

For the first time I looked away and found that my foot was tapping lightly to the sound. The screams echoed in chorus. "I —"

"Your mother would do the same," he said. "A cruel, fiery woman, intelligent, beautiful, and the only one who understood my humor. I had never enjoyed company. Then I met your mother. She was just a pup at the time ... yes ... yes, she is dearly missed. She even nicknamed me Ripper."

"Ripper?"

"Yes, for the way I rip out the souls." His thin face grinned and revealed the sharp, jagged fangs that lingered beneath his slender lips. He glided to me with an outstretched hand. "Dance with me to my music and we will discus."

I hesitated, remembering all the times I slammed down on Quade's toes, his silent yelps and curses. I glanced down at the bottom of his robes. Maybe he didn't have feet to step on. I reached out my hand, and the instant my skin touched his, a chill ran up my arm. I reached up with my other hand. His boney shoulder under the thick robe made me cringe.

He took his first step and pulled me into the tempo. Miraculously, my feet moved to his lead. For a while, we moved in silence. The cruelty of his music faded into a dark classical tune. I closed my eyes and allowed the wicked melody to take me.

"You're much like your mother, child."

My eyes blinked open. "How so?"

"For one, you enjoy my music. A rarity that only you and your mother share."

"How well did you know her?" I asked as my feet moved with his.

"She came down many times to visit from the surface. There were many things she liked to talk about. You and your brother were her most favorite of topics."

I let my hands slip away from him and backed. "My brother?" The ball of rage found its way back into my blood, burning at my skin. "Tell me about him."

"Your brother's name is Bruin. Your mother's firstborn. He has proclaimed himself the king of Sin. I wonder, how much do you know of the time you spent here with your mother?"

I bit my lip. I know nothing, I tried to say but couldn't.

Ripper released from our dance. He glided to a bench that jetted out of the stone wall. Steel tools and equipment I couldn't name filled the surface. "Ah..." he breathed. "You are still unable to recall the past, just as I assumed. Bruin is only your half-brother. His father was second to yours, but that was found out after the birth of your brother. Your brother was born without the tails, and with that, a truth was made clear."

"Truth?"

"Yes." He sighed. "The power that you inherited from your mother can only be passed down by the first mate's seed. When your brother was born deprived of that power, his father became enraged and taught the boy to hate his mother, your mother." He picked up a small box from the bench before he floated back to me. "Your mother was betrothed to Bruin's father, and his offspring was to be promised the power of the Nine Tails. He was crossed to find out that your mother had given herself to another."

"Doesn't deceit happen here all the time?" I asked with a raised brow. I thought it to be a fair question, it was Sin after all.

A flicker of annoyance twitched on his face. "Yes, child, although when it comes to the Nemasa, there are rules that mustn't be broken. The law states for the Nemasa to be given a worthy mate due to the magic that surrounds the Nine Tails.

The boy who is chosen undergoes an extensive amount of training to gain the status of Nemacoy. The bond between the two is unlike any other. A sharing of mind, body, and soul. Bound together in life and death." Ripper bent to retrieve a small box that hid behind another of saw blades.

"Master …" Soleil's voice broke through the tension. "You wished to be informed the moment they returned to collect Nemasa."

We both turned to see the twins bowed, one knee rested on the stone ground and their arms were crossed over their chests.

"They have come with haste," Ripper breathed. He floated to me within a blink to hand me the box. "A gift from your mother. She wished that I give it to you in case she was unable to see you age. Soleil, Lune, take her deeper. Keep her hidden at all cost."

"Yes, Master," they said in unison and rose.

I slipped the box into the bag and rushed to the twins. "I have more questions."

He bowed his skeleton face low. "And I have answers. Until we meet again, our discussion will need to be placed on hold."

Soleil and Lune took me in past the machines. The tortured men and women cried out in agony. I scanned over each that I rushed passed. The fire's light danced on their skin. Their faces were covered with wounds and blood. Limbs had been ripped from their sockets. Metal rods and spikes protruded from torsos and limbs.

"Come!" Soleil urged and held fast to my arm. He tugged me past the rest of Ripper's play.

A collage of faces whisked by. Their pain made its way into my soul. My dry tongue became moistened by an unknown sweetness. I pulled my arm back and licked my lips. They, too, had a candy-like flavor.

"What's wrong?" Lune asked, as he stopped to observe me thrashing my tongue around my mouth.

I licked my candied lips again. "What is that?"

They both gave a wicked grin. Without a reply, Lune grasped my hand and pulled me on.

We came to an abrupt stop. The area appeared the same as everything we had already passed. Lune released my hand and crouched to the ground. He rapped his knuckles on the stone floor five times, then stopped. A square wooden door appeared with an iron ring handle. He took hold of the iron and lifted the door upward. The rusted hinge's high-pitched squeak stung my ears.

"Down here," Lune said as he jumped in.

I followed, then Soleil. The door slammed shut and vanished. Darkness swallowed us. I could have stayed there in the dark. My skin vibrated, fingers wiggled. *More!* My mind screamed. I rubbed my hands over my arms. *No. I don't want to go back there. I don't, but I do. No.* I curled down and wrapped my arms around my legs. *If Hope was here with me, she'd know what I should do. Hope, where are you? Please, oh, please, be safe.*

Lune lit a silver orb that washed away the dark ideas. He brought it back to his ear and tossed it ahead. "We need to move fast. They'll do anything to know where we are. Ripper told us to choose any way we see fit, that way they can't get the information of where we have gone. He has no idea. Just deeper."

"Deeper? I need to go to Hope. Take me to her," I demanded.

Soleil shook his head not pleased by my order. "We can't. They will catch you there."

"Then you go on without me, and I will find my own way to her."

Lune crossed his arms. In the silver light his eyes shined like two tiny moons. "He did say at any cost. If you go to the castle, we would technically have to follow."

Soleil punched his brother hard in the arm. "You moron. Don't be saying it's an option, brother. You know what *he* would do to her? Kill her. That's what," he barked.

Lune slugged him back. "What did you hit me for? It's a great idea. They have every warrior the castle has on the lookout for her. The castle is empty."

"The king is still within those walls. He'd sense her instantly."

"*Tsk!* Fine then. You stay here, and we'll go to the castle."

Soleil pressed his face close to his brother's. His golden eyes were lit by the orb. Finally I had a way to tell them apart from one another. The silver-eyed twin was Lune and the golden-eyed twin was Soleil. I couldn't stop the upward twitch of my lip that formed from my discovery. "You just want to rescue *the girl*, ain't that right?" he teased.

"Save the girl?" I had to ask.

Soleil leaned back on his heels and crossed his arms. "Yep," he boasted, "save the girl."

"We should keep going," Lune muttered and bashed his bother with his shoulder on his passing.

"Fine, fine, I agree. Let's move on toward the exit. If we make it to the door, we can go to the castle, and if … *she* stops us, then we will have to play that game instead." Soleil laughed at his own joke. I didn't get it.

I tried hard to keep up with their fast pace but found it difficult. My head hit the roof of the narrow tunnel, my feet tripped on the uneven ground, and I gasped to catch my breath. They navigated the passage with ease, keeping their bodies small, using their hands as if they were another pair of feet. I mimicked their movements as best as I could, but my best wasn't good enough.

Irritated, Soleil grabbed my arm and tugged me on. After a while, my legs just couldn't take it any longer and my knees gave. I crashed to the floor. Shamed, heat rose to my cheeks.

"Crap," Soleil cursed. "You're really pathetic right now, aren't you?"

I refused to answer. He was right, I was weak and helpless. My ignorance hounded at me, and made me hot with rage.

Lune lowed himself to the ground with an understanding smile. "It's fine, really. We're just not used to the lack of energy given to you by the mortal body." He dug into his pocket and withdrew a pouch. "Here," he pulled out a chuck of dried meat and handed it to me. "This should fill you."

I took the food and tore a piece off. "Thank you." I ate it in silence. The small bit filled my stomach and dried my mouth. "Do you happen to have any water?"

They each shook their heads. I didn't think they would, but it was worth a shot. My eyes blinked closed, heaved by a sudden impulse to sleep.

"Hey!" Lune hollered and gave me a little shake. "Whatever you do, don't fall asleep here," he warned. "Up on your feet. We'll move slower."

The narrow corridor led into an immeasurable room: no floor, no ceiling. Doors floated, suspended by their own magic, each lit by a single torch. Thousands, maybe even millions, of old decrepit doors scattered about.

"Each doorway enters into a personalized torment," said Lune as we came to a stop at the curved edge. "It's tricky to get to the doors. Keep in mind where you want to go and step toward it." His foot fell over the edge and stopped as if the edge continued. His other foot followed. He strolled out onto invisible ground with a laugh. "Soleil and I have many jobs out this way and have gotten the hang of it. Took some time to master."

"Our teacher wasn't one to wait, if we failed, he would let us fall into the abyss." Soleil laughed as he joined his brother. Their bodies levitated over the uncountable doors. "We won't be as cruel. Here. Take my hand," he said.

The space reminded me of the void within my dreams, empty and yet filled with endless possibilities. I ignored his hand and stepped out on my own, my foot landing on unseen ground. My other foot followed at a steady pace to pass the twins. "What are we looking for?"

"Each door has its own torch. We need to find the one with two. Two is the exit. A torch to the left is a gateway to a world with many creatures. A right torch indicates one creature." Lune came to my left. "Don't fall. If you fall within this level, you will never stop."

I scanned each ancient door. Splintered wood was held together by rusted iron braces. A solid, but rusted iron ring handle hung heavily in the middle of each door. The cold space absorbed the heat from my body and left me chilled. No matter which door my eyes met, I couldn't see one with two torches.

"This way," Lune stated as he stepped upward and passed me. "We have to go higher."

From deep within the void of gateways, the child hummed her lullaby. It found its way into my soul and twisted my mind as we traveled. I bobbed my head to the tune, hardly able to keep myself from humming along with her. The twins seemed unaware of the melody. It was all in my head; that had become clear to me.

The door with two torches came into sight as the hum became louder. The twins' pace began to slow, their eyes twitched around the empty space, aware of a hidden danger that stalked nearby.

"Come to play, have you?" a voice whispered from behind the door. A pairs of claws gripped the top. "I do, *do* love games." The twisted creature raised its head. A few hairs stuck to the monster's greasy scalp. A mad wicked smile twitched on its narrow face.

A shiver ran up my spine as the child appeared to my left and her tiny hands gripped my shirt. Her blank face lifted toward the creature that peered down at us with its distorted eyes. Flames flickered in the depths of its pupils as its head bobbed left and right.

The twins stood transfixed, their heads turned away.

"Don't look into her eyes," they whispered together.

It was too late — my eyes found hers and the world around me seemed to shift into a kaleidoscope of reds. The creature blinked, and dropped down the back of the door. Her claws scratched the wood and iron as a shiver crept up my back. Her sickly body trembled and twitched. Long fingers poked out underneath the door. She lifted her whole naked body and sat, upside down to us, on the thick edge of the door. Her head seemed to bob to the melody the child hummed.

"You can hear her?"

"Don't talk to *her* ..." Soleil snapped as his eyes kept away. Both him and Lune shook with fear.

"This is a question I need to ask." I stepped forward. The creature tilted its head, the few greasy strands of hair fell to her shoulder. Its long arm reached out and wiggled its clawed fingers. "Can you see this child?" I placed my hand on the little girl's head.

The twins scanned over me. They're eyes moved past the child they couldn't see.

The creature placed her foot flat onto the front of the door and crawled up on all fours as if the door were regular ground. Her head tilted up and her eyes found their way into mine. Her mad smile reached her eyes, the thin almost transparent skin wrinkled on her forehead and around her ever-shifting eyes.

"My, my! Isn't this nice?" she whispered, her voice echoed through the void. She reached back with her hands and placed them level with my feet, then flipped to the plane where I stood. She turned and stretched her legs and rose to a towering nine feet.

The child detached herself from me and skipped over to the horrifying woman. She wrapped her tiny arms around the beast's legs and turned her mutated face to me. Her dangling jaw twitched as her cheeks lifted to the empty, blood-crusted sockets.

"Let's play a game, you and I," the woman's voice echoed. She turned her head down to the child. "If you win, I will give you a key to one memory, the one you wish to know the answer to the most. If you fail, I keep the child."

"Just me and you, right? They are free to leave?" I waved to the twins who still refused to steal a glance.

"Yes, I have no need for these rodents."

Angry growls found their way out of them.

"Go," I said to them. "Save Hope and the others. This is something I need to do. Once you save them, come back to this door, and I will be waiting on the other side. I will not move till you come back."

The woman and child stepped to the side in unison to allow the twins by. "Better go before I change my mind, *weasels.*"

Their shoulders raised at the word weasels, but they kept their heads low as they walked past, to the door. Lune withdrew a key from his pocket and opened the heavy door with ease.

"Don't fail!" he barked as he crossed to the other side.

Soleil gave me one last glare, his disapproval struck home. Hope would have given me the exact same look.

"Bring them back."

The door made no sound as it slammed shut, but a click let us know it was locked. *How was I supposed to get out if the door was locked?* I sighed. *Trapped.* The waking void swallowed me whole, with no intention to spit me out again.

"Now that they are out of the way …" her echoing voice boomed, "we will get started. Take this key. It will open all the doors around you, even the one that those two vermin have exited. Within one of the worlds that lay beyond, you will find a demon that used to have two horns. Bring me his last one, and I will give you your prize. Fail, and the sweet child will belong to me."

"How do I know what door to go through?"

"You will have to find out yourself. I'm not one to give hints."

I bit my lip and took in the sight of the thousands and thousands of doors. *Right has many, left has one. No … right has one ... or ... crap. Two is the way out.* I sighed. "And who am I making this deal with? You know who I am, but who are you?"

"Ah!" Her yellowed fangs crept out from behind her grin. "I have many names, and many faces." She crept closer. The child moved as she did, seemingly happy to be at her side. "I am commonly known as Madness or Fear. Yet no one speaks my name. Shame, shame." Her eyes shifted and swirled. "You do not fear me. I wonder ... will you let me find the fear that torments your soul? I would like that. Then we could venture into your mind together." Her grin dropped to the bottom of her jaw. "I doubt you would be the same after." Her lips twitched up and spread from ear to ear. "That's okay. Who needs sanity anyway?"

I didn't fear her. I gazed deep into her sinister eyes. Death and pain. My mind remembered every time I had ever felt frightened. It recalled the memories from the fire; my parents' screams as they burned alive, trapped in their bedroom, unable to escape the grip of the flames. I didn't feel pained by the emotions. I stood before her strong and sturdy.

"Take this key. It will open all doors that you see." Her body bobbed and wiggled. Her arms flung around mindlessly, and the child skipped and hummed at her side. "Be careful to lock the doors behind you. Don't want anything to get out now, do we?" she lied.

Chapter Ten

Madness and the child left me alone in the chilled, dreamlike space. If only I could remember what Lune had told me about the doors. I didn't want to find myself alone, surrounded by creatures as they drooled over how to play with me. With the child gone to the house of Madness, I felt a knot tie in my chest as abandonment set in. Alone and without aid.

I paced the void to examine the doors. I noticed that the doors had aged at different rates. Some seemed less splintered and worn, almost new. The ring in the middle was shiny and new. Other doors had rot and faded color; the ring was rusted and barely hanging on.

A torch to the right, one creature? No, many ...

The silence wore on me. I missed the child's soft hum of our lullaby. My loud thoughts scratched at my skull. I felt like an idiot for not being able to remember simple instructions that could save my life. I changed my direction to the door closest to me.

My fingers slid over the dry wood, the torch to the left. "My left or its left? One creature, I'm sure of it. Find the creature that once had two horns and bring her the other. How am I to fight these things?"

I slipped the key out of my pocket, careful not to drop it. My eyes scanned for a keyhole. There wasn't one. I circled the door. There was a ring on the back but still no keyhole. Now the torch was on the right. I circled the door again. Unsure of how to unlock the door, I tapped the key on the wood. *Click!* My eyes widened. I heaved the door open.

Bright sunlight beamed from the cracks. The scent of wild flowers flooded out on a breeze. The blinding light caused my eyes to snap shut. I forced them to flutter open. Vibrant green grass and azure sky reminded me of summer days with my mom, sister, and dad out on the trails in the mountains. Us and nature. Pure bliss.

Drawn to the beauty, I stepped into the new world. I pushed the door closed behind me. A rap of the key on the wood … *click! Locked.* I slid the key into my pocket and turned to the enchanted world I entered.

The ground squished under my feet, puddles pooled around my shoe hinting to a recent rainfall. I listened for birds — none — only the breeze through the trees rustled. I breathed in through my nose, the smell of the wet mulch, the fresh water, the sweet aroma of flowers brought me back to the Earthly Realm. For a moment, I forgot about the danger. Forgot about the creatures that might attack. I breathed in again. I missed the scents of the world I left behind.

A sharp snap of a twig to my right caught my attention. My hand drew Quade's broad blade without a thought. My eyes bounced from tree to tree. Whatever it was, it hid well behind the lush greenery.

From behind the low bushes, a deep growl warned me that I was no longer alone. A yip and reply echoed through the woods. A polished-horned woman dressed in furs crawled out on all fours. She growled and barred her fangs, warning me not to move. Her long ebony hair fell over her shoulders in knots. At the top of her head twitched furry, triangular ears. A thick fur tail swished over the ground. Another woman soon joined at her side. A deep growl escaped their throats.

"Hello," said an unseen man. My head whipped to the left and saw a tall, broad man, half-dressed in brown fur from his waist down. His curious eyes studied me as he strolled closer. He raised his hand to the two women. They nodded. Their lips closed, shoulders relaxed, but their hateful glare stayed fixed to me. The man's brown fur ears twitched as the wind blew into them. His tail wagged happily as his lips curved up to his eyes. "You are new to these parts. Let me welcome you, traveler. I am Kenna, the leader of the tribe behind the woods. I welcome you to the bounty of my table."

My eyes darted around the lush greenery. A part of me longed to be back home, on a hike with Hope, scheming pointless plans to get back at the students who bullied us.

"None of my wolves will harm you. You are a welcomed guest to our village. Come, please. I would love to hear where you have traveled from and the many stories that you have to share." He held out his hand and offered it to me. "What is your name, woman? We can spread word to the others that you aren't an intruder."

"My name …" I paused, unsure if I should tell him.

"Oh, dear!" His face saddened. "Have you no name? We will give you one to be called by. The clan will choose a proper name for one as beautiful as you."

I nodded. His tail swished over the grass as his smile returned to his face. My gut twisted as my eyes locked with his. Kenna reached out his hand as I sheathed Quade's sword.

Kenna led me to his village of wolves, and the two women followed closely. Their eyes were fixed to my every movement, one hand lingering on the hilt of their blades. He explained his world to me. For the first little while, I must remain by his side until word of the traveler spread to the pack. Intruders were normally killed where they stood. Kenna had caught wind of my scent, the "enticing aroma," as he put it, and sent him to investigate.

The small village crept up a hill on the outskirts of the forest. Straw, wood and plaster made up the structures. Eyes watched as I passed. A few members of the pack licked their lips as if I were a passing meal. A woman mended clothes on her porch, another crouched on the path-side, whittling a thick chunk of wood, and another strolled past, holding hands with two small girls.

"There're a lot of women here," I noted. Each bore characteristics of a wolf. Brown, gray, black, or white fur coved their ears and tails.

His hazel eyes shimmered. "Yes, we will discuss that at my place. There are things about this village you need to know about before you decide to wander." The wolves bowed their head in respect as Kenna passed.

A large plaster hut stood in the center of the village, and smoke seeped from the middle. A curved wall had one narrow door but no windows. A woman with gray ears and matching cold eyes stood guard, her hand tight on the hilt of her blade.

"Ta'la, this is our honoured guest," the sternness of Kenna's voice caused her to straighten. "Alert the others that she isn't to be harmed, or they will find themselves next in the arena."

Ta'la bowed and rushed off, stopping at everyone she passed.

"She's a wonderful warrior and servant. She takes every order I give with great passion." He smiled at me and nudged me in.

My nerves bunched. It didn't seem right, being in an individualized hell and finding a peaceful village with respectful citizens. I had expected violent, thoughtless beasts to attack from all of the shadows. I'd swing my blade wildly. Bloodied and broken. Barely surviving the depths behind each door I opened. But there I was ... bright blue skies, green leaved trees, vibrant colored wild flowers, and the wolf pack — all unexpected.

"Is there something wrong? Should I call a healer?"

"No, it's okay," I apologized and entered the dark space.

The scent of burning cedar and pine filled the room. The back wall held a thick banister. The fire roared in the middle of the room, surrounded by a floor of pillows. Five women laid out on them and greeted their master with a slight roll of their shoulders, drawing attention to their naked breasts.

"Leave us," he ordered, and the women bowed and obeyed. I raised an eyebrow.

"Being the alpha has its perks," he said with a wide, conceited grin. "Now, about that name." He melted into the pillows and patted the space beside him. I hesitated. "Sit. You must be tired after your journey," he commanded. His voice revealed he didn't like to be kept waiting.

I sat where I stood. His eyes narrowed and lit with anger. I had denied him. His expression softened and he shuffled closer.

"Where are you from, traveler?" he asked with extra charm, scooting closer.

"I'm from far, far, away." I breathed in through my nose. The fire smelled much nicer than the magic flames that Sati and Quade used to cook our meals. Kenna waited for a better explanation. My fingers traced the detailed stitch-work on the pillow beside me. I glanced to the banister. "What's beyond there?"

He glanced up and eyed the dark wood. "That's the arena."

"I wanted to ask you about your arena. You mentioned that if anyone harmed me that they would find themselves there. What is it used for?"

He sat up and pressed his lips into a hard line, unsure if he should answer the question. "You see, there is no food here. Not an animal to hunt or fish to catch. We carnivores needed to create a way to eat. We use the arena to feed the pack."

"You eat your own kind?" my stomach turned.

"There is a tournament every month, ten fighters. One survivor will remain. A battle to the death, the winner advances to the next round. The males are trained to take on the task and the women give birth to the opponents. Women who are no longer able to conceive pups find their way there. Law breakers and the deformed, they all become fodder for the arena."

I made a mental note not to eat anything he offered, but how else could they survive without that system? I rose to my feet and stepped on the soft pillows to the railing. The arena was painted with dried blood. Rows of seats encircled a bloodied stage that lingered twenty or thirty feet underground. I'm sure the depth was to keep his warriors in. All could observe and cheer on the cruelty of Kenna's sport. The once yellow sand was now a mix of brown, red, and gold.

"I should go now." I turned to the door.

Kenna grasped my arm. "It's been a long time since the gateway has sent us anything. You may wish to leave, but you will never escape my house. You belong to me now. You will obey my command. Do you understand?"

He slid his hand down to my waist and placed his other on Quade's belt. "You will have no need of this."

I backhanded him. His lip split and leaked a small bit of blood. "Don't you dare touch my things or I will kill you where you stand, understood? I'm not some bitch you can claim for your own."

He straightened. "How I have waited for a woman with a backbone." Desire filled his tone. "You belong to me. I have claimed you. In time, you will obey me. I will enjoy every moment of teaching you." He licked the blood from his lip, and his wound healed.

"Finally, this place makes sense. I was wondering what wicked creature lingered in this world. It's you. You sacrifice all the males to keep your alpha status. No one can challenge you if there are no males."

"Very true. If I am the only male, then I can never lose my throne." He stepped closer and reached for my cheek. I slapped his hand away. "We think alike. You will be my female."

"I'm not a wolf. Why would you want to do that?"

"Ah, yes. All females give birth in this pack or there would be no food to feed the survivors. You're new. Different. A treat, you see. The pups you would bare would be —"

"I'd rather die." I glanced at the door.

"Ta'la is back to her post. There is no way for you to leave. If you enter the arena, I will not be able to stop the males from challenging you." He lowered his eyes. "I will give you time to think about this, dearest. And while I'm out, I will ask the pack what your new name should be. They are great with names." He laughed as he exited.

I flopped into the pillows and covered my face. I wanted to scream but knew the effort would only please my captor. I rested my hand on my bag. *If only Quade was here, he'd know what to do. He'd rip the head from Kenna's shoulders*, I thought. I rolled to my side and my watery eyes stared into the flames. I hoped Soleil and Lune had found Hope, Quade, and Sati, and gotten them out.

"My brother?" I whispered. "I wonder who he is. I've got the power he desired?" I looked over my hands. They seemed ordinary. I ran my hands through my hair, no horns or fancy ears decorated the top of my head. As I did this, I thought, *I'm human. That's all I have ever been and ever will be.*

"The lord sent you a bountiful meal." Ta'la entered and lowered a silver platter.

I sat up. I wondered, *Does this woman know whom I'm about to feast on?* The woman kept her eyes cast down. "Thank you. Want some?" I asked, curious of the answer.

"I mustn't."

I pinched and picked up a small potion of the tender meat. I placed it into my mouth, the juices moistened my parched mouth. The smoked meats I had eaten over the past few weeks were good, but they had dried me from the inside out. This melty, juicy, sweet meat boosted my mood. I tried not to think about where the food had come from as I shoveled in more and more, till I had devoured the entire platter.

"A woman with an appetite. You surely are a rarity," Kenna whispered from his seat beside me.

When did he get here?

His thick fingers grasped my chin and pulled my face close to his. I recoiled and gave him a sharp elbow to the chest. He pounced and pinned me to the pillowed floor. Kenna held down my wrists as he straddled my hips.

"You will never strike me again," he ordered. "I will teach you to have manners in my house."

I pushed my head back as far as the pillow under me would allow. Our heads cracked together when I head-butted him in the nose. "Get off me!"

Ta'la gasped and the platter dropped. "Milord!"

He rose to his feet and waved her out. She collected the platter and scurried from the house.

"I do find your fight intriguing." He rubbed his nose with a wide smile. "It's been a while since I've had to fight to fill my own lust."

"I will never stop fighting you. I have a job to do, and if you get in my way, I will kill you. Though …" I rose to my feet. "I've never killed before, I'm finding the thought of it quite … enjoyable." A fire lit in my chest as my mind created an image of Kenna lifeless on the ground, blood pooled around him.

My face must have shown my thoughts, because for the first time I tasted his fear. A sweet candy-like taste tingled my tongue. He took a step back.

"Who are you, half-breed?"

"Half-breed?"

He recovered from his fear as I showed truth to my ignorance. "You smell of both human and demon. A half-breed."

"Hmm …" I thought about the new information that I had just received. "Remember this as I take my leave. I tasted your fear and will indulge in it if you try to stop me from walking out of here. First I have a few questions you may be able to answer."

Interested, he went closer to the fire and sat down on a blue pillow. "I'm all ears, my love."

I rested myself down beside him. "What is Nemasa?"

He jumped at the name; his tanned face paled. "Never speak that name."

"Master!" Ta'la called from the door. "Your drinks!"

"Ah, yes …" His charmed confidence returned. "Bring them here."

She walked the few steps, head lowered. She bowed and offered him the two wine glasses. He lifted the cherry red wine from the platter. "Leave."

She nodded her head and left; her gray tail swished over the cushions.

"They serve you well."

"They serve us well, my sweet." He offered the drink. "Blood wine, the best we have. A toast to our new *friendship*," he said, choking on the word *friendship*.

I took the glass and clinked it with his. He drank his in gulps, and I sipped, in fear of poison, only enough to wet my lips. The nectar-sweet wine slipped down my throat and calmed my mind. Soon my arms tingled and numbed, the room faded dark. The last thing I saw was his wide, fanged grin.

Chapter Eleven

Tight pains in my wrists and ankles woke me from a dead sleep. The darkness smelled of wet earth and burnt cedar and the slight scent of flowers, but I couldn't make out which kind. The blackened room started to show silhouettes. There was a shelf over to the left, two feet to the right from where I lay, a table with jars scattered on top. I attempted to lift my hands, but they were bound tight to my chest. A click from a door made me stare down past my feet at the wall that cracked open.

"She should be awake now," a female voice whispered. "She showed no sign of injury to the drug. She is a full creature, soul element and form unknown. Her human appearance might be used as a lure."

"I will take it from here," Kenna's unmistakable voice answered and flipped my gut.

The door opened; my eyes snapped shut. I could hear his footsteps as he entered the room and wandered over to the shelf to the left of me. My eyelids lit as a light turned on. The lower half of the bed sunk. My body froze as his hand grasped my knee.

"Are you awake yet, my love?" he whispered. "I do wish to change your mind on wanting to leave me. It's been so long since I've had anything other than wolf and would love for you to make me something new. I can hear your heart beating fast, my dear. You can't fake this sleep any longer."

My eyes cracked open, his ears twitched with joy. "There you are, my sweet. You've slept for a little over five days now." He crawled over the bed. "Did you sleep well?" I tried to reach out and push him away, but my hands were bound to my chest. "Sorry, dear. I had to. See, I won't let you leave me, and I will do anything it takes to keep you here forever." His mellow and calm voice tried to soothe.

Kenna's hand brushed away the little bit of hair that had bunched over my face in my struggle. "I have a few questions for you, my sweet." He stood and walked to the table. His hands moved over an object I couldn't see. "This surprised me. I never thought I'd ever see such power in a half-breed, though we both know you're not," he said as he flashed me a smile. He lifted the book from the table, and my heart stopped. "What is this, my love?" he asked, his voice honey coated. "Ta'la opened it and is now bedridden." A fire lit in his eyes. "I hate sick wolves. They're useless in every way possible."

"She opened it?" I asked, shocked. "She read out a passage?"

"Yes, this morning. What is this?" His hand slammed down onto the shelf.

"I don't know …" It was the truth, but I doubted he'd believe me.

His shoulders dropped as he released a calming breath. "Do you know anything about yourself?"

Kenna lowered himself back onto the bed with the book resting on his lap. I clenched my jaw, slightly grinding my teeth. When I lifted my eyes to him, he stared at me awaiting an answer.

"Nothing. I know absolutely nothing about myself. Everyone I meet knows the answers to my questions but is too afraid to speak the words aloud. Even when I asked the confident and strong Kenna, you cowered from my question."

A sharp pain crossed my face as he struck me. "I cowered? *Ha!* I fear nothing."

"Then tell me, tell me what Nemasa is. What is in the name that caused you to react so fearfully?" His eyes, once again, widened at the mention of the name. With no reply I continued, "When I talked to Madness —"

"That is enough!" he hollered and struck me again. My cheek stung. "I will hear no more. You are crazed. If you have spoken to *her*, then you have been touched by insanity." He backed away from the bed, his ears pulled back and his tail stilled.

"I can help Ta'la. Let me help her. Ignore my rambling and let me help her. She meant no harm. I can tell the book that. You must let me."

"You are touched by *her* and, therefore, are more damned than us." Kenna's hazel eyes darkened. "I'm sorry, my love. You'e told me too much. Tomorrow you will be placed in the arena with the other crazed."

With a sharp turn, he opened the door and left with the book. It was nice of him to leave the light on, so I extended my neck as high as it could go to see onto the shelf. Unfortunately it wasn't long enough. My belt and bag were gone, and from what I could tell, so was the locket and key. Defeated, I flopped back.

All I wanted were answers, and Madness seemed the best choice to get them. I didn't expect my own name to cause such fear in the creatures. I closed my eyes tightly and tried to force myself to remember. Without the child, I had been unable to enter my personal void. I bounced my head on the pillow in frustration.

"The one touched by *her*, I am entering your room," a shaky girl's voice called through the closed door.

Soon it swung open and a child no older than ten walked in carrying a tray of cooked meat. "The lord apologizes for not being able to make it to dinner. He says he will be down before night fall." The child entered, kneeled at my bedside, and held up the tray. Her ears pulled back and her tail wrapped around her leg.

"Um, sorry." I wiggled my bound hands, a rope held them to my chest. "I can't reach …" I flushed. "Just eat it for me."

"That would be wrong," the child said, weakened by her shaken nerves. "I will feed it to you then." She rose and balanced the heavy platter on one hand.

"That's a beautiful tail you have. I wish I had one," I said, with a smile to calm the child.

Her tail wagged once, and her head bobbed in a confused bow. Her little fingers pinched a pile of the meat and placed it into my mouth.

I had eaten half the platter of delicious melty meat when Kenna appeared in the doorway. He watched as the child fed me. I couldn't read the expression he wore. My mind warned me that he had a new plan for me. His hand clenched the book tightly at his side. I bit the inside of my cheek. The need to have my book back resurfaced, making bile sting the back of my throat.

"Leave," he ordered the child. "Feed the rest to your family."

"Honored, milord," she chirped, her tail wagged. "Milord, I sense she has not succumbed to the craze."

He nodded and dismissed her with a wave.

"Know what that means, my love? I get to keep you. There will be no battle in the arena for you, yet."

He slipped a tiny knife from a sheath hidden in his fur. "You will heal Ta'la, and then you will take your place at my side." A thick dagger cut the ropes from my limbs. "If you choose to defy me, you will return to this room. Each time will be longer and without food."

He offered me his hand, his eyes commanding me to take it. Not wanting to end up with my arms and legs wrapped in rope again, I placed my hand in his. He guided me out of the room. We walked past thick wooden beams, plaster walls, and a few cracked wooden doors. He stopped at a short staircase, and nudged his head up the narrow climb. It led up to a sealed door that he waved open.

"I am the only one who can unlock the doors from the lower levels," he boasted. "Keeps the warriors from escaping to the surface and causing a ruckus."

"Oh, we wouldn't want that now, would we?" I rolled my eyes behind his back and stepped onto the main floor. He closed and locked the door, and then started us down a wide plaster hall.

"You will learn, my sweet," he said as he raised my hand to his lips. "After we aid Ta'la, we will bond, and you will be mine forever. You're okay with it and that makes me happy. We will rule with open hands."

We passed doorways covered with leather as we made our way over the hardwood hall floor. The plaster walls were cracked in many places and decorated with candles. At the end of the hall, Kenna stopped and caught both of my wrists, pinning me to the wall and pressing his body into mine.

"Maybe we aid her after ..." He leaned his face close to mine.

"Now," I responded before his lips touched mine. He blinked, confused. "She doesn't have much time left. Did you hear what was read?"

"No," Kenna answered. "She was alone, found later with the book open over her." His breath smelled of the wine he used to drug me.

"Then we must hurry," I urged. "If you really want her well, then you need to let me go to her now, or she will die."

"I can't have that." Kenna's palm hit the wall by my head, and the plaster cracked under the pressure. "She is our prime female. We can't let her die."

I took my hand he no longer held and placed it on his cheek. "Then we must go to her," I whispered. I let my fingers brush against his ear. "You can save this passion for later. It can be our way of celebrating."

Charmed, he grinned and pulled me from the wall. "This way," he said with a skip.

Kenna led me into the backroom where Ta'la lay on a thin straw bed coved in a light fabric, her face a ghostly white. Herbs and potions lined shelves that were nailed into the plaster walls. A few unoccupied beds cramped the tiny space. Clean, sharp instruments lined the top of a desk where an old lady sat grinding a few chosen herbs.

"Milord, she is not well. We don't know if it is contagious. Guests, and you, milord, should stay out," the older wolf suggested.

"She knows more about what happened and has promised to give Ta'la aid." Kenna encouraged me in front of him.

"I need the book to see what she read." I held out my hand, thinking up a plan of escape on the spot. He refused and hid it behind his back. I smiled and swayed toward him, my fingers traced his hard abdomen, "Please, you need to trust that this is what she needs. I have to know what she did to undo it. I need all my other belongings as well.

"This book has a seal. I need to unlock the seal to be able to read it without harming myself in the process. If I read it with the seal active, I will die along with your best female, along with Ta'la." I batted my eyelashes twice. "And," I whispered, peeked over my shoulder to the healer, then back to him, "the faster I get this done ..." I scanned his body, hinting at our conversation we had before we came into the room.

"Healer, gather the things we have collected from my sweet and bring them to her with haste," he commanded the woman with an aroused grin, his eyes fixed to mine.

The moment the healer left the room, I didn't trust the closeness I had created between Kenna and myself. I hurried to Ta'la's side. I listened to her breathing, her heartbeat, checked her eyes; flashbacks of Noah rushed in and caused me to gasp. Kenna kneeled beside me and placed his hand on my back, worried that the change of heart rate and breathing was due to his beloved pup-barring queen.

"Sorry. I just remembered what happened to the last creature that read my book without permission. He almost lost his eyes."

Ta'la's physical appearance seemed fine. There were no bursting veins; her skin was a normal healthy color, and she had no swollen limbs.

The healer joined us. She was carrying my side bag, belt, and sword. She handed them to me. With haste, I pulled the bag open; inside was my locket, the little key, and, *the black box*. I had forgotten about the gift from my mother. The belt slid onto my lap, the blade still cozy in its sheath. I pushed it aside and grabbed the little key from Madness. It felt lighter.

"This is the wrong key —" I tossed the fake key to the floor. "If I open the book with the wrong key, it will kill everyone in this room," I lied.

He withdrew the key from a pocket in his fur and handed it to me. "I didn't trust it in the open."

I took the key and started to slip it back into my pocket. Kenna grabbed my hand. "Don't you need it to unlock that book?"

"Watch. Trust me, milord." I blinked a slow blink and let my free fingers brush against his arm. "I know what I am doing."

Hesitantly, he released me and let me slide the key into my pocket. I ducked under the strap of the bag, securing it to my body, and placed it on my lap.

I retrieved the locket from within the bag. "The book, please." An alluring smile crept up my cheeks.

He placed it into my hand. I unfolded the chain of hearts to form the key. Quade's warning not to open the book without him crept into my mind. I told myself that it was okay, my only way out. The book opened and I flipped to the first page. I placed one hand on the page and closed my eyes.

The abandoned house that Hope and I played in as children appeared around me. Its floor was missing boards, and the walls were knocked in and spray painted with different works of art. Bright sunbeams shone through the multiple holes in the collapsed ceiling.

"Where are you?" Quade asked from behind.

I spun around, and my arms wrapped around him tight. Stunned, he stood there for a moment, and then his arms tightened around me.

"Where are you?" he asked again in a whisper.

"I have no idea." I lifted my head off his warm chest and marveled at his amethyst eyes. "Someone read the book and has been put into a sleep. I need to wake her to be able to get away. I also need a way to make sure this man can't touch me anymore."

His eyes narrowed and his lips tightened. "Who?" he growled. His jaw clenched.

"Please, Quade, I don't have —" My head twitched to the side. Kenna shook me, trying to pull me out.

Quade whispered a spell into my ear, a warmth gripped my body. "Place your hand on her head and your skin will absorb the poison. No one can touch you after. It will last only for an hour —"

Quade vanished and I was back in the room with Ta'la, Kenna and the old wolf.

"What did you do that for?" I snapped at Kenna. "Crap! Well, I hope it works now."

Kenna's eyes widened. "I wasn't sure if you were okay, my love."

"I'm fine. I told you I know what I'm doing," I barked.

Irritated, I placed my hand on Ta'la's forehead and closed my eyes. Quade's spell whispered throughout my mind and heated my hand. The warm heat turned hot and spread up through my arm and over my chest, flooding into my body. My skin turned green as Ta'la's eyes opened. A sour-acidy smell filled my nose. That was my clock — when the smell vanished so did the poison.

"Ta'la ..." Kenna kneeled down beside the woman as she put the pieces together of where she was. "It's okay. She has healed you." He turned his excited grin to me. His expression dropped when his eyes locked with mine. I glared at him with all my hatred. He swallowed hard before he opened his mouth to say something, but I cut him off.

"Kenna, if you touch me, you will be placed under the same spell she was under. If anyone touches me, they will be placed under that spell. Do you hear me?" The green entered my veins and mapped my arms. I grabbed Quade's belt and stood. I lifted my foot to the door. Kenna went to grab my arm, then withdrew. I tightened the belt around my waist with a wide grin.

"You tricked me." Kenna's eyes watered, attempting to pull on my empathy.

"I did," I announced cooly. "I never wanted you, never will." I grinned. "I will take my leave." I bowed my head to the lord and exited.

The wolves didn't try to stop me as I left the village. They sniffed the air and backed away, able to smell the poison that pumped though my veins and leaked out my pores.

"You! Girl!" a woman called from the trees. "Come here!" A hand waved out from a vine-covered spruce. "I need to speak to you. And I can take you to the door you seek."

I cautiously strolled to the voice and peeked around the thick branches to find a wolf woman, a huge scar across her face. Her lower lip was split in two. "I have been planning to help you escape, milady, but I failed you. Forgive me."

"You know me?"

"No, I know the one you carry with you. The soul of my grandson travels with you."

"The soul of your grandson?"

"Yes, yes, milady. Please, how is he?" the woman asked with a huge smile, her hand waving me in the direction of the door.

"His mother escaped this world many moons ago. I have kept them in my thoughts. How fares my daughter? We get no information of the outside world. When I saw that book and touched it with my own hands, I knew it was him, my grandson. How is he?"

We quickly navigated through the trees, bushes, and shrubs as the woman asked questions with no room for answers.

"You say that your grandson's soul is in that book?"

"Yes."

"Do you know his name?"

"No. Nemasa said if my daughter bore a son, he'd be the guardian of her daughter. It was wonderful that the Nemasa befriended my daughter. She removed them from this place. I feared my child's temper would have caused her to fall victim to the arena after she bore her pup ..."

A door came into view. "I am sorry to tell you that my mother and your daughter have passed. Does the name Quade mean anything?"

"Quade? Yes, if I were ever allowed to keep my sons, I would have named one Quade."

"That is your grandson's name. I will let him know about you."

"Please, milady. I'm glad that he is okay, that he's alive and well. You're kind, milady, like your mother. Thank you." She bowed to the ground.

I turned to the door and tapped the key to the wood. The door unlocked with a *click*. I turned to the woman. "What should I tell him his grandmother's name is?"

"Zanda," she whispered. Joy filled tears streamed down her cheeks. "Fair well, Nemasa."

With a nod of my head, I vanished into the void and locked the door behind me.

Chapter Twelve

I rested my back on the door, the key in my pocket. My eyes searched the doors around the vast space. Thousand upon thousands of doors, and I needed to find a single creature with a missing horn. Every beast behind me wore their horns polished. Kenna liked his women polished, graced, strong, and attractive.

A huge sigh left my lips as I pushed away from the door. I turned to glance at the torch. "Torch to my left has many creatures lingering behind." I rested my forehead on the rough wood and shivered. "I almost became his ... his mate." Another disgusted shiver ran down my back and over my arms. "Yuck. Never again will I enter into this world."

I turned and walked toward a door with a torch to the right. I spotted three, each aged differently. I chose the closest. While I walked, my conversation with Zanda came to mind. *She was Quade's grandmother! His mother was from there. If she had stayed, Quade would have been eaten.*

I raised the book and stopped. "His soul? This is his soul?" I placed it back in the bag. I glanced around to make sure no one had seen me with it. "No way."

I continued on my way to the door. *I will have to go through every door. It's going to take forever …*

I tapped the key on the gray wood and heaved it open. The world on the other side was darker than the void I stood in. I placed my hand on the inner ring and pulled the door shut behind me as I slipped into the darkness. I kept my hand on the ring and hit the key to the door. *Click.*

Afraid to release the iron ring, in fear I would never find my way back, I held it tight. The darkness swallowed the world. My eyes were unable to adjust. I listened, no sound. I tucked the key into my pocket and crouched to the ground. With my nose closer to the ground, I could smell the wet, soft earth.

I crawled and swept my hands over the ground as I navigated over sharp and mushy needles that jabbed at my fingers while my hands slid over flexible barbs. Soon I could hear a constant splash ahead, and smell freshness as water filled the air, batted at the distant banks. The twigs I knelt on snapped as I crawled over to the river's side. The moist ground turned to rough stone.

The loud river rang in my ears. I bathed in the tranquility of the water gushing over stone. The sound of wind through the trees joined in. I breathed in the scent of the wet stone and humid air.

A snap of a twig caused me to tense. My head turned to the sound. The wind tuned out as I focused, the river quieter. I listened for a while but heard no more.

I ventured away from the river, back onto the mulch, over the tiny spikes. Time after time, my hands got pricked. I began to avoid them as I noticed the sickly odor.

Once the river was at a distance, I stopped and leaned my back against a smooth, hard substance that had no scent or warmth. My hands throbbed and were covered in tiny scratches. My knees hurt, and my shoes were soaked. My wrists stung from the bite of Kenna's rope. I began to wonder what possessed me to enter into that lightless world. I could see from the doorway what this place was. I raised my hand in an attempt to make an orb like Quade and Lune. As the sour odor from the poison wore off, I let my hands drop to my side. I knew no magic.

My eyes dropped closed, exhausted from all that Kenna had put me through, the spot was comfy enough to let my mind drift to sleep.

I toyed with the emerald dress I wore. My tiny hands were as big as the foxtail emblem embroidered into the hem. The woman's long, thin arms wrapped around my puny body, and I was warmed by her closeness. I lounged in her lap. Her crimson sleeves draped over my shoulders and collected on my knees.

"Mommy, Mommy, I can't see my pretty dress," the child I possessed spoke, unaware of my presence. (I realized that I was reliving my own childhood within the form of my three-year-old self.) Her tiny arms shoved at the rich material. "Look, look!" The child's body bounced on the lap of her mother's. She pointed to a boy, no older than seven. He pulled away from the tall, black-haired woman who had held his tiny hand. He straightened up at the sight of us and his lips cracked in a smile from ear to ear.

"Yes, sweetheart, you both did very well today." The woman petted the hair of the child.

"Nemasa," the woman and boy said in unison and bowed.

"You're three now. What kind of mischief do you have for my son this year?" the black-haired woman asked as she and the boy raised their heads. Her fine hands worked her dress around her as she knelt onto the wood. The boy flopped onto her lap. "What you both did today was very grown up. You're now the Nemasa. How do you feel?"

"Um ... " The girl turned to her mom, confused by the question.

The mother cradled her daughter's tiny face in her palm, the pressure and warmth of her hands warmed the girl's cheeks. "Do you feel like a princess?"

"Yep, I do. Look at my pretty dress." She jumped up and jolted to an open spot on the balcony to twirl. The long emerald dress lifted from her legs and encircled the child. She giggled and laughed as she watched the foxtail ripple.

"Beautiful," the boy announced as he stumbled to his feet. "Come, Nemasa. Let's go play in the woods."

Nemasa ... they called the child that. Me. I had drifted into my memories. I tried to turn the child's head to get a better view of our mother.

Her playful gaze stuck to the boy and his wonderful suggestion.

"Quade, please make sure she doesn't get too dirty. She has a ball to attend tonight, so do you," my mother warned.

"To the pond." Quade waved his hand through the air. "Short walk."

He grabbed her young hand and guided her toward the staircase off the deck.

"Wait!"

He stopped and glared at the girl, "What?"

"I am Nemasa." Her little hand waved, and then gripped the sides of the dress. The rim of the dress rose off the ground to keep it from dragging.

"Oh, bother ..." Young Quade smacked his face with his hand. "Girls ..."

"Hey!"

"I know. I know. Can't get dirty."

Young Quade led her by the hand to the pond, their little fingers twisted together. The girl's heart sang, the lullaby hummed out of her throat. Even Quade joined in with his boyish tone.

The pond, surrounded by large rocks, was a small circle of water that reflected the fiery sky. Quade released her hand and rushed off behind a large stone. The girl gasped, her eyes widened. Her heart picked up its pace. Once his head popped back out, her body calmed and grinned.

He caught her distress and flung his arms around her tiny body. "I will never leave you, Nemasa. Never, ever."

Her arms tightened around him.

"Look what I found." He leaned back, keeping her close but far enough to show her what he had. His little fist appeared in front of her. One finger peeled open, then the next, until he revealed a small white pebble. "Mama says it's a moonstone. I found it for you. Mama says it helps with dreams."

The girl opened a small slit behind the black velvet ribbon wrapped around her emerald dress. Underneath was a small pocket. She crammed the stone in.

"Isn't this cute? Nemasa and her guardian out for a stroll by the pond."

The child's eyes peered up. The one who spoke appeared as nothing more then a shadow.

"Brother," the surprised little girl sprinted to him with open arms. He caught her in his, picked her up, and spun around. His shadowy figure took on more of a solid suited form. His face remained blurred.

"Little sister, you look stunning. A true Nemasa! You deserve the title." His hand rose to offer her a crimson candy. "I brought you a gift." The child let him pop it into her mouth.

"Happy birthday, little sister. Three now. Time really does fly when you're having fun." He balanced her in one of his arms, his claws traced the fox emblem. "I have another birthday present for you. I made it myself, believe it or not. I am quite skilled."

"You do?" she asked with a candy-filled mouth.

"Yes, meet me by the Old Tree. Bring Mommy along. She'll die to see what I have for you." He lowered the child to the ground with a deep chuckle. "There will be another candy waiting for you, too, little sister."

"You're the best big brother ever."

"I know, I know. You remind me everyday. I will always look out for you. Remember that." With a wave he turned and headed back down along the dirt trail.

"I don't like him," Quade growled. The girl's watery eyes met with his glare and smothered it. "Sorry, Nemasa … I … "

"You big meanie," she barked and chased down her brother as tears flooded out.

A damp shiver woke me. Thick liquid rained down through the blackness. I slid over to the left and wedged myself in the rock, getting most of me out of the rain. My stomach growled and my hands stung. I was lost in the darkness.

The droplets created a barrier of sound all around me, a tranquil music of rain. The pitter-patter of the drops hit the wet leaves and turned up the soaked mulch. The river rushed in the distance.

"Brother!" the girl called as she searched the path. "Brother? Please, come back."

The blurred-face man appeared around the bend and knelt, with his arms open. "Oh, dear, little sister, did that mean boy do something to upset you?" His thick hand wiped the stray tears.

"He-he, a big meanie. That what he is. Mean, mean, boy."

"I know I'm not supposed to give you too much candy, but that mean boy made you cry. Don't tell Mommy," he whispered and held out another crimson candy. "Our little secret."

The girl took the candy and licked it a few times. The sweetness tingled her tongue. She popped it into her mouth.

"Don't forget to come see my gift. I have an idea. Go get Mommy right now, and I'll give it to you early. Don't tell anyone that it's from me yet, or someone may ruin my surprise, and I can't have that."

185

He wiped away the last tear. *"What in Sin did that boy say to you to make you cry? No Nemasa should ever cry."*

"He said he didn't like you."

"Do you like me, little sister?"

"Yes, big brother. You're the bestest ever."

"And that's all that matters. I don't care what the boy thinks, only you, little sister, only you." He brushed her hair behind her ear. *"Now run along. Go get Mommy. I'll get my gift ready."*

"Okay." She hopped down from his arms and skipped along the path toward the castle.

Her mother sat on a chair, legs folded under her. Beside her sat Quade's mother. She smiled while she sipped her hot drink. The girl's mother's lips moved, and they both laughed at an unheard joke.

"Mommy!" the child yelled out with a wide grin, *"Mommy, come."*

Quade's mother's eyes searched the trail. *"Where is Quade?"*

"He's a big meanie."

"Oh, little lady, did you two have a fight?" the girl's mother, my mother, asked, her face clear for me to see. Her long crimson hair reached her lap, her soft face sported lightly rose cheeks. Her eyes were the color of evergreen trees. *"We should go get him. He's most likely searching the whole woods for you."* Her smile warmed the dark corner of my mind that I couldn't seem to fill. This was my mom. I spotted her white horns, and behind them twitched red fox ears, tipped black. Beautiful, I remember thinking.

"Come with me first. I have something to show you."

The mother's face lit as she took in the wonder in her daughter's eyes. Her rose lips grew into a gorgeous smile that showed off her white fangs. "Quickly then, we have to go set things right with Quade. You know he's not a big meanie. Whatever it is he did, you shouldn't be calling others rude names. It's not very ladylike." Her soft laugh filled the air.

"I know, but he made me mad." The child stomped her foot on the wooden deck.

"Boys tend to do that, little one." She bent down and swept the girl into her arms. "Now where are we going?"

"The Old Tree, by the caves."

The forest became quiet the closer they got to the Old Tree. It towered over the lush green ones that accompanied it. The twisted, ash-covered branches jutted out of the trunk like broken boney fingers. A shadow from the short mountain on the right darkened the rest of the trail. The girl clung to her mother, scared of what might be lingering in the mountain's shadow.

"Would you like a nap when we get home, little lady?" her mother asked while she brushed her fingers through the child's hair.

"No, I too big."

"How about you put me to bed? I'll have a nap and you watch over me."

"You're too big to have a nap, Mommy," the girl stated as she pulled back to search her mom's eyes for a clue that she was joking.

"Oh, you think adults don't like naps? I love naps."

"You do?"

The mother and daughter arrived at the Old Tree. The grass and underbrush died off closer to where the tree stood. The mother put the girl down and stepped over to Old Tree. Her hand swiped the ash bark. "What is it you wanted to show me?"

"Brother told me he had a gift."

"Your brother?" Her voice cracked, her eyes searching the surrounding trees. "When did he speak to you?"

"Today," the chipper girl said. "He gave me a candy."

"Why did you and Q —"

Out from the shadow of the tree, our brother slipped out and leaned his shoulder against it. "Hello, Mother, miss me? You banished me, remember that, Mother? I was utterly hurt." He pushed from the tree and stepped closer to the shaken woman. "Come, little sister. I have your gift."

The child rose to her tiptoes and hopped to him. Her mother intervened, dropped to her knees, and held the child close. "Happy birthday, little lady. Mommy loves you." She began to hum the lullaby.

The song gurgled. A wet splatter sprayed down their bodies. The beautiful woman's face turned a sickly white, and her head fell forward, rolled off her shoulders, down her body, and stilled on the ground. Her body limp.

"M…m…mommy! No!" I hollered out into the dark world around me.

I woke from the nightmare.

The sound of the rain vanished as I jumped to my feet and drew Quade's sword. I hacked forward. I didn't care what was ahead of me. The blade was embedded into the nearest tree. Again and again, I hacked and slashed. Over and over. My body heated; my rational mind switched off. The black world around me danced with thin crimson streaks.

The thud-thud of blade against wood rang in my ears. Tears flooded from my eyes, my body trembled. I screamed a loud, long, pained screech. One final swing and the tree I had beaten snapped, and the crackle of tree branches filled the air. The thud of the tree crashing to the ground made me scream out again as I fell to my knees.

The ground cooled my knees as they slammed into the puddled soil. My shoulders slouched forward and my head drooped down onto my chest. Tears dripped straight off the lids of my eyes onto my lap, the hilt still squeezed by my fingers.

"You shouldn't wake her. She still needs to sleep," a man coaxed from behind a white door. A yellow light seeped in from the crack between the door and cream-colored carpet. "It's midnight, sweetheart. When she gets up in the morning, you can give it to her."

"I know how late it is," the woman argued.

"Then let her sleep, honey."

"It will only be a minute. She will be back asleep in no time," she begged.

"How about you slip it around her neck and when she wakes up she will see it? It will be a nice surprise, like the tooth fairy. We could turn it into a birthday tradition."

"Oh, hun," the woman almost sang. "That's a fantastic idea. I love you."

"I love you, too."

The warm blankets felt like they had swallowed me whole. Cozy and warm. My head lay on a bright pink pillow, underneath an army of unicorns, dolls, bunnies, and cute dragons. Pink ballerinas danced on the top of the purple walls.

The door clicked open. My eyes snapped shut.

"Oh, dear, look at our angel. She's asleep," the woman whispered. "I can't believe that we were blessed with such an adorable child."

"I know, dear. We really have been given an angel."

"When the doctor told me … we couldn't have a child, I told him. Oh, I let him know that no one could tell me that. And now here is our little miracle."

"Give her the gift quickly. We don't want to wake her. I'm sure even angels get cranky when awakened too early."

The woman laughed. "Yes, sweetie."

Quiet footfalls pressed into the carpet and over a few squeaky floorboards. My head was lifted and cold, thin metal was slipped around my neck. A warm, loving kiss pressed against my forehead. "Happy birthday, little lady," the woman whispered into my ear. "Mommy loves you."

A painful heat boiled under my skin and erupted as the flashes of memory of my brother's betrayal blew through my mind. My eyes sprung open. The purple room shined red from the flames that seeped from my bed to the white nightstand, melting the plastic princess toy that waited there. The stuffed animals that protected me from the monsters I feared failed to tell me that I was the monster.

My wide eyes scanned the flames, and on the floor beside my bed were two charred bodies. Their arms reached for the bed of flame. My heart pounded. I flung off the blanket. I leapt off the bed. As the last bit of me released the covers, the bed turned to ash.

My little feet torched the carpet as they carried me forward, out of the burning room. The flames flickered, taking on the form of large, monstrous foxes. Their tails, which were made of flame, lit all they touched. They gnashed their fangs and lunged out the door.

I followed the trail they left in their wake. Burnt paw prints imprinted in the hard wood floor. Framed pictures of an infant in the arms of a loving mother and father filled the light green walls. A bookshelf topped with wooden frames which held images of a toddler smiling in the sun, filled the nook by the stairs. The tracks led down and around the corner. I followed.

Gnash of fangs and growls echoed with the crackle of the fire. I held tight to the hand rail as my little legs struggled with the large steps. The smoke and heat didn't seem to bother me. The fire hugged my body as I walked through unharmed. The white dress I wore repelled the flames, glistened in the dancing light. The lace played against my knees as I jumped off the last stair, landing on both feet at once.

I peeked around the corner, with a grin. A game of hide and seek with the foxes came to mind as I peeked under the tables and chairs. Around the corner, I peered into the fiery room. I spotted one of the foxes jumping on the couch. It glanced at me, and with a happy bark, it scurried off into the next room.

"There's a child in there," a booming voice called from outside.

I ran back into the hall to see if I could find any more of my fox friends before the voice came in and took me away.

"There you are," thick yellow arms wrapped around me. "Don't be afraid. You're safe."

The firefighter removed me from the house. I was able to grasp the extent of the fire. Flames billowed out from the second story windows. The structure cracked, and collapsed. A gust of heat hit my face, then I was chilled by the early morning air.

"Just the child?" another firefighter asked.

The one that held me removed his mask. His dark eyes watered. "Unfortunately … she's the only survivor."

"What happened here?" the other asked and removed his mask. "I've never encountered a fire like this one. The water isn't working on it. It's not even spreading to the trees or other houses."

"You'll be okay," the firefighter that saved me promised.

Chapter Thirteen

My eyes sprang open. Blood rained from the black sky. It soaked the world and flickered with the glow emanating from the fiery orange flames that engulfed my body. Tears streamed down my cheeks as the memories clawed at my broken heart.

"I lost my bargaining chip," Madness announced as she made her way into view, tailed by the wicked-faced girl. "Seems the deal's off. You recalled it all on your own. Well done, Nemasa." Her lanky form wiggled as she spoke. Her arms slung behind her head. "Go to her now, child. I will have to plan another way to make you mine."

The child curtsied then dashed toward me. Her body absorbed into mine when our bodies collided. A hot heat lingered where her body met mine. The sensation spread throughout, seeping into my limbs and face. The flames flickered from orange to a deep red.

With a twitch, Madness turned to the darkness and vanished. "Let's play again."

A loud noise from the distance sparked my attention. Finally the demon hidden in the dark sensed me.

"Come to me," I whispered. I lifted my arms, embracing the sin that had laid dormant within me for too long. I glanced around at the black sky, Quade's sword in my grasp. My lips twisted at the corners, amused by what might happen when the creature reached me.

The image of my mother's headless body caught me off guard. I swung wildly at the nearest thing to me, a tree. The blade embedded deep into the wood. The flames around my body spiraled down the cool steel and began to bite at the wet wood.

A great snap of trees and a loud groan filled the air and warned me of danger emerging from the forest. A whisper tickled my ears, but my mind was too preoccupied to listen. I wanted the beast to find me. Fresh meat. A brutal kill.

"Come get me!" I growled and withdrew my blade from the bark. Wildly, I hacked at the tree. Over and over. My hands and body trembled, my face hot from the memories of my brother's hateful deed. Over and over. Each hit slammed deeper and deeper. "Find me," I yelled again.

A close-by snap, my tense body halted midswing. The air smelled of rotted meat and foul body odor. My guest had arrived. My guest ... no, my meal.

"The light. Where is it? I know it's here. Where?" the creature's voice rumbled as it tore the trees from the ground. "The light ..." His head turned to me. "There it is." He reached out with his massive paw, its sharp talons reflected my flames.

"Give me your light. End my eternal darkness. I hate the dark," it whimpered.

Pathetic, I thought as the creature came into view. The light from the flames lit its patchy skin as he emerged from the trees.

"Give it to me," it roared. The creature cocked its massive paw back and launched over the ground. The trees in the way snapped like tiny twigs. My legs were too slow to react as the palm slammed into me and his fingers curled.

The creature's fist squeezed the air from my lungs. I gasped to fill them. I wiggled; he tightened his grip. "Don't worry, my light," the creature raised me to its snout. Blotchy hairy patches decorated its dark, sickly-gray skin. "I won't eat you or kill you. I need you. You will be my light, yes, my light. I finally have light."

The pressure around my body loosened. I tried to force the flames to devour my attacker, but every time my fire touched the creature, it sizzled as if he were made of water. The beast leaned back and held me up to its surroundings. I lit the crimson painted stone, leaves, and thick green underbrush. The creature's black beady eyes widened as he took his first look around.

"Oh, how wonderful! Look at that! What is that?" It moved me to the side. A stream that trickled down the stone had slowed. The creature was fascinated by the flowing red mass. "I'll bring you home to Mother. She hangs there, quiet, unmoving. That's why I love her. I do enjoy showing her my accomplishments. You, my light, are one. Mother will be proud." The beast let out a high-pitched shriek that caused me to cringe.

Mother? An image of my human mother's charred body flashed into my mind. Her hand forever reaching out for me. The smell of her burnt body stung my nose.

My whole body vibrated at the thought that my brother still breathed. *I trusted him, respected him, loved him.* My heart pounded, and the fire darkened in color. It licked my skin and clothes in their blood red furry.

"You're shaking my light."

My head snapped back then forward as the creature jerked me hard. "Turn your light back on ... brighter. Now!"

I ignored the roar from my captor. I felt a splatter of fresh blood on my face, and again, I watched my mother's head roll from her shoulders.

"Turn it up!" The beast tossed me to the ground. I bounced like a rag doll. The creature's fist collided with the stone wall, a boulder loosened and toppled downward, straight at me. I hopped to my feet and rolled to the left. The large stone stilled where I once laid. With my eyes fixed to the beast, I readied my blade. I would let nothing stand in my way. My thoughts created multiple ways I could tear my only brother's body apart. *Slow or fast? Make him feel the pain he has caused me or end his terror quickly?*

The creature's arm raised again, my grip tightened. Its paw swiped fast and low. I dashed forward and aligned with the massive, hairless wrist. I pointed the tip of Quade's sword toward the incoming paw. The creature jabbed the sword deep into its own flesh. The tip emerged out the other side. The force of his swing knocked me against a distant tree. Air was forced from my lungs and the world blurred. My eyelids squeezed shut and opened. The red glow from my flamed body deepened. My hands tightened to fists. Quade's sword stuck out of the beast like a bad sliver. The beast let out a high-pitched scream that rang in my ears.

"What's the matter? Can't handle a little cut?" I taunted.

The creature before me clawed at the sword in his paw. I held my breath with each inhale, hoping that it would calm the erratic gasps. The throbbing of my back and the pins-and-needles of every joint were forgotten. The creature would be my practice target. Every creature that stood in the way of my bittersweet revenge or fulfilling my goal would fall. My brother had to die, and I would be the one to kill him.

The beast, with his black glazed look, turned to me. His unwounded hand yanked the blade from his wrist, while sugary sweet juices dripped to the ground. Quade's blade gave a ting as it collided with the stone wall.

Kill it. Kill it, the child sang.

I lunged for the blade. With it tight in my grasp, I fed the hungry blade. The creature's flesh split wide open with each swing. The creature cried out, but nothing came to its aid. The rational side of me was cloaked underneath the wicked demon within me that desired the brutal punishment.

The creature lay still on the ground though my blade still hacked away. My heart pounded in my ears. Deep hateful growls rumbled from my throat, and blood poured from the wounds I could not feel.

"I'll kill him," I repeated several times before the final swing. I released the blade imbedded deep in the dead beast's hide. A vibration of pure rage shook every nerve within me. A wide, toothy grin had grown over the corpse of my saluter. Its greasy patched fur remained hidden under a thick layer of blood. The creature's skin resembled a well-used chopping block.

My tongue slid over the corner of my lips. The candied taste made my bottom lip turn in. I yanked out the blade, sawed off a chunk, raised it to my teeth and took a bite — sweet, tangy, and juicy.

My fire flickered out, and the world faded to black. The distant river sounded closer than it used to sound. Water beat the rocks and pounded my eardrums. The muscles underneath my skull hammered. My eyes were swollen shut. As my chest rose, streaks of sharp pain shot across my body. My fingers relaxed, the blade dropped and clanked against a few stones as it landed at my feet. During the battle the creature had slashed at my torso, its claws tearing open my front left shoulder down to my right hip. I hadn't noticed the throb of the pain.

The shirt I wore hung in threads. *The bag?* My eyes shot open as far as they could and searched the blackness. The pain from the battle was minimized as I felt for the strap. *It's gone.* I lifted my hands to call on the fox fire, but couldn't remember how I did it. I dropped to my knees, pain again forgotten, my hands patting through the dirt and rock. It had to be there. I pushed on over the ground, around the carcass, my hands getting jabbed by a sharp plant. My head was dizzy and light from the loss of blood and sheer worry that I had lost Quade's soul.

The book had to be here, somewhere. *How could I've been so stupid? Where is it?* I ignored the moments my body limped and when the world seemed to spin faster than it should. *Come on!*

My hands bumped a small, flat, smooth object. The box, and it was still sealed. I patted around it. The book lay beside the box and the bag. I cradled the book in my arms for a moment and dropped backward. The initial thud was painful as shock waved through every nerve after my whole body relaxed, and I let the natural process of my body's ability to heal take over.

The box. I bent my elbow and scooped it into my hand. The cube fit comfortably in my palm. I popped the top and let my fingers reveal the secret object. Without use of my eyes, it was difficult to know exactly what it was. A long, soft, velvety ribbon, in the middle of a cool metal ring. Attached to the ring hung an oval pendant of some kind. As my fingers rubbed its smooth surface, my eyes began to grow heavy, and with every blink, I saw a dim light. I let my eyes close, relax, and pull into the pendant. I could no longer feel the stings and throbs of my tattered body.

Bright candles coated stone walls. The round room was cut in half by dense, rusted bars that caged off the room. Behind the bars sat Sati and Quade. Lune slunk into the room from behind a thick wooded door. He withdrew a ring filled with keys and released

Quade and Sati. Sati followed close behind Lune with a limp in her step. Her foot left behind a thin trail of blood.

"We have to move quickly. We have to get Hope," Lune whispered to the group as he slunk to the wood door.

My heart sank.

Sati froze; her head turned to me. Those liquid crystal eyes locked into mine.

"Milady," she whispered and the others' heads whipped around. Their eyes searched the spaces around me. "What happened?" She swallowed hard as she took in my broken form. "Where are you? We are coming."

My mouth opened, but my strength failed. The room and everything in it disappeared.

Chapter Fourteen

Gasps of air attempted to fill my lungs. Every breath shot a sharp, hot pain across my chest. No matter how I breathed, I always fell short. I pulled up my right arm to push away the heavy weight on my stomach. I tugged at my arms, but they were pinned to my sides.

I pushed on my heels to lift my midsection, and *snap* went a rib. I bit my tongue to mask a scream. *Crack.* I bit harder. My eyes refused to open. They were swollen shut. I pulled and yanked at my arms and bucked up my leg. Every inch of me stung and throbbed.

Pressure formed on my chest again. I breathed in and prepared for another dose of pain. *Snap!* I released the trapped air in a scream. The sting lessened. Another breath in, and it hurt less. That couldn't be possible. *Snap!* I released another scream; I was not prepared for more instant pain.

The bindings on my arms released, though the weight on my chest remained. Warm tingles filled my face and traveled down my neck. I took another deep breath. My chest rose and fell with minimal pain. The warmth across my face cooled. My eyes fluttered open.

Hope straddled my stomach; her eyes drifted over me. I turned my head to the right and Quade knelt inches from me. *He must have held my arm down. If he held that arm.* I looked left but kept my head turned to him. Sati knelt poised at my side as she pointed out to Hope the massive gash across my torso.

"Hey!" Quade whispered. "Feel better?"

I went to open my mouth but failed.

"It's okay. Rest. You've been beaten up pretty bad. Broken ribs and a few fractures. Hope already healed all that. The cut is next. Just relax, it will be over soon." He placed his warm hand on my arm; his touch soothed my worries. My torso started to pulse, and the fusing skin stung. I tried to keep my attention on him to keep my mind off the rippling pain.

Stone walls arched over me, creating an enclosed narrow hall. A fire was burning a few feet away with a blue ring above to suck out all the smoke. An echo of drums pounded in my head. Crackles and pops startled me, snapping at my headache.

Hope had become skilled in magic and healed me as if she had known how her whole life. *When did she learn such things?* I wondered. With every painless breath I rejoiced that I wasn't still in the mud next to that carcass, unable to see my way back.

"Quade?" I turned my head to him. His elbows rested on his crossed legs, hands in fists over his lips.

Our eyes met, his tense shoulders released as his arms folded into his lap. "You had me worried, all of us worried."

"How did you find me?"

"I didn't," he said and scowled. "Lune and Sati did."

I propped up on my elbows. Quade placed his hand tight onto my shoulder and pressed me back down. "Sati spotted you in the castle. She said that you were seriously injured, then vanished." Quade bit his lip and turned his gaze away from mine.

"I remember seeing her before I passed out. How did I get here? Where are we?"

A smirk cracked. "That door over there …" He pointed to a door that was hidden by shadows. "It leads to all those crazy doors. Personally, I've never been there. Sati and Lune went and found you. Lune knows how to navigate through there, so he took Sati. They went straight for you." Even though his lips moved as if he spoke in bare whispers, it sounded as if he talked a bit too loud. His voice hammered on the soft muscle in my skull. My eyes squeezed shut, and my spine twitched as I pushed up onto my elbow. My body felt strange and new. "My head still hurts," I hinted. Maybe he knew why the world seemed loud.

"Well —"

"Oh, I'm jumping in on this!" Hope hollered, her mouth moved as if she released her words in a whisper. "I have to see her face when she finds out." She landed next to Quade. Her eyes sparkled; her teeth peeked through her lips.

"Find out what?"

"Oh, it's awesome!"

I glared at her, and then him. "What?"

Under the covers, a light flick hit my leg. Startled, I jumped to my feet. I glanced down at my legs. They seemed normal. Nothing moved under the thrown fur. A twitch of my spine and a swish behind me caused me to peek back. A bushy, white-tipped red tail swished with uncontrolled movements.

I twisted to take a better look. The tail was attached to me, and with the twitch of confused nerves, the tail flicked through the air. Soon settled, it curved an inch above the stone ground. I reached down and stroked the soft fur.

"Quade wouldn't let me touch it when you were wounded. Now you're not, so —" she reached over and took it in her arms as if my tail were a cat. Her hand pressed in. "Oh, so soft and fluffy. Just how I imagined it would feel." She shot a cold glare at Quade. "He didn't let me do this. But I did get to have a moment with those ever-so-foxy ears." Her mischievous gaze stared at the top of my head.

Her fingers through my fur calmed every nerve as they moved through the long hairs. The calm traveled up my spine and warmed the base of my neck. I managed to pull the tail from her grasp. Once the sensation faded, I moved my hand to my forehead.

Where it should have been bare, right above my eyebrows, my fingers hit bone. My mouth dried as they slid up to the pointed tip. *Horns.* I glanced at Quade. They felt the way his looked — rough and twisted. The fingers made their way up more, accidentally jabbed the inside of my triangular ear. They twitched, my whole scalp along with it.

"Holy crap," I gasped.

Hope swiped at my tail again. I turned so she couldn't catch it. "Yeah, you just went up on the awesome scale." She pounced again and missed. "I have a new and better way to bug you."

"Quade …" I shifted my attention. "Is this why the world seems loud?"

He pressed his palm into the ground and hoisted himself up. "Come with me." He nudged his head away from the door and down the dark hall.

When I lifted my leg to step over to him, I noticed that my clothes had been changed. It reminded me of something Krista would wear. Tight black shirt and pants that flared out at the ankle. Fitted and comfy.

Hope skipped to his side. "Where are we going?" she joked.

He pressed his lips tight. "You stay here. There are things I have to talk with Nemasa about. You're not invited."

"Don't be so mean," Hope whined.

Mean. That was the last thing I said to Quade before we parted as children, I called him "a big meanie." My heart pounded in my new ears. Tears filled my eyes. *How could I've been so cruel?*

"Nemasa!" Quade's eyes shot open as he spun to look at me. "Are you okay?"

I shook away the sudden wave of emotion. "I'm okay. Hope, I have to speak to him, too. Please understand."

She pushed out her bottom lip as far as it could go, then laughed. Her heart pounded in her chest, the air from her lungs whistled out of her nose. "Sure, I'll give you the space. But remember, this is a small, narrow space and sound travels well through it. Now you'll have to go far; you're going to be blocking my only way away from your … um … how should I put it? It would have to be in a language you understand, ah, canoodling. Hear me?" She wiggled her eyebrows.

Heat swamped my face. "Hope!" I barked.

Hope giggled while she spun on her heels and skipped to the fire. She plopped down in between Soleil and Lune. *Everyone is safe now,* I thought as a warm smile filled my face. *No one needs to know what happened to me behind the doors.*

Quade and I strolled down the corridor till the light of the fire dwindled away to a tiny spark. I could still hear the fire and the whispers of the others, though I didn't understand what they said. I followed close behind Quade. There was much I wished to say.

"Where were you?" he asked as his feet stopped. A low, quiet breath lowered his shoulders, but he kept his eyes cast away from me.

"When were you going to tell me that book is your soul?"

He swivelled his head around, then back. "I —"

"Wanted me to remember on my own? I understand. You could have, at least, told me that. It was hard to hear it from someone who we've never seen before. She knew who I was because I carried that book." My body shivered as the image of Kenna reached for me.

I stepped forward and rested my head on Quade's back. My horns kept my forehead from making contact, yet I could still feel his warmth and hear his quiet breath and heartbeat. "Thank you. You helped me more than you know."

He pulled his body away. I stumbled as I regained balance. The corners of my lips dropped. *Did he feel betrayed because I didn't want to tell him where I was, that I'd met his grandmother and knew the background his kind had? Was that the reason he hid his inner creature?*

He stepped further way. My heart snapped.

The crash of his fist into the wall caused my skin to jump. "I'm sorry you got hurt. I should have been there."

"If you had come with me, then who would have saved Hope? Kept her safe? Protecting her is like protecting me." My hand slid over his tense shoulder. "I would have been captured along with you, if I didn't think you'd be there for her."

"What is it about that human?" He pulled his hand off the stone and rested it on mine.

"She saved me. When I lost —"

The image of my parents' burnt bodies caught me off guard, and I stepped back, my heart pounding against my ribs.

"Nemasa?" He spun around and clasped my shoulders.

"Sorry. It's all fresh again," I breathed. "When I lost my parents in the fire, Hope was the only one that could reach me. She never left me when I lost control. She was right there, pulling me out, no matter what I did or said."

His hands slipped around my shoulders and pulled me to him. We stood in silence, my heart fluttering as his breath brushed my neck.

He released me and walked into the middle of the space. "Well, let's try out that new form of yours. You still won't have a chance against me, but who knows."

I laughed. "Yeah, sure, that's what you think. I have been practicing, you know." I jolted forward and swung my right leg.

He caught it with ease. "You're thinking too hard again. Relax. Have fun." He tossed my leg to the side, and my right foot stumbled back. His left foot hooked behind it, and I toppled to the ground. Quade lowered himself over me and straddled my stomach. His hands collected my wrists, held them above my ears. "See? Still too easy." He laughed as I attempted to buck him off.

"I was only joking but ... *ha* ... maybe I'll come back." Hope grabbed our attention. Neither of us had noticed her approach. Quade released my hands. "If you're hungry, food's ready."

Her cheeks tried hard to force the goofy smile from her lips. They wiggled and pressed. A laugh then burst through as she hopped back to the fire. "We'll put some food off to the side for you. Take your time."

When she was out of earshot, Quade lowered his head to mine, pressing the curve of our horns together, his nose, a hair's length from mine. "You're going to have to be careful now."

Heat flared over my face. "What do you mean?"

"Your sin is taking over. First you'll be able to hear the tinniest of whispers. That evens out after a while. Your headache should be gone by now. Next will be improved scent." His eyes locked into mine. I swallowed a dry lump. "When this happens, I want you to look directly at me."

"Why?" I whispered, surprised it came out at all.

"She's human. A drug. Most learn to control themselves at a young age. Pups are easier to train and do minimal damage. You're a pup in an adult's body. You could kill Hope before you even realize what you've done."

"You just said her name."

He sat up and frowned.

"Don't worry. I won't tell her." I let out a small laugh.

"You've never unleashed your demon yet. I might not be able to stop you." He crossed his arms over his chest. His face dropped. My tail that was pinned under my leg twitched. "Just be careful."

"I will. And … I think I did let out a bit of my rage before Sati and Lune found me. Did they tell you what they found when they came to me?"

"No, they refused to give me any details. I won't press you if you don't want to tell me. You hungry?"

"I could eat. What about you?"

He stood and offered me a hand. "Yes. Soleil and I hit up the kitchen in the castle. It's going to be a good meal." I placed my hand in his and let him pull me to my feet. "The human wasn't too pleased. She thought we were being reckless. She picked out our outfits — that was reckless."

"Sounds like Hope. I'm sure she enjoyed the thrill, even if she complained the whole time." I thought for a moment. "Where was she?"

"Krista's room. I'm sure Krista came back and noticed Hope was gone as we entered the kitchen. Guards flooded the halls. We lucked out. The hidden door we needed to exit through was located in the wine cellar below the kitchen floor. We were long gone before they noticed the cages were empty." A pride-filled smile took over his face. "Come on. Before the human gets any more ideas."

Soleil and Lune had propped their backs against the wall. Their hands held filled bowls. Hope and Sati took their seats by the fire. Their grins accused us as Quade and I entered the camp.

"What?" I asked.

The twins shifted their gaze to their food in sync and took a big bite. Quade served us each a bowl of stew and ignored the glances the others gave us.

"Milady," Sati said as she rested her bowl on the ground. "I collected your things from where I found you." She lifted the brown, blood-covered bag, reached in and pulled out a black velvet ribbon. In the middle hung an oval mirror. "This was in your hand when I found you." She passed it over to Quade, who then tied it around my neck.

"What is it?"

"It's a mirror that allows you to see whatever you wish to see. It will translocate your soul to show you what you are looking for. I was able to see your soul. Milady, if we had not found you when we did, you might not be here now."

"Thank you for coming for me. How did you know which door to use?" I scooped up and ate some of the stew. The textures and taste exploded in my mouth.

Lune leaned forward. "We are the keepers of the keys. It's our job to know what doors have been opened. All the doors," he hinted. "How did you manage to open them?"

I patted my pocket, then remembered my pants had been changed.

Hope reached back and lifted the tattered pair. "Is this what you're looking for?" she said with a mouthful of awful-smelling food.

"In the pocket on the right, can you see if there's anything in it?"

She placed her bowl down, reached in, and pulled out the key. "This?"

"Yeah, that."

Soleil and Lune gasped.

"You know that key?" I spooned in another mouthful, and with every bite, I felt renewed.

"We know all the keys," Soleil voiced, then snatched the key from Hope. "You did it, didn't you? You made a deal with *her*."

I swallowed my mouthful before answering. "Yeah, sure did."

"And what did you use to bargain with her? What did she want you to do?"

"She wanted me to bring her a horn."

"Do you know what that would have done?" Sati asked. "Milady, who did you make a deal with?"

"It doesn't matter. She called it off."

"She did what?" Lune choked. After he swallowed the food, he said, "She never calls off a deal."

"Who did you make a deal with, Nemasa?" Quade asked, his jaw clenched.

I threw in another bite. Soleil and Lune were there, they knew. *Quade and Sati … they wouldn't understand.* I chewed my food, even though I didn't need to anymore. Time was needed to think. *Should I tell them? They'll get pissed and lecture me for being reckless.* I swallowed, then sighed. "She called herself Madness."

"You made a deal with *her*?" Quade's jaw clenched tighter.

"Don't worry. She didn't have anything that I wanted. She came to me and told me herself. She let me keep the key, and gave me back what she took. It's all good now. I kind of like her."

"You don't mean that. You don't even know what she is," Lune said.

"Milady, do you know what happens when you take a horn?" Sati's watery eyes swirled. I shook my head. "Your soul becomes tainted, and you cannot ascend. You would be trapped in Sin. Never would you be able to be reborn in the Earthly Realm. You would be an eternal creature of the Sinful Realm."

I scooped in more food as I thought, I almost played right into her hands.

"Nemasa?" Quade nudged my shoulder. "Did you hear the human?"

I shook away my thoughts. "No. Sorry, Hope."

"I asked, how do you like your food?"

"It really hit the spot. I didn't know I was this hungry."

I watched as Soleil tossed the key into the bag. "You better keep a close eye on that key. If anyone knows you have it, they will stop at nothing to hunt you down and take it."

"I'll be careful."

I laid out on the hard stone wrapped in layers of furs. With my new tail, sleeping on my back had become uncomfortable. My side seemed tender to the jagged points. On my stomach, I rested my head on my folded arms, and my tail had room to move. It swished under the light fur cover. But my horns jabbed into my arms.

Sounds had dulled to a normal level like Quade told me would happen. He had left to scout down the tunnel. I offered to go, but he turned me down and told me I needed sleep. I tried to argue with him, but he was insistent that I stay. I wondered if he knew the troubles that came with sleeping in my new form.

"*Psst* ..." Hope popped up her head, followed by the rest of her body. She tiptoed to me and placed her hand on my shoulder. "Let's go for a walk."

As much as my body begged for sleep, it didn't come. The twins snored and poised Sati slept with legs crossed, back straight, her chin resting in her chest. They were all used to the dark, eery places in the Sinful Realm. Hope and I were still used to the comforts of the Earthly Realm. I missed my fluffy duvet and pillow. I sighed and climbed to my feet.

"Quade is making sure that it's safe all the way down there. As long as we don't go too far, he might not even know we went for a little wander."

She patted my face with her hand. An earthy smell floated from her skin, which confused me. Quade compared her to a drug. *How could her earthy scent draw me in and make me dangerous to her? Maybe, since I had lived in her realm my entire life, I'd become used to what the others were attracted to.*

"A slow wander, okay?"

Her right brow raised. "Sure." She breathed a laugh and skipped down the tunnel. I hesitated to stroll alongside her as she led the way though the narrow corridor.

Soon her feet settled into small strides. "I've been wondering … what do you think our families think we are doing right now? My mom might think I ran away —"

"She knows you wouldn't."

"I know — that's the problem. I could have been kidnapped, rapped, and killed. Or worse, kept alive. She'd never know."

The sting of salt filled my nose. I turned to see her watery eyes.

She sighed. "There's no way I can call home and tell them, 'I'm okay. I'm alive and fine, just on a crazy adventure in the Sinful Realm, hanging out with demons.' You know, a normal phone call."

My lower lip curved in, and my teeth closed around it. A tear spilled over her lid and trickled down her round cheek. I wanted to tell her I had a solution or that I could take her home.

"Blaze …" She pressed her shoulder into me as her feet synced with mine. "A day. Let's go home for one day to let everyone know we're off on a road trip. Then, we can come back."

I reached up and fingered my horns. "Do you really think I can go back? Look at me … maybe we've been away long enough that, if we pop back for Halloween, I'll have a killer costume."

She laughed. Tears pooled fell as she blinked. When she stopped laughing, she shoved my shoulder. "That's for sure. What would I go as?"

"A witch," I whispered, and then we both laughed. It felt good to laugh, even though it was small and the joke wasn't all that funny. I had forgotten and Hope reminded me how a small gesture could make life bearable, even in the darkest of places.

"You two are loud," Quade interrupted.

"Oops." Hope coved her mouth with both her hands. "Better?" she mumbled through her fingers.

"We should get back. We better move tomorrow. We could get cornered if we stay here too long." He stepped past us. "Come back soon, or I'll come and drag you both to camp."

I watched him as he left and wondered, *How much did he hear? Would he let me go?*

Hope pinched my ear and lowered my head to her level. She put her lips close. "Ooo …" She released her pinch. "Never in all my years …"

"And what does that mean?"

"Come on. Are you really that dense? He likes you, and I mean a lot." She waved her hands through the air.

"Really?" I crossed my arms and pressed my lips together.

"Do you really have to think about it? It's written all over you both." She linked our arms, and as she pressed her body close, a strong waft of earthy freshness filled my nose. "Do you think he would let you go back with me for a while? I'm just asking for a day. Nothing too extreme. We'd come back as soon as we let everyone know we aren't dead."

"I'm not too sure. I think it's more a question for all of them, and it's not to stop you from going. They might not let me back. Who knows what I could do if I went on a rampage. You weren't there … Sati and Lune, if they told me to stay, I would."

"What do you think your lover boy would say?" Hope wiggled her eyebrows.

My sight narrowed. She responded with a little laugh. "I don't know. Hope, I remember what happened before I left here. My brother … he … I have to stop him. And it's not for power; it's not for every creature here that hates him. It's for me, my revenge." My body heated, my heart quickened. I held my breath. *Calm. Breath in, and out.*

"Blaze?"

"I'm — I'm okay." The heat subsided. "It was horrible, Hope. Then, after I remembered what happened, the memory of the fire came to me. My mother sparked the memory of what my brother did, I lost all control of the fire within me and … I killed them. It was me." Tears spilled over and streamed down my cheeks. In frustration, I stood and walked slowly back down the tunnel. Hope followed, saying what her heart knew I needed to hear.

"You didn't. It wasn't you." She held me. "My dear Blaze, you did nothing but love them."

Quade waited for us by the fire with a far off gaze in his eyes. "How was your walk?"

Hope patted me on the back. "Foxy here needed to get some things out. She's all better now." She knew better though. She had tried to cheer me up, and she had comforted me, so I tried to smile.

Quade could see that, whatever it was, it still stung and twisted my heart. "You both should try to get some rest. It's a long way out of here."

Hope saluted. "Aye, captain." She bounced to her thin blanket and laid down. "Nighty night."

When I was comfortable on my stomach, Quade moved over to me and crossed his legs by my side, his right knee resting on my back. His warm touch caused my back to tingle. A smile crept up on my face as I peeked over my elbow and watched his eyes close. Soon, mine followed.

Chapter Fifteen

The void engulfed me while I slept. The faceless child skipped and twirled as she hummed our lullaby. Her dress lifted from her knees as she spun; white light seemed to sparkle off the laced hem.

I watched her joyfully play, back where she belonged ... with me.

"Nemasa, what do you think you're doing?" Her body vanished. My eyes twitched over the empty blackness. "Well?" She tapped my shoulder, hidden behind me.

"What do you mean?"

"You're sitting around doing nothing. Nothing. If you don't go after him, then I will start killing off those little friends of yours."

"Then you will be no different than him." I pivoted on my heels, letting my eyes stare into her empty sockets, immune to her brutal face. "I still don't know how to defeat him. I know nothing about him."

"You know more than you let on."

"That's what you think."

"That's what I know. You can go, kill him now, and then be back on your merry way to the Earthly Realm to slaughter and conquer that *world. Won't that be fun? I think it will be. You wouldn't have to leave that pathetic human, if you don't kill her first." She chuckled, her jaw wiggled, her meaty tongue flapped.*

"You think I'd really do that? You know that I could never hurt her."

"I know that you have it in you to peel her skin off as if she were breaded chicken."

I inhaled deeply through my nose, and let it seep out from my lips. "I have control over this."

"Do you?"

"I do."

"He doesn't think so. He sits close by because he doesn't believe you have the ability to cage your inner beast and tame it. Oh, how sad. You think he sits close because he wants to be that close."

Both my hands tightened into fists.

"That's cute, Nemasa. Really. Though it's a childish thought. Look where you are. You're in Sin. Creatures down here can't love the way you were taught in the Earthly Realm. They don't respect others' feelings or opinions. They are here for themselves, so that they can survive."

"You're wrong. These creatures have done nothing to me to make me believe you. They have all been right here by my side helping me."

"See? Now, isn't that the problem? 'Helping.' Since when have you ever read a tale in the Earthly Realm about demons and wicked creatures helping one another?"

"I —"

"You haven't!" Her hands swung up and slammed down onto her sides. Her tongue thrashed around her extended mouth.

"Wake up, Nemasa! You're in Sin. You breath Sin. You walk within Sin. Damn it! Open your eyes. You must ditch these hateful beasts and get back to your task."

"My task? What is that exactly? Go storm into the castle, face my brother, and get killed. It doesn't work like that, you stupid little child. Robin and Krista will be there. I will need back up. How could I possibly face all three without a weapon? Or have you forgot, I'm bare-handed and have no training with magic. Tell me! If you're so smart, how am I going storm in there right now, as is?" I paused, letting her think. I sighed and placed my hands on her tiny, cold shoulders. "I can't do this alone, and I can't do this without training. I know how much you want him to pay, I want it, too. I just need a bit more time, and I need you to see that."

She nodded her head. Her wicked face sunk back in, a blank smooth layer of skin took place of the dangled jaw and empty sockets.

"Okay, a bit more time."

She turned and faced the empty space in front of her. A version of me faded in. Her long dark hair draped over her naked shoulders. Eyes closed, chin hung low. Human ears poked out from the side of her head, where they should be. Strange sensations filled my body as I gazed at my imperfect human body.

"Why are you showing me this?" I asked, unable to break my awed stare.

"This is your human soul. She is here with me while you are Nemasa. Being born in both the Earthly and Sinful Realm, you were given two souls. You can switch between the two whenever you need."

I reached up and stroked my icy human cheek. Her eyes shot open and flowed into my arm. Needles jabbed and stung my arm as the soul took over.

I shot up to my feet. Every nerve throbbed. I stomped away from camp, and when I was at a distance from the others, I stared down at my hands. My nails had thinned and dulled. I ran my fingers though my hair where my fox ears should have been. Horns gone. Claws gone. Tail …

"Damn it!" I slammed my fist into the nearest wall. The rough rock split open the skin. Blood pooled at the open wound.

"Nemasa?" Quade said as his hand wrapped my bloody hand. "What —"

"Little bitch." I breathed. I ripped my hand out of his light grip and stormed further down the hall.

I kicked the wall, the hardness stung my toe. "Crap!" I tried hard not to yell.

"Nemasa." Quade grabbed both my hands and held them tight. I pulled to get away, but he didn't let go.

My knee hit him in the side, and his grip on my right loosened. I ripped my hand from his and cocked it back. He blocked my fist as it barrelled for his chest. He released my other hand and let me swing wildly at him. One after another.

Every punch and kick blocked. He never once tried to counter and hit me back.

"You going to tell me what's going on?" he asked as his fingers wrapped around each of my fists and held them still. I pulled and pulled, unable to beat his strength.

"I'm back in my human body, right? I can feel it." I panted. When he didn't answer, I leaned into him. His hands stayed over mine and moved, so I could rest my head on his warm chest.

"Do I have to worry about you trying to hit me again, or do you feel better?"

"I feel better."

His fingers switched their grip and intertwined with mine. "Who's this 'little bitch' that has made you angry?"

Of course, he heard that, I still didn't want to tell him. What would he think if I told him about the child within my mind? Maybe he'd believe that I've been touched by madness and he'd give me a door of my own. "I'm all better now."

His head rested against mine. His breath rolled over my neck. My skin tightened, and my heart skipped. I gasped as my heart continued to flutter. I lifted my foot to take a step back. I had to break the connection. I couldn't breathe.

He must have known what I was about to do as his hands released mine and wrapped around me. "Human form or not, I won't leave you."

"*Yes, he will.*" The child's giggles echoed from the darkest corners of my mind.

"Let's go back. I'm not the only one you woke up."

Quade had lit four orange orbs for our journey out of the cramped hall. I was excited to have something else to look at other than gray. Camp was almost packed, just a few stray things needed to be stuffed into a bag.

"You're human again! Woo-hoo!" Hope cheered, her hands pumped the air above her.

"Yeah, yeah, human," I sighed.

Being human around Quade made thing worse. Every time my eyes found his, my heart tried to leap out of its cage and attack him. The closer he was, the harder it tried. I felt it in my fox form, but it was mild compared to the waves of desire my human soul created.

"What? You don't like being human anymore?" Hope pressed her face up to mine, her one eye closed and the other glared into me. "Human ain't good enough for ya, eh?"

"It's not that. It's just … well … I forgot what it was like. That's all."

She lowered her face and peeked over her shoulder at Quade. Her hand cupped her mouth and pressed against my ear. "It's him, isn't it? Can't stand the human emotions of *love,* can you?"

I shoved her.

"Hey, you two!" Lune strapped on his backpack. "Packed yet?"

"Sorry, us humans …" She elbowed me. "We are a lot slower than you creatures." She had already had her backpack on before she came over and pestered me. She had been packed long before the others had started. "Oh, my weak and pathetic body! It's too heavy. You need to carry it for me," she pretended to whine as she stumbled around.

I laughed as I straightened out my straps. "I'm ready."

"Sure you don't want me to carry that?" Quade asked with a full grin. I was positive he had heard what Hope had tried to secretly whisper to me.

I nodded. I was human, not weak.

Everyone started down the hall toward the exit. No one mentioned what we were going to do when we reached the other door. Find another place to hide? Or maybe they thought I was good enough to toss in front. Bruin, my brother? Human form? That didn't matter. She was ready. *Ready or not here I come, I guess.*

Hope and Lune lead the pack. They chatted back and forth for the majority of the time. Hope laughed, and Lune smiled and added in witty comments. He gazed down at her as she spoke of the Earthly Realm. He questioned her about everything she would tell him, fascinated by a world ruled by *humans.*

Quade and Sati followed out of ear shot. Every time I peeked back they seemed to be whispering on purpose.

Silent Soleil walked alongside me. His short hair bounced around his eyebrows with each step. His eyes seemed to be fixed on his identical twin as he chatted up Hope.

"You don't care for the way he talks to the *human,* do you?" I asked low enough that he could just hear me.

His golden gaze shifted to me. "You've noticed."

"It's hard not to." My lip twitched up on the right. "It's all good. I understand. I'm sure, if you came to the Earthly Realm, you would be looked at the same way. Humans don't take to the unordinary very well. You'd be taken to a lab, most likely cut into pieces to see what makes you tick."

"That's barbaric."

"So you think Ripper is barbaric?"

"Worse than that. He's on his own spectrum."

I thought about it for a moment. "His garden. What's it like?"

"You will soon find out. We want to keep you safe. Ripper would use our heads as gnomes if anything happened to you. He might already be planning where to put our heads after what happened." He ran his hand through his hair, his golden eyes flared. "If you get hurt like that again, I'll have to kiss my sweet ass good-bye." His head dropped in defeat.

"How did you end up with him?"

His head lifted, and his eyes seemed to brighten. "He's like a father to us, found us abandoned in one of the tunnels. He said we followed him all the way home. He couldn't get rid of us, so he tried everything to scare us off. After a while he gave us tasks. Then, over time, he just kept us, until your mom found us with him. She offered to give us a life at the castle. From then on, we lived there in the walls as a secret security."

"You went back to him after my mother died?"

"Yeah, had to. The newly appointed King Bruin put a price on our heads. Not knowing what we looked like or anything about us made it difficult for him to capture us. We fled to Ripper with nowhere else to go."

"We aren't really going to the heart of the garden, just to a little trail that not many know about. It's called Crystallized. There is fear in being trapped, frozen, unable to move — anyway, you'll see it and know how it got its name."

The conversation with Soleil helped distract me from the whispers behind me. Sati walked with her back straight, arms still at her side. With every step, only her legs would move, her head remained even and unchanged by the bounce of her step. Her scales reflected Quade's orange light like the sun's light dancing on water. Elegant and beautiful.

I snapped my attention back to Soleil, and then to Hope and Lune. I needed something, anything, to get her closeness with Quade off my mind. *They're friends, best friends, and that's okay. Isn't it?*

Another old wooden door held together by rusted iron bars blocked the way. Lune stuck out his hand and summoned a little golden key to his palm. He held the key with his thumb and index finger. With a quick rap on the door, the key vanished and the door clicked open. I imagined that Lune had made a mistake and summoned the wrong key, that Kenna would burst out of the door and sweep me away. A shiver up my spine snapped me back to reality. Quade placed his hand on my shoulder and gave it a squeeze.

The door swung open as Lune tugged hard on the iron ring. A faint white light shone through the cracks around the door. I stepped through the open doorway into the next room. Awed, I froze.

Three times larger than our school gym, the rich cave was filled with magnificent masterful pieces. White crystal spiraled down from the ceiling into sharp points. A crystallized waterfall poured into the room from halfway up the gray stone wall. Its raw power solidified in glass.

Hope spun into the room, her eyes tried to absorb everything all at once. "Wow! This is amazing."

"Don't touch anything," Lune warned. "These structures are made of compressed souls. You could be added to the collection."

She walked up to one of the pillars and stared into its almost blue fractals. "These are all souls?"

"Yes. No one comes down this way. We should be safe here for a few days. No matter how remote this place is, we shouldn't linger here too long." Lune made his way across the room and behind some of the crystal. Hope and I gazed at the magnificence.

Lune found a place good enough to settle into and called us over. He had picked a spot under a circle of pillars that joined each other near the top. The glow of their light illuminated the middle in a brilliant white.

"Well done, Lune, this is a great place to camp." I tugged off the straps of my bag and dropped it. "Even if we don't stay long, I'm glad I got to see this place."

Soleil patted my shoulder. "Just don't try to make out what the whispers are saying. You can't. It's impossible, and you'll drive yourself mad."

"Thanks. I'll remember that."

"You can't hear them now, you know, with those human ears." His gaze shifted to my ears then chuckled. His fingers grazed my ear. "When you change back, the room will fill with them. You'll learn to tune it all out." He threw his bag next to mine, then joined his brother and the curious Hope.

"Blaze, you have to see this!" she hollered with her face inches from one of the pillars. "There's faces in there," she whispered more to herself.

Intrigued, I strolled over. "Where?" I asked and lowered myself to her view.

"There," she pointed into the glass pillar.

Thick white streaks were in the clear crystal. "You've lost it. Simply nuts."

"No, I'm not. Right there. Hundreds of faces."

"Whatever you say," I said while my eyes rolled.

"I'm serious. Men. Women. Hundreds of them crammed into the glass."

"You can see the trapped souls?" I couldn't hear Satis approach, and when she joined into the conversation, my muscles tensed. "You are a remarkable human. Your abilities grow stronger as the days pass. Being able to see into the crystal, to see the truth that lingers beneath, is a talent that even skilled magic welders have trouble with."

"Hear that, Blaze?" Hope stood and flexed her muscles. "I'm *remarkable*."

"I never doubted that for a moment, Hope."

"This gives me an idea." Hope twirled on her heels and grabbed Quade's arm. She dragged him far out of sight.

"Milady ..." Sati breathed. "I've been talking with Quade about your recent transformation. May I tell you what we have discussed?" The white glow from the crystals reflected off her scales. The calm ripple reminded me of raindrops on a lake.

She had always been kind and sweet. She never did me any wrong. Guilt twisted my heart. *How could I hate her as much as I did when she hadn't done anything to make me hate her?*

"Is that what you two talked about on our walk here?" My mind had created many stories, but I knew it would never tell me the truth. Sati had done nothing to ever make me truly hate her. I just envied her closeness with Quade.

"Yes. It troubled me the moment your aura changed." Her knees bent and folded over one another as she took her seat on the floor. "I have never heard of such skill. You are able to become completely human. Your aura, your essences, it all transforms." Her head bowed. "Forgive me. I don't mean to pry into your magic and knowledge. I understand and accept any punishment given. Forgive me."

Taken back, I plopped down in front of her. "I've come to know that I have two souls that are living in my body. Blaze, the human. And Nemasa, the demon."

Her head sprung up, "Two? How could that be possible? A body is only capable of sustaining a single soul."

"I'm beginning to think that I have adopted another," I mumbled. The child could also be a creation of my mind to help me down the path. Or an obstacle. I wasn't sure which.

Another theory was that she was a trapped alternate soul, a keeper of my memories, and was placed in front of the doors, so I could never open them.

"Another? Milady ... I do not understand."

"Never mind. Forget I said anything." My shoulders relaxed. "About Hope. She's asked me if there was a chance she could go home for a while. She misses her family. To be honest, they probably have a search party out, and haven't slept in days. They're a closely knit family, and I owe it to her."

"What do you think is the best thing to do?"

"I don't know ... she wants me to go with her, but ..." My eyes strayed away from hers. I couldn't admit I didn't trust myself.

She gave me time to think. I knew she saw the shredded creature that lay beside me in the darkness. "Your mom acted like an adviser to my mom, right?"

"Yes, milady."

"If I were my mom, and you yours, what would she say?"

Her face lightened. "She would suggest to seek the counsel's opinions."

"Counsel? Really?"

"Yes. Counsel members live on each level of Sin. She called on them through a looking glass. The room your mother used has many, one for each level. I've only been there once. I am positive that there was a single tall mirror for each. My mother passed before she could teach me the room's secrets."

"Counsel ..." My eyes fell onto Soleil and Lune. Hope was stubborn and would say anything to make me go. Quade knew me the best. I'd need to listen closely to what he had to say.

"Their ideas on the situation are valid." She nodded to the twins. "They both have learned much about you and Hope."

"I'll ask everyone later, maybe talk to Hope one more time. Hear what she really thinks."

A week flew past within Crystallized, or maybe it was longer. Judging days became near impossible without the sun. Hope refused to tell me what she wanted with Quade. Every time I asked him, he glared at Hope. She'd smile and make a tight fist and shake it at him. I pushed hard enough for an answer one night that he left. I questioned Hope about him suddenly leaving. She laughed and then shrugged off the question.

I chased after him wanting to know why he got so angry. He rounded the corner a few feet from the camp. When I turned, he had gone further into the cave. Thin pillars vanished behind thicker ones as I crept past. My eyes searched for the faces Hope talked about, but they never saw them.

A white shadow shifted out of the corner of my eye, too short to be Quade. I stepped toward it. My eyes darted around, pillar to pillar. The child's lullaby hummed.

"Neeemmmaaassaaa..." It was only her. My body lost its tenseness.

What do you want? I asked in thought.

"Go. Go to that human world. You know you want to. I am hungry. Always hungry."

My body heated. I gasped as if all the oxygen in the world disappeared.

"Nemasa?" My muscles jumped. Quade stood puzzled to the far left of me.

"Are you okay?" He stepped forward.

"Yeah, you just spooked me. That's all." I forced a smile. My heart slowed with every beat.

His eyes told me he didn't believe me. It was the same look Hope gave me when she knew I lied. "I thought I saw something, but it was just in my head." A not entirely true truth, but close enough.

"Please don't ask me to tell you. It's really neat, and you'll like it. Now I've said too much. Please, *please*, don't ask again," he begged.

Right. "Okay, I won't."

"Good. Now, this might sound weird, but I think I dreamt up a way to protect that book better." His cheeks reddened.

"Dreamt?"

His face flushed deeper. "Yeah." His fingers ran through his hair. "It's pretty neat. Just let me try. Ignore what I just said. Actually, forget I said it."

"Okay, forgotten," I said, motioning my hands to toss a handful of air. The bag did put a damper on things. A panic shivered through my nerves as the memory of almost losing it came at me in full swing. "I would like a better way to carry it around," I hinted.

He grinned. "Close your eyes."

My eyes blinked shut. The bag slid around my hip as he unclasped the buckle and pulled out the heavy book. His fingers tickled my hand as he guided it upward. Rotating my palm up, the rough leather balanced on my widely spread fingers.

His warm right hand clasped the left side of my neck. My lips tightened; my heart skipped. The child chuckled. Her shimmer flickered in the dark space behind my eyelids.

Right below my ear, under his hand, began to burn. The weight of the book lightened, then vanished. Again the child giggled, skipped, twirled up the void into view. Her tiny thin arms wrapped tight around the book. The empty black sockets mocked me. Her jaw rested on the top of the cover.

My eyes shot open.

"It worked." The spot on my neck burned as his hand slid back to him. "Where did you get that mark? I don't recognize the symbol."

"It appeared the same time the book did. I thought they were related somehow." My fingers traced the heat. "Aren't they?"

He shook his head. "Never seen a mark like that before."

Chapter Sixteen

nother week passed. I tried to catch Hope to talk to her about going back; however, she was too busy with her little secret.

The child enjoyed her new gift. She didn't feel the need to push toward my brother.

Quade took me away from the group to practice with the wooden swords. No matter how hard I tried, he blocked everything I threw at him.

Sati and Hope passed out early each night. Hope's secret wore her out. Sometimes she even skipped supper to pass out uncovered on her bed. I couldn't figure out what she was doing. Quade kept me occupied with training. I'm sure on purpose.

I had made myself comfortable wrapped in a light fur. The twins had done a supply run and picked up a few things to make our stay more bearable. Hope snored over in the corner. The twins slept close by her. She had asked them to make sure that I didn't go snoop around to discover what she had planned.

I was the only one awake, unable to sleep, my mind racing from everything that had happened and the uncertainty of the thought seemed to dig deeper. I lifted my head

Quade. His chest raised and lowered with each silent breath. His arms crossed over his chest, back against the rock wall, close enough that, if I leaned left, my side would touch his knee.

His eyes blinked open, my head dropped. I clenched my jaw, praying he didn't notice me.

"Can't sleep?" he whispered.

"No," I mumbled, face buried in my arms. "I didn't mean to wake you."

His clothes ruffled; then I could feel pressure on my back. I closed my eyes and took a deep breath in. I let my mind drift …

Bright light beamed in through cracks above me, my eyes taking their time to adjust. It seemed forever since sunlight had danced on my cold skin. I raised my arms to soak in the yellow sun rays.

Aged planks formed weak walls, topped with fragments of a roof. A few boards hung by a single nail. The lush-green outside world peeked through. I could smell the light fragrance of the morning dew. I did miss parts of the Earthly Realm. A floor board creaked from the doorway.

Quade lingered there, lit by the sunlight. "Here again?" he moved closer. With every step, my heart pounded harder. He was right. We were in the same building when I called on him to help me with Ta'la.

A dream. It's only a dream, I told myself.

"Where is this place?" he asked as his eyes scanned the rundown building. I stood within arm's reach. Still he moved closer. "Any one else here?"

My mouth opened to answer, but words failed me. The way the sun lit his skin and eyes had my tongue tied in knots. My eyes couldn't leave him while he took in our surroundings.

His violet eyes shifted to me, and I could see a thought or two cross his mind. "Must be." He breathed with a grin. He stopped inches from me. His rough fingers glided over my cheek and loosely caressed it. His eyes locked into mine as he drew me in. "Nemasa," he whispered.

It's a dream, I thought as his breath tickled my lips. A dream.

His eyes shut. My heart skipped, my body warmed. His soft lips pressed into mine, his arms tightened around me. I wrapped mine around him. I wouldn't let him go. Dream or not, he was mine and only mine.

Quade's hand slid down my spine, teasing every nerve on its way down. His fingers crept up under my top. My lips stayed locked with his. Heat flooded my cheeks as our tongues met and twisted. I tried to catch my breath, but he took it and held it tight.

My hands wondered underneath his shirt, traced his defined abs, his hips, and spine. He let go from our heated kiss. My lips begged him back. His quick hands peeled off his shirt then gripped the back of my neck, pulled me in once again. The heat of his body flowed out of him into me. My hands took on a life of their own and glided over his skin.

We travelled from the middle of the room to the wall behind me. A light moan escaped my lips from the pressure of my back *hitting the wall. A satisfied smirk filled my face. Finally I had him alone.*

Quade rested his forehead against mine; his narrow eyes gazed into me. I wanted him, and he, he wanted me, too. Just a dream, I reminded myself as our lips met again.

Fireworks exploded within. I let him lift my shirt over my head and drop to the ground. My hands slipped around his waist to close the thin distance that had been made between us. As our half-naked bodies touched, every muscle in my body tensed and begged for more.

Quade pecked a trail over my cheek and down my neck. His hands pressed firm over my skin as he traced the rim of my pants. I placed my hand over his and his palm glided over my skin. In its wake, my teased skin tingled, trembled, screamed for more. I breathed in his scent as his hand memorized my body. I lifted his face to press my lips into his, our tongues tangled. My heart pounded. Quade lowered us to the floor. His weight on my hips pinned my back to the ground. My fingers gripped his hair, bringing his lips back into mine. His bare chest graced my breasts; a shock wave pulsed under my skin.

"Nemasa," he whispered as his lips trailed down to my neck. I couldn't respond, paralyzed by the moment.

Quade's hand slid up, lingered under my breast. Our bodies tensed, eyes met. My fingers again gripped his hair, guided him back into another deep kiss. My fingers slid down his soft skin, trailing down his spine, beneath his pants. A firm grip tightened on my breast as my hand squeezed.

His face nuzzled into my ear. "Want them off?"

I bit my lip. Yes, my mind screamed. My tongue tried to say.

His teeth playfully clamped my ear. "I'll do whatever you tell me to, Nemasa." If only I could speak. My wrists found themselves pinned above my head. "If you don't, I'll do whatever I like."

My heart skipped. I attempted to breath, tried to say something, anything.

His soft lips touched my bare skin, down my neck and over my chest. I wiggled my hands, lifted, it was no use. He overpowered me. The warmth of his breath heated my already hot skin.

Lips clamped around my nipple, and my body pulsed. His rough tongue circled around, flicked. My pinned hands tried to escape. My gaze fixed on him, watched as he moved, grinned, the grip around my wrist tightened as his lips peeked down.

He lowered his body to my knees. "Keep your hands right here," he demanded. They obeyed. His fingers slid over my neck, gripped my breasts, then quickly removed his pants. Even though seconds passed, it felt as if we had parted for a lifetime.

He clasped his body around mine, our lips locked. My hands disobeyed him and wrapped themselves around his neck. I felt his lips crack a smile, his hand gripped my chest, the other supported his weight. A pressure on the inside of my knee separated one leg for the other, firm fingers glided down as my other leg was pushed to the side.

Our tongues twisted, his finger pressed in. My hand squeezed around his neck, the other gripped his side. Each movement intensified the next. I breathed in deep, intoxicated by his scent. "Quade," I panted as I gasped for breath.

He lifted his head. "Yes?" I bit my lip. He kissed it free. "If you do that, you won't be able to tell me what you want."

I pressed my lips back into his. "You … I want you." A slight sting hit the back of my head as he pressed his lips against mine. His hips thrust him into me.

My eyes shot open, lungs gasped. Heart slammed against its cage, heat radiated, body tingled. Every sensation carried over from the dream, teased my senses. I peeked up over my elbow. Quade slept next to me fully clothed. Piece by piece, my mind undressed him. Flushed I turned my head away.

It had to be my imagination. *Was he panting?* I peeked back. His chest rose and fell rapidly. His eyes squeezed shut. Face reddened. Again I turned away, not wanting him to catch me as I mentally undressed him.

A deep breath filled my lungs, my heart beat slowed.

"Nemasa?" he whispered. My heart skipped, his breathless voice triggered a swarm of images. "You awake?"

I swallowed the dry lump in my throat. "Yeah."

"Um … wa-want to go for a walk?"

It was a dream. No way he could just hop into my dreams whenever he pleased. My eyes tried to find him, afraid that once they did, my body would pounce and make the dream a reality. "Sure," I gasped. "A walk would be great right now."

My feet wobbled as I stood. "Um, how was your sleep?" I attempted to act normal. Not being able to look at him made it hard for me to walk behind him. Two green orbs that formed in his hands grew, shifted, and stretched into wooden swords. He tossed the two sticks at me, then created one for himself.

Quade said nothing as he put up his guard. I smirked as I thought, *This I can do.* I struck fast and hard. He blocked. Over the past few weeks, I had never been able to hit him. Ever since that incident where I stabbed him, he always stayed on his toes. Right. Left. Block with one, attack with the other. Whenever my eyes found his, his hot gaze triggered the sensation of his touch. I couldn't keep them on him long.

He struck down, the sound of my block rang in my ear. "You seem distracted," he stated. "Maybe you should go back to bed."

Our eyes met for a moment. "I'm fine."

The wooden sticks clashed together, over and over. Still unable to tag him, I was irritated by my unskilled hands. My strikes became stronger, though sloppier. He grinned as his foot slipped behind mine while I stepped back to regain my balance. I toppled backward; my elbows and back stung on impact.

He stepped over me and gazed down. For the first time since I woke up, my eyes stayed with his. He lowered himself and sat comfortably on my stomach.

"Are you sure you're fine?"

"Is 'I'm tired of losing to you' a good enough answer?"

"Maybe I'll come back," Hope interrupted.

Both our heads snapped over to Hope as she giddily chuckled to herself. All my attention had been on Quade. *How long had she been there?*

He released his breath and frowned. "What do you want, *human?*"

"I woke up and heard *bang bang* from down here. I wanted to know what it was." She put her hand to her lips. "Could have been an enemy," she whispered. "Then I found you two all like on top of each other and what not. Sati woke up, too. She wasn't as concerned as me. She said that I should stay at camp. But I didn't know if you were being attacked." A grin grew. "Then I caught you like this, again."

Heat rose to my face as I realized Quade was still straddling me. I watched as his eyebrows pushed together and his lips tightened.

"Anyway, breakfast is almost ready, and the twins are up, too. Just so you know, you're both very loud. If you're going to do the naked tango, be a little quieter." She turned and walked back. "Oh, and, Blaze, when you get back, after we eat, I want to give you your surprise." She gave a wave and strolled around the bend.

The weight of Quade's body lifted as he stood. "We best get back."

I sighed. *Everyone ... we woke them all up ... crap.* "What's Hope surprise?" I pushed myself up off the ground and began to dust off my pants.

"Please, Nemasa, don't ask." The sound of my name made my heart flutter. "I want to tell you, it hurts not to. You'll like it. I know you will. I'm sure you'd be more upset if I told you." He gripped both my shoulders, "Just wait a little longer."

"Okay," I nodded. I stepped forward into his arms and rested my head on his chest. I could feel his heart pound as mine did. "Let's get back, so we can eat. Then I don't have to wait any more. I hate waiting. It's not fun." He tightened his arms around me and held me for a moment. "Quade," I lifted my head from his chest, his eyes shifted to mine. "Why were you up so early?"

His face reddened. "I … umm … I had an interesting dream —"

"Oh! And I forgot something." Hope bounced around the corner, her eyes widened as she spotted us. "Um … it can wait till later."

"What?" Quade tried hard not to snap at her, his tongue clenched in between his teeth.

"Sati wants to talk to you when you have a moment." She looked directly at me, then left.

"A dream?" I turned my attention back to him. *There was no way we could have had the same one.*

His lip curled. "Why were you awake, Nemasa?"

"Umm …" The heat intensified. "I had a dream, too," I mumbled.

His cocky smile dropped a little. "There's no way," he whispered to himself. "Come on. We better go back. Your human is excited to give you her gift."

"You think?"

"Well, she's never come over here twice in a row. Normally she leaves us be." He shifted but kept close.

I turned toward the narrow pathway through the crystal pillars. "That's true. She's good like that." A strong urge to pounce on him bubbled to the surface. I bit down hard on my lip to keep it in.

His arm slid over my back, fingers curved at my hip. In the dream, he said "must be." *Could we have had the same dream, both thinking it was a normal dream?* All of a sudden, it became hard to breath.

"You okay?" he asked, his breath graced my ear. A shiver ran up my spine.

"Yeah, yeah, I'm okay." *More than okay*, "Hungry. I can almost smell the food."

The camp came into view, and Quade's arm glided off. Every part of me that he touched tingled.

"There they are." Soleil laughed and elbowed his brother.

"Food is just about to come off the fire, perfect timing." Lune struggled to keep his face under control. "A little early to start training today, don't you think?"

"I don't think they were just training."

"Be nice now, brother. Even if she's human right now, she is still Nemasa."

Soleil's lips tightened, and he lowered his head.

Sati stirred a pot filled with thick brown gravy and a few chunks. Hope gawked at me from behind her.

"What's for breakfast?" I asked as I dropped to the ground beside Hope.

"A mix of whatever was left, milady. I saved things that we can eat later, might last us a day or two."

"We have to move?"

"Yes, milady, or go gather supplies," Sati stated. Her straight lips pulled down the corner of her eyes.

"Are you okay, Sati?"

She kept her wide-eyed gaze of the brown mush. "I am fine, milady."

My eyes shifted between her and Quade. I could feel that a new tension had formed.

"It's ready," she said as she scooped the mush into a bowl.

"I like the idea of moving," Lune announced as he filled his bowl. "We've been here too long. Someone is bound to find us. There is a possibility that we have already been spotted, and now they're just watching, waiting."

"Where will we go?" asked Soleil.

Lune spooned a load into his mouth, stumped.

"Blaze, I can't wait anymore. You want your gift?" Hope stated, bouncing on her knees.

I chewed the food I had just stuffed into my mouth, and my eyes shifted from my bowl to her. I swallowed the mouthful. "Hell yeah, I've been waiting too long."

"I know, me too. I had to use everyone here to make sure that it was made right. I even got better at hand-to-hand combat, too." I raised my eyebrow at her. "Don't look at me like that, I'm amazing and I know. Anyway." Hope turned around, pulled up her bed, and withdrew a long, thin object wrapped in a dirty fabric. "Before we decide where to go next, I figure you might want to know what you're getting. It may help you … anyway, just open it."

I stretched out my hands, and waited. I had an idea by the shape, but then it was also too bulky at the base. *What could have taken her weeks to create?* She placed the light object into my hands.

"Thank you."

"Don't thank me yet. Just open it." She waved her hands toward me. "Go on, don't be shy."

I let the fabric slide from the object that lingered underneath. It drifted down into my lap. In my hand, I held two identical masterful leather sheathes. Engraved into the leather work were the symbols of a hornet, ant, and butterfly twisted around the moon's cycles. One-handed hilts wrapped in thick tight leather poked out of each sheath.

"These are amazing, Hope!" I said in awe as my hands traced the fine craftsmanship.

"Oh, and here." She turned around and heaved out a thick leather belt that matched the sheaths. A small dagger hung on the left a few inches before the metal clasp.

"Hope ... this ... this is —"

"Awesome!" she interrupted. "I know, right? After you freaked me out by almost getting killed, I thought you were going to die. I didn't think that I would be able to heal you fast enough to stop your bleeding. Then I noticed that you had stopped your own bleeding. Even though you were covered in blood from head-to-toe, your wounds weren't that bad.

"That got me thinking. You really can't be wondering around without a proper weapon. Quade's is nice. It suits him. These, now these babies, they suit you."

"Is this why you had to take Quade away?"

"Yeah, and about that. The glares and jealous snorts you gave me ... well, you didn't need those. I wasn't taking your man out back to get a taste of his action, all right? But I couldn't tell you what I was doing out back, now could I?"

"You were right, Quade," I said as my head lifted to him. The instant our eyes met they shot back down to the swords. Heat filled my cheeks as I remembered the touch of his lips. "I didn't want to know. Thank you. I'm sorry for hounding you."

Hope rested the belt beside me. "Now what? Finish eating, then where are we off to?"

I squeezed the swords in my hands, eyed the delicate detail. She knew exactly what I needed, down to my core. Every night she had come back exhausted. "Where to next?" she asked. I needed to give back to her. All I've done is take, take, take.

"What do you all think if Hope and I go back to the Earthly Realm for a day or so?" The blunt flat words trickled from my lips.

"You really think that's wise?" Soleil pressed his face forward. "You may look and smell it, every bit of you at the moment seems completely human, but you're a creature of Sin, Nemasa. You're like us. Do you care for all the humans in that world like you do Hope? None of them make you angry?"

"Hey!" Hope barked. "I'll be right by her side!"

"What if you can't be there?" Lune's silver eyes met with Hopes'. "Say you have to leave, even for a moment, and something triggers the Nine Tails. You haven't seen it yet." Lune saw what I had done to the beast in the dark. "If she doesn't care for those around her, she could easily pick off a few. Once a creature has tasted humans, it's hard to come back to the way things were."

"Sati?" Hope's eyes shifted to the woman next to her. "What do you think? Do you think she can control herself? Or do you think that she will go on a blood-hungry rampage and slaughter everything in her wake until nothing is left breathing?" Sati's gaze fell on me.

"Sati and I talked about this already," I stated. Quade grunted beside me. I glanced at him, his eyebrows pressed together tight, his jaw clenched. I looked away. Did he really think that I couldn't control it? Did he really believe that I would kill a human? "She said that it would be important to ask all of you." My gaze fell onto Lune.

"It's hard to say," Lune responded. "You could have a wonderful time and be welcomed back by your family with open arms and proceed on living the way you had been."

A deep breath exhaled from Quade. His arms crossed around his chest. *How could he have so little faith in me? Did he really object to Lune's idea that strongly that he had to tense right up?* I bit down hard on my tongue.

"On the other hand, you could have a run in with someone you hate and devour them whole. It's tough to say." Lune pinched his chin with his finger and thumb. "Quade, you've trained with her the most. What do you think?"

Again he grunted.

"Hope could contain her," Lune continued. "I've seen her work on those blades. For a human, she is quite skilled. I'm sure it helps that Sati trained her. Do you think she could go and handle it?" Lune turned his attention to Quade.

Abruptly Quade rose to his feet and stormed off, away from the group.

"Wow, that's harsh," the child's voice echoed. *"Told you."*

Told me what?

"That no one here really trusts you." She giggled.

I watched as Quade twisted around the corner and disappeared out of sight.

"What was that about? You're coming back with me whether he likes it or not. I won't leave without you, just like you didn't leave without me," Hope declared.

"What if I do lose control and people find out I'm not fully human. I don't want to end up on some scientist's table."

"You won't. I won't let you," she promised.

"You don't know that, Hope. How could you? What if I attack and my family found out? They took me in, raised me. Even after all the hell I've put them through, they still love me. I won't add this to the weight they already carry. I can't. I owe them, at least, that much. Could you imagine the looks on their faces if I have a run in with a bully at school and massacre every one of them? The stress that would put on them? They'd be disowned by the town, by the county. I can't do that to them. If Quade really feels that strongly about me not being able to control my demon, then I should listen to that. As Lune said, Quade knows this new me better than anyone."

"Don't talk about yourself that way. I know you better than he does. You have great self-control. You haven't harmed me."

"And I won't —"

"I won't let you lose control. I'll be right there."

"And what if you aren't?" Heat flooded my face as I let her think about the question. "What if we end up in some office with a police officer's face pressed into mine asking, 'Where have you been these past months?' I give the truth as an answer. 'That's a lie. You're a lunatic.' Bam, I'm dressed in all white, caged in a padded room. All control that I have over myself, thrown out the window." I jumped to my feet. "I don't want to risk it."

"You should go talk to him." I didn't expect that from Sati. She seemed to be upset by the closeness that had formed between Quade and I.

"Why? He has made his point. He made it clear to me that I shouldn't go. Bad idea. I'll get there and fuck everything up."

Hope collected the belt and stood. She fit it around my waist. "You attach the sheaths like this." She placed the sheaths in each of my hands, then moved my hands close to each hilt, pressed my left knuckles to the left side of the belt, my right to my right. "Pull your knuckles away. The friction will activate the magic and seal the sheaths to the belt. To release them, just wedge your fingers back and they come off. Cool, eh?" I nodded. "Now go to him." She pushed.

I breathed, and admired my new appeal. "I don't see how talking will help. He's pissed me off. I don't think it will end well."

"Just go."

I found Quade with his hand bloodied against a stone wall. The crystal around him lit his hard-pressed face. He shot me a sharp glare that sliced through my heart. I drew my blades and attacked. Rage fueled my strikes. He unsheathed his sword, blocked, and countered each blow. The clash of blades rang throughout the cavern. Every time I swung, my blade seemed to vanish. His steel pressed into the clear glass edge of the swords Hope made for me. Not a chip dulled the blade. No matter how hard he struck, it didn't break.

"When were you going to tell me?" he snapped and knocked my left blade from my hand.

I countered with an upward right. "Did I need to?"

He knocked my other blade from my hand. I struck him with a left fist to the ribs. He tossed his sword to the side, caught my right fist as it came for a second. He kept his grip firm, then pressed my back to the stone and held me there.

"Do you truly think that I have that little control?"

I hooked my foot behind his heel and pressed, knocking him off balance. He fell back, pulling me down along with him. My hands switched and pinned his wrists above his head. I held him down by straddling his chest.

"Little control?" he whispered. "I think you'll be fine. That human could contain you, you'd be fine. Although … have you noticed yet?" His eyes locked with mine, zapping every once of anger out of me.

"Noticed what?" I barked.

His heart pounded against his ribs. I let his wrist lift from the ground, his fingers brushed my cheek, past my temple, and petted my ear. "Did I make you that angry that you didn't even notice that you transformed?" His hardened face melted. Eyes softened. "Your Earthly Realm, it smells fresh, bright colors everywhere. There's much more than gray and black." His fingers tangled in my hair, guided me in. "You glow in the sunlight. If you leave, why would you want to come back to a world of chaos when you can live in peace?" Our horns rested on each other; his breath teased my lips. "I'm afraid if you leave, you won —"

The smell of fresh air and sunshine wafted all around us. We both turned our heads to see Hope lingering in the entrance. "I'm sorry … really … I didn't … I'll go."

I straightened my back. His hand, reluctant to let go, released my hair, slid down my face and shoulder, found a new place to rest on my lap. "Hope," Quade said with a grin. I gasped and stared at him. "You're not interrupting. Come here. What do you need?"

My muscles twitched to get off, but he held me on him. Hope squatted by us. With her eyes fixed to him, her jaw dropped a tiny bit. It opened at the sound of hearing her name come from him.

"I … did you just … no … never mind. I came over here against Sati's orders to make sure you weren't mad at Blazey. It was my idea. She was torn when I told her. I could tell she wanted to stay, didn't give one thought to going back. We'll come back, that I promise. That brother of hers deserves what's coming. No one can do that to my Blaze and get away with it. She can control herself if she tries. Here she doesn't feel the need to contain herself." She reached up and pinched my ear between her fingers. My head dropped closer to her, a waft of luscious grass and morning dew radiated from her skin. I took a second sniff, unnoticeable to Hope while she kept her eyes on him lying comfortably under me. "She's got this. I know she does."

"I know she does," he agreed with her. His hand moved inward on my leg. My heart fluttered. I couldn't break the fixed gaze he trapped me in. The scents of fresh earth were again lost to the spiral of images from the dream.

"Then why are you so upset? Everyone back at camp is trying to figure out what happened."

His face reddened. "I ... um ..."

"Never mind. Don't answer. If it's what I think it is, I best leave you two. Sorry again for intruding on whatever this is." She twirled up and skipped out of sight.

"You're human is a strange one," He mumbled and then reached up to grab the collar of my shirt. With his other arm, he propped himself up with his elbow.

A slight whisper filled the air. I looked to see if Hope had forgotten something, though the sound seemed all around me. I listened. As I did, more and more voices filled my head. Thousands and thousands of voices whispered all at once.

"Don't listen to them." Quade's voice overpowered them all. His lips pressed into my ear. The sound of each breath he took and released tickled the inside. "Concentrate on me."

With both hands, I pressed him down and rested my ears onto his chest. His heart boomed in my ears, silencing all the voices.

"They are the whispers from the souls imprisoned in the crystal. No matter how hard you try, you can never hear what they are saying. The crystal muffles their voices. You'll go insane if you try. Ignoring them is the best way to quiet them. Keep your mind preoccupied and you won't hear them."

I breathed in through my nose. He smelled as he did in the dream. "Quade ... why were you awake so early this morning?"

"I was going to ask you the same thing." He stroked my head.

"I asked first."

"Apparently I was having too much fun." His thumb traced the back of my ear as heat flushed my face. "You?"

"Did we have the same dream?" I chanced a glance up; his hot gaze had returned.

"Yeah, I think —"

Soleil and Lune burst around the corner; frantic eyes searched the room. "Have you seen Hope? We can't sense her anymore."

My head shot up. "She went back to camp."

"Well, she's not there." He sniffed the air.

Not as noticeably, I did the same. I couldn't tell her fresh scent from the old. Quade could, and he leapt up. "We better go look for her."

Chapter Seventeen

"Hope was right here." I pointed to the spot where she stood. "She left back to camp. It's only a few steps away."

My spine prickled as a creature made its way into the cavern from a hidden tunnel to the left. "No need to fear," a voice boomed. My eyes strained to make out the form. "Your little Hope is fine. For how long? That I can't say. That's up to Nemasa." A cloaked man entered into the light. "Nice to see you again, traitor."

Quade smirked, then stepped in front of me. "So you're doing his dirty work. How long did he get you to be me? The king missed me that much? It's nice to know that I made that big of an impact."

"He didn't get me to be you for that reason," the cloaked man raised his fist. "It was to get her to think I was you, to ease her into this world. To trust us."

"And how did that go? Did you do a good job? No, wait. She's here with me. What was your punishment for your failure?"

The man removed his hood, three monstrous scratches ripped down his face, the edges tainted purple. A patch over his left eye hid the damage underneath.

"Ah, I bet you're riddled with marks like that. The king sure enjoys using those poison claws of his now, doesn't he?"

"It's been hard living in your shadow … he wants me to be just like you."

"Ah, yes."

"You talk too much, Wilder." Robin made his way in from the darkness. "Where's the girl? I'm ready for her."

Wilder bowed his head low. "Master, she's here, waiting for your torment." Hope materialized beside him, her body bound by an invisible force. Her mouth moved as if she were trying to say something to us. "She's a feisty one, just the way you like it, Master."

Robin gripped Hope's face tight in his right hand. "I'm allowed to kill you any way I please. I'm sure Wilder gave you all the details." His eyes burned into hers. "I won't be the one getting my hands dirty. That's the runt's job."

He turned to us, a full fanged grin filled his cheeky face. "I waited till you brought back that demon of yours. She's hungry. Can't you feel it, Nemasa?" He turned and nodded to Wilder.

Wilder reached up and sliced Hope's face with his razor-sharp claws. Her cheek burst open. Blood streamed down her jaw and neck. The smell … it filled the air … my nose … straight to my head. Sweet, oh-so-sweet, tickled my tongue. A crimson glow teased my eyes as my mouth pooled with saliva.

Quade grabbed my shoulders and attempted to lock eyes with me. My gaze was fixed to Hope. My heart raced, pounding in my ears. I couldn't hear Quade's words. Wilder reached over and dug his claws into Hope's hip and dragged them up to her collarbone. The spell that held her voice was removed, and her scream filled the cavern. The taste of her pain tingled my mouth. Quade shook me, but I was lost.

A hunger grew, slaughtering all rational thought. I breathed in deep through my nose. My whole body vibrated ... I shoved Quade out of the way and lunged at Hope. Wilder scooped Hope up into his arms and ran down the tunnel behind him.

Spiders emerged from the tunnel. I ignored them, and they ignored me as I jolted past them. My thoughts, my body, fixated on one thing and one thing only — the desire to feed the festering hunger.

How long did I run for? I do not know. I followed the scent, the pools of blood that trailed behind.

"Over here." Wilder snapped my attention to him. Hope lay bloodied on the ground. Red orbs lit the tiny tunnel around her head. "You can have her back," he said with a wave of his hand over her.

Hope pressed her weak hands into the ground. "Blaze," she said, blood gurgling in her throat.

Wilder helped Hope to her feet and propped her up against the wall. I stepped forward. My tongue tingled, my mouth watered. Uncontrolled beastly growls escaped from deep inside me. Her arms wrapped her torso, attempting to hold all the blood in. Her eyes fluttered, her knees wobbled. Wilder backed

259

off and watched. I blinked. My body had moved on its own, my face ending up dangerously close to hers.

"Have a taste," he tempted. "It's like no rush you've ever felt before."

"B-*Blaze* ..."

I tensed. My hands tightened into fists ... slammed into the wall beside her head. Her tangy fear watered my mouth. I repeatedly punched the space around her. Her wide eyes watched as each fist grazed her head.

"What are you doing? Give in!" he hollered.

My attention on Hope broke. I pounced at Wilder. My fist connected with his face, and he staggered backward. Another split his lip and sent him smashing into the wall behind him. I cocked my elbow back. His knees buckled, my bloodied fist crumpled the stone behind him. Wilder rolled to Hope, scooped her up into his arms. "She will pay for your disobedience." The cramped space turned black as Hope faded away in Wilder's grasp.

Over and over, my hands connected with the stone.

A single faint light lit behind me. My wicked shadow cast on the cave wall with an ominous flicker. "Well, isn't this a sight to behold?" a ghostly voice cackled.

I spun around. Madness crouched low to the ground, her knees in line with her pointed ears. A single candle suspended in the air behind her cast a flickered shadow. I collapsed to the ground in front of her. I hadn't noticed my exhausted gasps for air.

"Now he has her," she whispered as her voice echoed. "Come with me, child. Let me take away all thought and emotion. Let yourself give in to me. I will make it all go away. Come child, come."

The little girl peeked over Madness's shoulder. Her small hand reached out for me to take it. I lifted my hand to take hers. Madness's eyes swirled with pleasure. Her crimson and black irises mixed with flakes of gold. "Yes, child, come and play in the madness with us."

"Nemasa!" Quade called out from the darkness.

My gaze broke from the wicked pair and searched the dense void. A silhouette shifted. My eyes glanced back at the space Madness and the child had occupied, then back to the blackness.

"Nemasa?" Quade panted as his eyes searched the area around me. His orange orbs lit the bloodied space. He dropped down to the ground beside me. "Where's Hope?"

I shook my head, disgusted with myself.

"Did Wilder get away with her?" I nodded. "How are you?" He glanced at my tattered hands. "Your hands..."

"Fine."

His arms flung around me. "Come. The others need our help. They made a space for me to slip through, but there're too many for them to handle on their own. After that we will go after Hope." He helped me to my feet and towed me by the elbow toward the others.

Soleil's scythe cut deep into one of the spider's back. The creature screeched from pain, and dropped. Another spider fell to the ground near Lune. Quade intercepted one of the arachnids, which had lunged at Lune's back.

I drew my blades. There were two on the ceiling and one crept down the crystal pillar behind Soleil. I shifted toward one of the creatures. I remained out of sight as it twisted around into view.

As sore as my hands were, I tightened my grip on the hilts of my new blades. The sound of my foot on a loose rock gave away my position. A string of web spat passed my head from the creature I stalked. I crouched right to avoid contact. My left blade swung down past my ear and severed a leg. The creature screeched for a moment before my right came down and removed its head.

When I turned to see if there were any left, the twins had already finished off the others.

It was all over, and Soleil and Lune stood still in the middle of the battlefield. They eyed me with a gaze that shook my soul. I knew what they thought. Hope hadn't come back out with me.

"Wilder got away with the human. We need to hurry," Quade said as he made his way to my side. "Where is Sati?"

The others glanced around. Their eyebrows pressed together, jaws clenched. They peeked around to see if she was out of sight. When she didn't respond to our calls, the four of us raced back to the camp. Sati was on the ground near the gear. Her watery scales had lost their shimmer.

Quade dropped to his knees and turned her onto her back. "Sati?"

I joined him on the ground at his side. His hands moved over her body, *checking for wounds*. I held my breath. *He's checking for wounds, to save her. He'd do the same for any of them.*

"Look. Snake bite." He flipped her arm up. On the inside, two small holes punctured her scales.

"How could fangs that small harm her? She's practically made of diamonds. Nothing should be able to puncture her scales," Soleil stated as he joined us by her side.

That smell ... I leaned in closer and stiffened. I knew that smell.

"Has she been poisoned?" Lune asked as he formed a silver orb in his palm.

"You going to find out, brother?"

Poison?

"I don't think my magic will work over her, but this should tell us if there is any in her."

"Poison..." I repeated out loud. "That's it." It smelled just like I did when my body absorbed the poison out of Ta'la. It was the same spell the book used. Robin mentioned he needed my demon back. I then remembered the snakes at his feet at Ripper's. The two puncture marks on Sati reminded me of a snake bite.

This must have been Robin's doing, I thought while I examined Sati. Her limp body seemed frail, as if a single touch might break her. All the horrible thoughts I cast toward her while she was near Quade felt petty and childish. If only I had given her a chance and learned from her as my mother did from hers.

"Quade, I need you to tell me the spell you used when we were separated. The one you used when I talked to you through the book."

Lune closed his hand around the orb he lit. It burst and rained down to the ground. "You know what this is?"

"Yes, it's the same spell that was placed on someone I know. She fell into this sleep and her breathing was shallow just like this. And the smell. That sour smell is the giveaway."

Quade leaned over and whispered the spell into my ear. Words of a language I had long since forgotten. I placed my hand over Sati's forehead, and a warmth rose through my hand, up my arm, filled my veins, heating my entire body. A sickly green mapped my skin.

I pulled my hand away. Sati stared up at me with her bright blue eyes. "Milady? Hope! They are after —"

"We know," I interrupted. I backed up to avoid accidental contact with anyone of them.

"They're after Hope! Robin! He's here!" She tried to get up to her feet.

"Hey! Hold on," Quade pressed her down. The contact caused me to bite my tongue. "Let your body heal for a moment. You've been out for a while."

"Milady … I heard your voice."

A faint smile grew. "I'm glad you're okay."

"Robin!" She grabbed Quade's hand. I bit the inside of my lip. "Quade, he's here!"

"We know. He brought spiders with him, and Wilder. They tried to get Nemasa to kill Hope. It didn't work, and Wilder ran off with her. My guess is that they are at the castle."

"Tried …" Her watery gaze fell onto me. "Milady … I am sorry that I was not there for you."

"I'm okay. Hope, on the other hand, she —"

"She will be fine." Lune slapped the ground. "We will get her back."

"Let's pack only what we absolutely need. We'll travel light. If we're going to sneak into the castle, we'll need an in. Since our last adventure into the castle, I'm sure the king has upped his security."

"Let's give Sati time to regain her full strength and the poison to run its course through Nemasa." Quade stood and walked over to me. I backed up. "Nemasa?"

"We don't know if it's the same. If you touch me and get sick … I can't withdraw the poison by myself."

He reached his hand out to touch my hand. "You could—"

"Don't."

Quade let his hand drop to his side, his eyes shifted to the ground.

I turned, released my sheaths from the belt, and sat down against the far wall. Hope's fearful face flashed into my mind. I could've cried. *Never before had she been afraid of me.* I lifted my blood crusted knuckles into the air and wondered, *How could I have let myself go so far?*

Soleil and Lune sat down on either side of me. Lune crossed his legs and leaned his head back onto the jagged rock. Soleil stretched his one leg forward, bent the other up, and let his chin hang close to his chest. They, too, felt the failure.

"We will get her back." Lune turned his head to me. His turned-down lips and narrowed silver eyes reassured me.

"So are you going to tell me what's been going on between you and my human?" I cracked a smile. Lune's jaw dropped a bit. "Come on. You're always beside her. You tail her everywhere." I glanced at Soleil. "You, too." Soleil's face flushed. "So, there is something that I missed. When did this happen?"

"I don't know what you're talking about," Lune mumbled.

"I have a great punishment planned for liars. Do I need to try it out on you?" His eyes widened. "Kidding. Or am I?"

"Is she even human?" Lune questioned. "I know humans have spiritual powers. I just never thought that one could be that strong. The way she built those swords … I've never seen anything like it."

"Maybe humans from the Earthly Realm are naturally more powerful than the ones here."

"No," Soleil jumped in. "Humans have been brought here against their will for ages. They go to traders, get branded, and can never go back. Happens all the time. Those humans have no power at all. Hope's another story." His eyes shined like tiny suns as he talked about her.

"Wow! You two got it bad." I laughed. It felt good to let it out. I watched Quade stand up and stare at the three of us. I smiled and waved, unsure if he could hear us.

"Got what bad?" they asked in unison.

"You're obsessed."

"I am not," they replied again together.

"Sure." My smile faded. "Hey … how come none of you got affected by what happened?" I gazed at my hands. "What I did … that impulse? It was *so* powerful."

For a moment, there was silence. "We have been like this our whole lives. What you're going through is new to you." Lune breathed. "We all went through it as pups, though. I've never seen self-control to that extent. Normally, no matter what the age, the first outburst … the human doesn't survive."

"I showed self-control?" I asked as my tail flicked at my side. I scooped it up in my hands and petted it the way Hope did the first time she saw it. The thought made a smile grow.

"I don't smell a single drop of her blood on you. From what Quade said, they gave you a chance to kill her. Presented her to you on a silver platter and you resisted."

Chapter Eighteen

Sati's legs wobbled with an odd form of grace as she attempted to walk. Every time she stumbled Quade caught her. My body tensed. The contact between them knifed at every piece of me. I tried to control the urge to storm over there and beat her senseless, but she was frail, and there was nothing to be jealous about, merely a friend helping a friend. He'd do the same for the twins if he had to; then again, if they touched him, I would have felt the jealous urge.

"Sati is ready to walk. We best make our way as undetected as possible." Quade crouched down by my knees.

"That means we need to take the long way," Soleil joked. He placed his hand on my shoulder and let it linger. Quade shot him a warning glare.

"Brother, stop that. You need to ask Nemasa before you can lay a hand on her."

I turned to look at Lune as he shook his head at his brother. "Really?"

"Yeah. There's even a punishment for it," Lune announced.

I placed my hand over Soleil's. "That sounds fun."

Soleil withdrew his hand. "I don't think so."

"And since what you were doing got under Quade's skin, maybe he could carry out the sentence." Lune nudged his head toward the enraged Quade.

"I'd like that," Quade said with a smirk. His attention shifted back to me, and he extended his hand. "Ready to go get your human back?"

I placed my hand in his. "Yeah. How long is the 'long' way?"

"A few days. We'll have to travel without the use of the doors. We're quite a distance from the Keep. Sati won't be able to walk full speed for a while yet. She should be okay tomorrow. Your brother knew this would slow us down."

"Wasn't it Robin who poisoned her?" I asked as I attached my blades.

"It was through Robin's snakes that the poison got to her. It was your brother who created the poison. No one else can mimic the magic of that book other than your bloodline."

I gave a hard stare to the blue crystal beside me, but still I couldn't see the faces Hope described. "Do you think she will be okay? She might not have a few days."

Quade placed his hand on my shoulder where Soleil had placed his. "He needs her alive. He will keep her that way."

"How come he can touch you without asking?" Soleil crossed his arms and raised a brow.

"Hush, you pup," teased Quade as he pulled me forward toward the space where Hope had been kidnapped.

"I'm not a pup, just think it's not fair."

Hope's blood had pooled on the floor and led the way into the blackness of the tunnel. Quade wrapped his arm around my waist as the sweet intoxicating smell filled my nose. I held my breath to keep as much of the smell out of me as possible. Hope's terrified face haunted my mind.

Giggles were heard soon after as the child tiptoed onto the pool as we walked past. She reached down, ran her finger tips though the blood, her distorted face twitching at the cheeks. Her crimson finger tips met with her meaty tongue. *"Have a taste … you'd like it … you know you want to try. Come and play with me."*

I peeled my eyes away from her and focused on the darkness.

"You okay?" Quade whispered into my ear.

"Yeah, just can't believe what I did …"

"You did better than me," he admitted. "There was a human child at the castle before you were born. His mother worked as a housekeeper and he helped her. Once in a while, they would come in and clean my room. He cut his finger when he cleaned under my bed — I don't remember what happened after.

"When I came to, I was with my mom. She wouldn't tell me what happened or let me in my room for a few days." Quade's body began to vibrate, eyes locked with mine. "You're the only one I know who succeeded in fighting the desire."

"Could have something to do with your bond with her," Lune jumped into the conversation, throwing his arm around my neck. "You have a strong connection with that human."

His palm created three silver orbs as we entered into the dark. "Though her power over you is very suspicious. She could have you under a spell. She could be controlling your actions. Have you ever considered that you may be her pet?"

Quade released my waist and lingered behind Lune and me. He didn't seem pleased that Lune had butted in.

"She never let's me forget. I really don't mind. She has never treated me poorly."

"What?" he gasped. "You're Nemasa, not some human plaything."

"She's not just some human. And I'm sure my brother is finding that out right now … though I think that might get her into more trouble with him than it did with me." Tears rimmed my eyelids. "I really hope she's okay."

Lune's arm tightened around my neck. "Me, too," he whispered. "I better let go. Seems I've stuck a nerve." I giggled, Lune was right. Grumbles and growls came from Quade as he tailed behind us. "Though," Lune said lower, "I think it's good for him."

"Me to," I agreed. We both ended up letting out a quiet laugh. I stole a glance at Quade. His brows pressed together and eyes shifted away.

"Do you remember much about my mother?" I asked as the gray walls lit up in a silver unsteady light.

"She gave us candy, lots of candy. Your brother really didn't like how much your mother cared for us. I don't blame him. She ignored him most the time. He was too much like his father."

"His father?"

"Your mother was betrothed to marry his father. He was her guardian, but nothing like you and Quade. He kept his distance from her, and if anyone came near her, he killed them without question."

"Your guardian is slacking on the defensiveness," joked Soleil as he walked at par with Lune and I.

"I could kill you both now, if you'd like."

"How many spiders have you killed? One?" Soleil challenged.

"If you really want the count ..." Lune grinned. "I've killed three, and you have both killed two. Nemasa, one. Better step up your game before Nemasa and I take the lead."

I glanced back and smiled at the hard-pressed-face behind me. Then my eyes shifted to Sati, her natural brightness dulled by the poison's effects. I slipped out of Lune's arm and made my way to her side.

"How are you doing?"

"I'm okay, milady. I am sorry I failed you."

"I already told you that you didn't fail me. One of the twins mentioned that they couldn't believe a snake could puncture your scales."

"Yes, my body is not like others. It is very unique. I was born to a mother without a father, as my mother and her mother before her. Our kind is still very much a mystery. We have always served the Nemasa, and I am proud to be in your service."

"Oh..." My eyes shifted to the back of Quade's head.

"You know, you have always been that way with him."

"What way?" I could think of many *ways* I've been with him that confused the hell out of me. I waited quietly for her answer.

"Even as children, you hated when anyone other than his mother touched him." She stumbled. My arm caught her's and linked. I let her put pressure onto me for support. Where her skin touched mine felt as if I had dunked my arm in a cool refreshing stream. "There was a time he slipped off a branch of a tree and I caught him by the hand. After he was safely back in the tree, you climbed down and ignored us for the whole day. You were only two at the time."

"Really, that young?"

"I recognize the look you have been giving him when he helps me or I help him. It is the same. I will keep my distance, milady." I couldn't look at her. I thought I had been hiding my envy from all of them, but they saw right through my mask. "It is part of who you are. You are the Nine Tails. Possessiveness is in your nature when it comes to a ... um ..." She paused then whispered in my ear, "A mate." I swallowed hard. "I mean not to be disrespectful. You two were always meant to be."

Quade, the twins, Sati, and I traveled on and on through the caves. Quade and the twins strolled comfortably in the lead. There were times when we all talked, then were silent. The thought of what my brother and Hope were doing tormented every moment. I knew him to be cruel and heartless. *Alive, that's what Quade said,* I thought. *He will keep her alive. Not safe or unharmed. Alive.*

After what seemed like hours of walking, we took a break. Sati seemed run down and the further we pressed on the more she needed my support.

We sat on the uneven ground to rest our legs. Sati laid out on one of the bags across from me. She seemed peaceful as she slept.

"Nemasa," Quade passed me a chuck of dried meat. "There's an underground market nearby. A couple hours walk. The twins are wondering if you want to go there and stock up or spend the night here and go tomorrow."

"Let's see how long she sleeps. We won't wake her. If she wakes soon, then we will go. If not, we will go in the morning."

"You should try to sleep." He shuffled beside me, resting his back against the rock wall.

I eyed the stone behind him, a dull, life-sucking gray. He was right. Gray, gray, and more gray. The Earthly Realm had much more color: greens, yellows, reds, blues, purples, oranges, and every shade in-between. Colors of life. Not the wicked life that dwelled in this sinister land. Glorious pure color that warmed life, soaking in the light of the sun. Hunter green grass eaten by the delicate deer, stalked by the patient mountain lion resting on a sturdy branch, hidden by broad healthy leaves. The unseen ocean splashed against the rock bank of the shoreline as predator and prey enjoyed the summer breeze. The Earthly Realm was alive; Sin seemed bare.

The Earthly Realm had much to offer when you thought about the life outside the towns. Then there were humans, thieving murderous beasts that manipulate and backstab. How was any of that different than what I had experienced in Sin? I'd rather be in Sin. With him. With Soleil, Lune, and Sati.

"Did you really think I wouldn't come back to you?" Quade breathed out. "I came back, didn't I? Didn't even know there was a place to come back to. I even knew that Wilder wasn't actually you."

"That's because he was a horrible copy of me." He slung his arm around my neck and eased me close. "Maybe we could send the twins for supplies."

"Why would we do that?" I searched his eyes for an answer.

His face flushed. "Never mind. You should sleep."

I lowered myself down and rested my head on his lap. "Mind if I use you as a pillow?"

"He won't mind, Nemasa," Soleil teased as he plopped down beside Quade.

Lune joined by my feet. "Nope. He won't mind at all."

I squeezed my eyes shut as my face heated. "And about trying to get rid of us, Quade, tell me, what was your intention with the Nemasa while we're away?" Quade, didn't answer. "I thought as much," Soleil snickered.

The cool void wrapped me like a black blanket as I slipped to sleep. The child hummed somewhere far off. I could see her light flicker, a single star in the night.

Star light, star bright, first star I see tonight ... no. I had no wish that would be heard. And wishes were only granted to those who deserved them. Me, I didn't. What I did to Hope — if I did see her again, she'd run. Or was there a chance she'd come to me?

I had no idea. No matter, I needed to go to her. Save her from my brother's grasp.

I stretched out my arms and let my feet drop. I floated on the void's thick air. The blackness above me brightened, the light forced my eyes shut. Slowly I reopened them, the blue sky took over above me white cotton clouds drifted on the breeze.

A cool splash of water over my naked chest tightened my skin. My hands squished the liquid in between my fingers. A huge breath of fresh air filled my lungs, relaxed my body. My eyes closed. The rustle of the leaves from trees at the distant shoreline sang as the breeze filtered through their thick canopy.

"What are you doing down there?" Quade asked.

I opened my eyes. He stood tall on the water's surface.

"Swimming." Another wave sent a few droplets onto my skin, I dropped down into the water. Even though the water was chilly, I could feel the heat rise to my face. I popped my head out to breathe.

"Swimming? Where are we?"

"We're at a lake, but I don't recognize it." My eyes searched for a similarity but found none. "Come in," I coaxed.

"I'd much rather stay dry."

I pressed my hand over the surface of the water, a small wave that soaked his feet. He skipped back. "Hey!" He pouted.

I held my breath in, dropped down, and could hear my name through the water. Quade dropped to his knees and scanned the water.

I sped upward and splashed. "Come on, scaredy cat. It's just water."

"You're a fire fox. I don't see how you could like being wet."

I bit my lip, lifted my hands, and firmly placed them on top of the water's surface, as if it were the side of a pool, and hoisted myself up and sat on the surface. My legs dangled in the water, splashing the water with my toes.

"Come in with me. I won't let you drown."

His arms crossed. I dropped back into the water and swam underneath him. On the other side, I crawled back on to the surface and joined him.

"What's a lake?" he questioned as my hands lifted his shirt over his head.

"This is a lake. A gigantic puddle of water, great for swimming in." I dropped the shirt into the water. Like a rock, it sank to the bottom.

"We don't have lakes," he stated as I unclasped his belt and dropped it. "We used to have ponds. You wouldn't want to swim in them. Something might eat you." His fingers brushed my neck; his eyes darted over the water beneath him.

"Nothing will eat you here." My fingers traced down his chest. "I won't let them." I slipped his pants down and let them sink down with the rest of his clothes.

My hands gripped his hips. His heart raced as I stepped away. My hands slipped from his skin.

"Wait! I ... I'll try."

I smiled and let the tension of the water break under me. The rush of water swallowed me whole. The soft smooth liquid graced my skin, pulled my hair up around my head. My hands and feet moved to keep me in place. I paddled backward and poked my head out of the water.

He kneeled and tested the water with his fingertips. *"It's cold ..."*

I grasped his hand and tugged him in. The lake splashed up around us. He struggled to keep his head above the water.

"Slowly." I moved my hands to show him how. *"Move your feet and hands like this."* After a few tries he treaded water clumsily. *"Welcome to my element."* I ducked under the water and swam a few feet from him and resurfaced. *"Try to catch me."*

"That's not fair!" He pouted again.

"Why not? You made me chase you around when I had no idea how, and you made me dance. Now I'm making you swim. Plus, you'll like what you get if you catch me."

Quade's eyes shined in the sunlight as his hands awkwardly paddled the water. With every passing moment, he became faster and faster. I ducked under the water a few times to escape his reach.

Soon he had me by the arm. *"Caught you!"* He panted.

I lifted myself out of the water and sat on its surface. He crawled over me. His hand teased my skin as he lay me down. *"I'm curious. What do I get if I catch you?"*

My fingers entwined in his hair, his lips pressed firmly to mine.

I could feel a hand firm on my shoulder, I peeked over, but nothing was there. *"I think someone's trying to wake me."*

His lips pecked mine again. *"Ignore them."*

Our lips locked, tongues twisted. *"Sorry ... "*

"Milady," Sati whispered.

"Yes," I yawned.

"It's your turn for watch."

"Oh … right. I'm up," I said as I raised myself from Quade's lap. I knew Quade was awake even though his eyes remained closed. "Go ahead. Get some sleep."

She bowed her head with a smile. "Milady," she said as she found a comfortable place to sit, "may I ask you a question?"

"Sure."

"Have you tried to use the mirror?" Her legs were crossed, her hands folded loosely in her lap.

"No, I haven't even thought about it."

"The king is a powerful magic wielder. He took interest in my mother's work at a young age. He read every book she owned hundreds of times. Memorized each word. By the time you were born, he stopped. My mother thought it was strange that he took interest in magic when he was already a master swordsman. If you use the mirror, I think, he would be able to see you if you go looking for Hope. He might trap your soul."

"Could he really do that? Trap my soul?"

"Yes. There are ways, and I think he might be able to do it."

Quade's clothes ruffled as he rested his elbows on his knees. "He could."

I twisted my head. He stared deeply into the low burning fire. "How do you know for sure?"

"I was his right-hand for a time being."

My eyes widened. "What? Why?"

"Sati and I fled to the tunnels as children. When I was old enough, I joined the royal ranks as a simple warrior. It had been years since he last saw me. I was sure he thought I was dead. No one could recognized me. Ever wonder why Robin and Wilder call me traitor?"

"I have wondered about it."

"When I was in training, one of the masters called me weak and pathetic. He challenged me. He did it every few days or so to scare the new meat he collected into his ranks. Needless to say, I won. When you kill a higher-ranked officer, you inherit their status. The king was informed about what happened and summoned me."

"Why did you join in the first place?" I questioned.

"To find out more about you. I wanted to know if he knew of your whereabouts." Quade tilted his head back.

"When the king summoned you, what happened?"

His lips widened. "I tried to remain in the shadows, investigate without drawing attention to myself. My will to live was a lot stronger than reason. I should have fled, but didn't." He reached over and placed his hand on my head. "A story for another time." He glanced up at Sati. You should rest. You're still weak from that poison."

"You should rest, too, Quade." Sati's eyes closed, and then opened again. "How long have you two been dream walking together?"

"Dream walking?" I turned to Quade.

"It is a skill normally used to visit the Earthly Realm beings through their dreams."

"What makes you think we're dream walking?"

"Your heartbeats and breaths are synced. I noticed it when I woke you."

I remained silent, and Quade followed my lead. The time we spent in our dreams together was our business. She didn't need to pry into the only time we had together. She didn't need to know.

"If you are to continue, be sure that you get an adequate amount of actual sleep, to keep from passing out. Dream walking has the same effects on the body as being awake."

"Go to sleep now, Sati," Quade said as his eyes locked with mine.

"Quade?" Sati's gaze burned into him. He shook his head. An answer to a secret question. Her eyes closed once again, and soon she fell fast asleep.

"Going to tell me what that last thing was about?"

"Later." He smiled and ran his fingers over my hair. "Are you tired?"

"Not really? You should sleep. Your shift is next."

His lips parted like he wanted to say something else, but the words never came out. My ear tingled as his fingers grazed it. Heat filled my body as I realized that he had the same hot gaze on me that he used in the dream. Lune shifted in his sleep and knocked over Soleil's sword. Both blinked awake, kicked each other, then dosed off. There was always someone that kept us apart, even though we were close enough to touch. "Good night, Quade."

He grumbled, then laid out on the floor, his head resting in my lap. That moment was the first time I had seen him sleep laying down. Sati, Soleil, Lune, and Quade all slept with their backs resting against a wall or propped up somehow. If I didn't know them and stumbled onto their camp, I would have mistakenly thought they were awake.

As my hand brushed his soft hair, I wondered, *What is it that they're hiding from me?*

I suddenly felt the mirror bounce off my skin. *Sati had warned me not to use it. But what if my brother waited, wanting to make a deal with me? Hope would be safe back with us where she belonged.* I reached up and fingered the cool metal. My eyes twitched around the empty corridors. *Only a peek, should be harmless.* I thought about waking Quade. *He could watch over the others while I left. Then again, he would only try to stop me.* My hand tightened over the small pendant. My thumb pressed into the mirror as my eyes fluttered shut.

As soon as my eyelids sealed, they opened in a grand golden room. Marble floors glistened under an extravagant candle chandelier that hung down from the domed ceiling. Golden pillars equally spaced stood proud. Etched into the pillars, thousands of faces displayed an emphasized expression.

"Welcome, little sister. I knew you would come." A bold voice boomed from behind me.

I whipped around. It was him. My brother, Bruin. My heart pounded in my chest. He stood fully cloaked, face hidden by a thick black hood. His crimson eyes peered out with their own wicked glow. "I expected you sooner. Your human was quite the vocal one. Don't worry. I fixed her for you."

My mouth dried. "What ... where is she?"

"Alive. Would you like to see her? There will be a price. And if you don't see her, there will be a punishment."

"What's the price?"

A heavy moment hung between us. His body shifted closer, his robe slid over the smooth marble. He clasped my chin between his thick fingers. "Let us discuss the punishment." My jaw tightened. "I will kill her."

"Then let me see her."

"Ah! Do you have payment?" He raised my chin, his face inches from mine. Still I could not see past the shadow. His wicked eyes burned into mine as he studied my features. "You look just like mother did when I —"

"Careful. I might just kill you."

"I will leave your human unharmed for an extra fee, if you so choose." I nodded as best I could. "Come back tomorrow night." He removed his hand and stepped back. "I am a busy man, you know. And I can't keep my next appointment waiting." He began to unclasp his robe. "Where you are about to go, they will kill you in an instant. I do not wish to give that luxury to anyone other than myself." He flipped off his hood, and long black horns stuck out above his eyes. His red irises floated in an onyx sea. I could feel the warmth drain from my face as his handsome features set in. Then it struck me. He was the one I had drawn in art class. It was his image that got Mrs. Hritz killed. The robe slipped off his broad shoulders as he unveiled the simplicity of his clothes.

"You know where I am?"

"Yes. I've been watching you, always."

The robe wrapped around me. "How are you able to touch me if I am not actually with you?" I pressed my arms through the large sleeves.

"There are many things I am able to do." His fingers pinched at the shoulders and withdrew a blue thread from the material. The robe faded from solid to transparent, the weight of the heavy fabric sunk onto my shoulders. "Your friends are about to wake. Do not speak of me or your human will pay dearly."

I let the pendant drop against my collarbone as a hot breath of air filled my lungs. *He knows where I am,* I thought. My eyes searched the walls for a clue how. My ears twitched as Quade moved his one hand off the other, but everything else remained silent.

Quade's head lifted from my lap, I wondered what he would think of my new item of clothing that appeared from nowhere. I tried to think of an excuse; however nothing came to mind. His eyes met mine, then spotted the robe.

"Did I miss something?" He yawned.

I shook my head. His eyes narrowed. "You should rest."

"I think I've had more than enough of sleep for the night."

"Didn't you hear what Sati said? It doesn't count as sleep. Two nights in a row, you haven't had any *real* sleep." He lifted the sleeve of the robe and sniffed it.

"What are you doing?" I pulled it away from him. "I thought it would be good to hide my form from whoever is in the market. Unless a fox creature is a common sight?"

285

"No, you're right." He sniffed it again. "The Nemasa is the only fox born. It just doesn't smell like your magic made it. Where did it come from?"

"Well, if it wasn't me, where would it have come from?"

"I ... just ... get some rest." His arms and legs crossed in one swift motion. Eyes slitted.

"You know for me being the Nemasa, you sure order me around a lot."

His lips tightened; air escaped through his nose. Moments passed and he said nothing. My shoulders slouched forward. "Sorry, I guess I am tired." I leaned back to the wall behind me. Quade seemed to want nothing to do with me after my outburst and random item of clothing. I let my eyes close and made sure no part of me was touching him.

His hand pressed against the back of my neck, pulling me onto his chest. "I won't do it again. Forgive me."

My body melted into his as I shifted my weight to lay completely onto him. "Forgiven."

* * *

Before I knew it, his hand stroked my cheek. "Nemasa," he whispered into my ear, "it's time to wake up." I yawned, his arm warmed my side and stomach. His gentle touch stimulated my skin. "Nemasa."

"I'm up. I'm up ... no ... five more minutes."

His chest vibrated as he laughed. "If only I could. Any later and there will be more creatures than you can handle at the gate."

I buried my face into his chest. "Five more ... meanie ..." My eyes sprang open. *That was the last thing I called him before we separated. I still hadn't apologized for that.* I lifted my head from the comfort of his chest. I could see the hidden hurt in his eyes. "Sorry."

"For what?" A smile tried to form.

My eyes drifted from his deep gaze. "I called you that the last time I saw you before I left for the Earthly Realm. I'm sorry." I didn't care that the others watched us. My arms tightened around him. "You're not a meanie. I'm sorry."

His left arm wrapped around my back as the other patted the top of my head. "It's okay, Nemasa. You always called me a meanie. Most of the time, I deserved it. It's nice to know that, even though you were reborn in the other realm, the old you is still here."

The image of the child filled the black space behind my eyelids whenever I blinked. "Yeah, she's there all right."

Chapter Nineteen

Home was a distant memory. The softness of the Earthly Realm hardened to stone, love twisted to wickedness, and the colors faded to gray. The creatures that joined me were fragments of what I had left behind. Loyal and communal. Unlike Madness, Ripper, and the creature I left to rot in the mud, whom seemed to only want to feed their loneliness and self-desires. Whatever part of me that lived in the calm of the human realm hid itself in the deep corner of the void. I had forgotten what happiness felt like, even dreams alone with Quade were more to fill the hunger to touch him and control him.

"We are almost at the market," Soleil said. The end of the tunnel was lit in a fiery shimmer. "You better cover up now."

I lifted the hood up over my face. Quade helped me lift it over one of my horns that refused to go under. "You must ... I mean ... try ..." He stumbled.

"Just say it," I barked.

"Stay on your feet. If you hit the ground, you're fair game to the beasts around you. Stay close. If we get separated, head for the iron wall. You won't miss it. Most likely it will be the first thing you notice. It stands at the back of the swarm."

"The swarm?" I pictured a black wave of wasps buzzing toward me. I gasped. I hated wasps and hornets. It hurt when they stung.

Soleil's arms wrapped my chest. "Yeah, the swarm. Those who are unable to meet the qualifications to enter the market gather outside the wall, feasting on whatever hits the ground. They're mindless beasts that only think to feed and fuck whatever they dig their claws into."

"Brother," Lune warned, "don't scare her."

"What? She will see it either way. It's helpful for her to know what she is getting herself into."

"I must agree with Soleil." Sati lifted a black hood over her face. "Milady, don't let any of them see your face, even in the market. They will kill you or worse."

"I'll be fine!" I snapped, arms crossed.

The hood rippled as her head lowered. "Of coarse, milady."

The glow brightened as we neared. The smell of brimstone and sweat stung my nose. Screams filled my ears, pain and joy-filled roars, grunts, and hollers. Quade was right. The first thing my eyes saw was a massive, sharp iron wall. Little creatures scurried around the top lip. They stared down at the beasts that pressed up against the hot metal. A few nimble creatures clawed their way up the iron close to the top. The little creatures waited in a pile, their tongues moistening their blood soaked lips.

My eyes drifted down to the swarm of creatures that pushed and shoved. One lost its footing, and the beasts around it pounced. Their claws tore open the grounded creature, shoving fresh meat into their dripping jaws. The fresh sweet smell of blood drifted to my nose. Intoxicating.

"Keep on your toes," Lune whispered as he shifted behind me.

Sati and Soleil led. Quade pressed into my side, and Lune followed close behind me as we stepped into the swarm. Shoulders bashed against mine. A skinny creature grabbed onto my robe and heaved me toward it. I tried to tug my sleeve back, but it wouldn't let go.

A small dagger severed the beggar's hand from its body. Lune bashed into my back. I stumbled forward as a creature pushed me sideways. When I tried to regain my balance, my foot slipped. Air rushed around me as the ground became closer. Before I hit the ground, Quade grabbed my arm and stood me back on my feet. My heart pounded so loudly in my ears that it almost masked the screams from a creature that wasn't as fortunate as me. Blood sprayed through the air as claws ripped into it.

Then all sound vanished. I spun where I stood, the others nowhere to be seen. I glanced at the wall and quickened my pace. If I fell, there would be no one to save me. Another scrawny creature grabbed me. I mimicked Lune and withdrew the small dagger from its sheath and jabbed into its hand. The creature let out a high-pitched squeal. Those passing by jumped to another feast.

A tight grip seized my arm, and I turned to please my dagger once again. Lune caught the hilt. I gasped. There was too much going on. Too many creatures. Too much death. My breathing turned to short gasps.

Lune kept his hand on my elbow the rest of the way, pushing and shoving me through the crowd. He led me to a gate carved into the wall covered in razor wire and spikes, guarded by two, broad, hairy creatures. Long snouts snorted as we closed the distance in between them and us.

"Lune?" one bellowed. "It's been ages."

"Have you seen my brother?"

"Not since the last time you both delighted us with your presences." He rubbed his hands together and grinned. "Bring anything good for the boss this time?" His round yellow eyes searched me over; his nostrils flared.

"Not this time. This client seeks passage through the tunnels. I come as a buyer. We need supplies. I told it I knew the best place for that."

My dagger was still unsheathed under my robe.

"I smell blood on its hands."

"Yes. A dweller tried to have it as a snack. Needless to say, the dweller lost."

The beast's grin widened. "A feisty one. You sure pick spirited clients."

"And this one deserves to shop at the best."

The beast lowered his eyes to my level. "State a name." I remained silent. "A name or no crossing. And I know if you speak a true name or a lie." His eyes filled with a swirl of magic.

"Blaze."

"Hmm ..." Its back straightened and it twisted to Lune. "You may enter."

The doors cracked, creaked, and then burst open. Lune led me into a much less pushy market. Poorly boarded stands pressed against one after the other. Creatures filled the wide walkways in an unorganized fashion. Venders' and buyers' voices fueled the atmosphere.

"We should find the others. If I were my brother, where would I go? He would want to go ... so ... he'll be over here."

I tailed Lune as best I could. His feet carried him fast through the bends of the market. My eyes tried to take in all the hand-crafted treasures, trinkets, food, clothes, and glamorous riches. One food vender caused me to stop dead. The smell made my mouth water, a delightful smell of roasted seasoned meat. My eyes stood fixed to the buffet laid out before them.

"Come on. I don't want to lose you here." Lune dragged me away from the temptation.

"Hey!" a voice yelled from a ways away. "Thief!"

"That could be Soleil." Lune pulled us toward the commotion. We passed a small stand filled with pendants, hats, dried meats, and clear gel jars. I watched Lune swipe a bag of meat on passing. The creature behind the booth was too busy up-selling to a hairy customer to notice.

"Lune?" A creature clicked from behind us.

"Ah," Lune turned, a huge smile showed off all his fangs. "Boss, how goes business?"

"When the guardsman told me my favourite sinner was in the market, I had to set out to find you." His long, dirty ears twitched on the top of his head above his horns. Fine fur covered every inch of his body, resembling a filthy jack rabbit. "Your scent is an easy one to follow."

"Speaking of scent, have you sensed my brother? He travels with two others."

"Nope. I would have been told if both of you had entered." He leaned his thin head in close. "I found what you've been hunting for." He slouched forward and winked. "I have another potential buyer, but I like you boys. You do good business."

Lune looked at me, then back at Boss. "I—"

"He would be pleased to see what you have to offer," I said in a flat tone.

Lune's eyes darted back to me. "I would?"

"Yes. I am interested in things you hunt for." A grin filled my face. "This place, I've come to like it." My eyes shifted to a meat shop. Behind the clerk hung different types of carcasses to bleed out. At the end of the row hung a human corpse. I swallowed the saliva that poured into my mouth.

"Who is this, Lune?"

"A client."

"We've been pals long enough to —"

"Just as I do when I work for you, I respect my client's privacy."

"And that's why we do business, you greedy rodent. Now come, see what I have for you, old friend."

On the furthest side from the gate, built into the stone behind the market, Boss led us into his home. The inside wasn't as extravagant as I thought it would be. A small den crammed full with trinkets of all shapes and sizes, with one thing in common. Gold. He had an eye for anything polished to shimmer. In the center, a roaring fire had been left unattended.

Boss sunk his thin muscular body down into one of the pillows by the fire. His long, leather-wrapped feet stuck out from underneath him. "Now, friend. That *item* you've been searching for. A book, right? More specifically, a journal?" Lune lowered onto a red embroidered gold pillow, crossing his legs while his lips tightened. "Let's say I found it. The journal your greedy hands long to hold."

Lunes eyes met with Boss' gaze. "It's a myth."

"It's gibberish. That's what it is. I couldn't crack the code no matter how hard I tried. Now I'm passing it off to a creature with more brains than I."

"That must be hard for you to say."

"Indeed." Boss rubbed his chin, scratched behind his flopped ear and then stood it back up. "Look, if timing is an issue, let me send a messenger to find your brother. I'll give you time to hold the journal."

"That's unlike you."

"I know, I know. I feel like I'm getting too soft in my old age."

"You're not old." Lune turned to me. I nodded. "And send the messenger."

Boss's hand clenched into a fist and slammed it into the metal cabinet that hid under statues, a rolled rug, books, and many other random gold trinkets. The door creaked open. A small, bruised hand pressed into the layer of carpet that made up the floor. Soon a human boy, no older than seven, curled into a ball bowed before Boss. My mouth tingled as his fear set in, pools of saliva filled the empty spaces. I swallowed, and breathed in deeply.

"Having trouble?" Boss's eyes were on me. I had been too distracted by the human to notice he had moved to my side; his nose twitched at my ear. "You have no scent. That's what's wrong with you. Who is this, Lune?"

"It is new to humans, finds them tempting."

"New?"

"Yes, the boy is its first human it has encountered in a small space."

"Don't lie to me, friend. No one can control themselves with their first human."

Boss sat back onto his spring-loaded feet, bouncing slightly. His hands clenched his stitched pants and pulling them up a bit. "Human. Find Soleil and tell him his brother is here. Bring him to me."

The boy nodded, then scurried across the floor, keeping his head a hair's width from the ground, and pointed at his master. At the door, he bowed again before he darted out.

"First human. Don't believe it." Boss turned and pushed a few trinkets out of the way. He lifted a statue of a frightened bear and placed it onto another shelf. His paws grasped a thick metal box, sealed closed by razor wire tied tight around.

"I said, 'first human in a small space,'" Lune said as his body inched closer and closer, his shaky eyes transfixed to the box. "Can't be ..."

"Oh, but it is, friend. You weasels owe me big for this one."

"Just because it has fancy packaging doesn't mean I will like what's inside."

"True." Boss poked his finger around the wire in a coded sequence. The wire snapped and collapsed to the ground. "Guests first." He extended the box over to Lune.

The silver in Lune's eyes brightened as his fingers touched the box. "Have you been able to crack a word of it?" He lifted its lid, jaw dropped. "There's no ... no way ..."

"It's the real deal. When I came across it, I believed as you did. Then I saw it. The magic practically grabbed my throat and left me speechless. It cost me a fortune and two of my best business partners."

Lune lifted the skin-covered book from its case. "I ... I can't ... how much?"

I leaned forward. The book seemed ordinary, for Sin, to me. The simple cover, not a mark on it. Lune knew what it was, and wanted it badly. His mouth moved between gnawing his lip to his tongue and back to his lip again.

"Well, with a face like that I should steepen the bargain."

Lune's face hardened.

"Friend, this won't come cheap. I'm sure you weasels would understand."

"Let me see," I said and held out my hand. Both of them glared my way. "Who knows? I might just pay early."

Lune moved the book my way, then pulled it back. I reached to him again. His eyes rolled and the book's soft skin cover touched my fingers. A surge knocked the wind from my lungs. My hand gripped the cover tighter.

Noise from the entrance drew both Boss's and Lune's attention.

"Boss? Hey, Boss! Your human gave us your message."

Both Lune's and Boss' eyes sprang to the cloth door. I slipped the book into my robe and opened the box.

"Hey! Hands off!" Boss snapped the lid closed and cradled the box in his thick, long arms. I nodded my head in respect. I didn't want to risk a fight. He slipped the box under the shelf and moved the statue to hide it. My hands slipped into my robe and loosened my belt.

"Yes. Yes. What do you mean *we*?" Boss stared at the cloth-covered door.

I slipped the book to my back and cinched the belt tight enough to make each breath difficult to take.

"I have two companions with me. I know you don't like uninvited guests."

"Ah, yes. Come in." Boss moved his body back to his original seat. Lune shifted closer to him to make more room in the small space.

Soleil entered first. "Crap. There you are. We searched everywhere for you." His eyes shifted to his brother. "Decided to visit an old friend instead of finding your panicked brother?"

"I sent a messenger." Lune let out a small laugh.

Sati, covered by her robe, entered next. She found her seat between Boss and me, nodded to me. I could see a faint smile fill her thin lips. I grinned back.

"Quade!" Soleil called.

"Too cramped, I'll wait here."

"Come in," Boss demanded.

Quade's irritated growl caused me to chuckle.

"Something funny?" Boss's attention shifted back to me. My silence irritated him. The veins in his forehead bulged.

"This is a lot of people in your den, Boss." Soleil's cautious eyes studied him.

From under the brim of the hood, I watched Quade's legs cross as he leaned closer. The weight of his hand lowered my head. "You're a hard one to keep track of."

Boss shifted, his eyes darted between each of us. "Now weasels, tell me why my *friends* are being hunted down by the king?" The air stilled — silenced. "I think it has something to do with those you travel with." He turned to Sati. His paw tore her hood back. "The High Sorceress's daughter? Now this is a surprise! I knew, when Quade walked in here, you'd be one of the creatures I'd find hiding behind the shadow. Then, if this is you…" I slid my hand over the hilt of my dagger. "Who are you?"

The curtain pulled back at the door. "Now, now, Boss. Don't be going at finding that out." Krista lifted her heeled boot and pressed it into the other side of the door frame to block the exit. "The king wants this one as is. Hidden away. He explained it clear enough when he gave you your gift, didn't he?"

I unsheathed my dagger and twisted my body upward. The dagger speared her above the hip. She fell out of the doorway with a screech. "You bitch. I'll kill you for that!"

I withdrew and stabbed her again in the arm. "You know he wouldn't give you that pleasure." I turned to the creature-filled streets and jolted into the crowd. Everyone soon followed.

"You're crazy. You know that?" Quade said to me with a chuckle.

"This way." Lune pushed me toward the wall. His hand slid a stone down and pressed a few more in. The wall cracked open. The space opened just wide enough to squeeze through. Once we were all in, he closed it.

"That was close." Soleil placed his hand on my shoulder. "That was quick thinking."

I gasped to gather my breath back. I raised my bloody blade as Lune ignited his silver orbs. Krista's crimson blood soaked the blade and dripped down my hand to my elbow.

"You should have seen it, brother. He had the journal."

"There are many journals in the world."

"*The* journal. The one that we have been searching for. It was beautiful, and the magic ... wow! I could feel it throughout my body."

Sati stepped closer to me. "Here, I was able to get a bit of food while we looked for you, milady." She placed a chunk of balled ground meat in my hand. "I think you will like these. They have all sorts of flavors blended into one."

Lune showed off the meat he swiped. "See, I wasn't just roaming around shopping for me. I got some food, too."

"You stole that." I plopped the ball into my mouth. Bursts of flavours exploded in my mouth.

"Milady, I stole these."

"No way," I said with mouth still stuffed.

"I apologize."

"Oh, yeah." Quade pulled out three leather bags of food.

Soleil withdrew his cache, his mouth widened as he noticed he had stolen the largest quantity.

I unbuttoned my robe and reached back to stabilize the book in my hand. My free hand loosened my belt. "Sorry, I think I have the biggest steal of the day. If you really wish to make it a competition."

"Yeah, right Nemasa. You don't have the reflexes and stealth. We grew up down here. Though you are the Nemasa, and we will let you win. No need to show us."

"Really, but Lune seems so in love with my object." I narrowed my eyes at Lune and let my wicked grin bare all my teeth.

"You didn't …"

I shifted the book out from behind my back. "I did. Are you going to tell me what it is?"

Quade stood silent as he processed what was before him. Sati's face grew long, her eyes widened and fixed.

"That's a myth. It doesn't actually exist." Soleil gasped.

"As shocking as this may be, it won't take long for them to find where we have gone. We need to keep moving." Lune placed his hands over mine. "Nemasa, let me translate it. I will tell you everything I find in the pages. Never before has it been decoded. Give me a chance to be the one to do it. They say it's a journal from your brother's father. He wrote every spell he ever learned and manipulated. His Book of Shadows. Please let me crack the code."

I let the book fall into his hands. "The task is yours then."

Chapter Twenty

Hours and hours and hours passed before we all felt safe enough to stop. The twist and turns of the jagged tunnel dragged on. Lune seemed to know where to go. At every turn off or minor split, he didn't stop, sometimes right, others left.

"You think we lost her?" Soleil whispered to Lune.

"I hope. Nemasa slowed her for sure. Those weren't minor cuts."

I strolled a distance from the group, then stopped. My hands moved on their own. *She had threatened my safety, and worse, I enjoyed hurting her.* The ease that it took for my swift blade to pierce her frail body. *And that smell . . .* it caused a shiver to run down my spine. I enjoyed every bit of it. *Did that make me a horrible human? More monster?* I no longer cared. *I'd do it again if given the chance.* I smelled the blood that coated my skin. The sensations of the slaughtered monster tickled beneath my skin.

"Nemasa?" Quade stopped behind me. I stayed silent. My hands formed into fists and pressed into my chest. "You reacted faster than I thought you could. Holding back on me?"

The muscles in my face loosened. "No." My shoulders slouched.

He took a step closer. *Why did he keep his distance? Did he fear what I was becoming?* "Lune said that he never noticed you take the book. He was sure you placed it back into the box."

"It was Boss who let me know that I had no scent. I was sure that my robe would hide the book's scent as well. Worked like a charm." I chuckled as I thought, *My brother, ha, Bruin gave me a lucky charm. Wouldn't he be pleased to find that out?*

"Risky." The rocks under Quade's feet crunched.

"I know. Where did you go?"

"I lost you in the swarm. I feared that you fell ..."

"You caught me. I almost hit the ground that time. After that, we got separated. If it wasn't for Lune pushing me all the way through, I'd still be in there."

"I didn't know he was with you." My body tightened as he threw himself around me. "I shouldn't have been worried. You've done well on your own. The swarm can be intimidating. Many creatures from the Keep think they can make it through and end up losing themselves."

"I'm fine."

His grip tightened. "Have you had any candy yet?"

"What?"

His chest vibrated as he chuckled. "That's what I collected from the market. You should try a piece. It might calm you down."

"Who said I needed to be calmed?"

He let out a sharp exhale. "I didn't mean it that way ..."

"Why are you pussy footing around me?" I broke out of his arms and spun around.

"Nemasa, I ..." He turned his face away.

"Leave me be. I'm fine."

He bowed his head and left. I turned back to the darkness of the tunnel. Madness creeped at the edge of the shadow. Her hand stretched out to welcome me to her world. I stepped to the edge of the silver light and sat. The spiral of insanity swirled in her shifty eyes. The skin beneath her eyes wrinkled as she showed off her jagged fangs.

After a few seconds, Quade crouched beside me. "Nemasa? Would you like something to eat?"

Madness's head twisted toward her shoulder, then further, until soon the back of her bald head faced me. Her neck wrinkled as her face came back to view.

"Sure."

Her head snapped back, then started its twist. Her chin rotated sideways past her eyes that remained fixed to mine.

Quade rose. I clutched his sleeve. "Candy. I want to try the candy you got." I tried to look up at him, then her head snapped back to its original position and held my attention.

"I'll go get it."

I released his sleeve and let Madness entertain me more until he returned, only minutes later.

Quade handed me a chunk of sticky green candy. I didn't hear him come back or sit down. His hand rested on my knee and still I hadn't notice. I didn't know how long he sat there and watched me. Did his arm get tired of holding the candy out? I didn't know.

"You seem troubled."

I looked down at the cracked, uneven candy pinched between his fingers glistening in the light. I glanced back at Madness. She had left. "Maybe a little." I took the candy and popped it into my mouth. My lips puckered when the candy touched my tongue.

Quade laughed. My fist hit his shoulder. "That snapped you out of whatever dreamland you entered."

He was right. The candy perked me right up. Sour and sweet.

"We'll get her back, and she will be fine. She already forgives you for your outburst. The human is strong. She won't give in to any of his lighter deeds that he will try first."

"That's comforting." I rolled the candy with my tongue. "Quade, what happens when something is touched by Madness?"

His shoulders drew back. He raised his hand to his chin as he thought, then rested it back on his leg. "Well, not many creatures that are touched by her are around long enough to talk about it. Rumor is she drags them to the Pit. The creature willingly goes with her, and then she devours their soul."

"Does she normally stalk her food?"

"I don't …" His hand rested on my cheek. I tried to pull away, but he wouldn't let me. "You've been seeing her. She's been following us. You should have said something. Have you looked into her eyes? You have, haven't you?" My head bobbed.

He glanced at where she sat, then back to me. "She was here, tempting you." Again my head bobbed.

He scooted to the wall and opened his arms to me. I crawled over to him, my head pressed into his chest. I let myself melt into him. He felt warm, safe, as if nothing could hurt me when he was near. The lids on my eye shut, the smell of him filled my nose. Soon I drifted into a comfortable sleep.

The child hummed the lullaby off in the void somewhere. She seemed to be in a cheerful mood as the merry tone sailed on the still air. She adored her gift, Quade's soul. She hadn't mentioned our brother, or killing my companions. It was nice. Just the lullaby, a happily hummed tune.

"Who's singing if you're not?" Quade asked as his head nuzzled into mine. I shook my head, not ready to tell him. "You've unlocked a few of the doors." His cheek brushed into mine. "You going to take me anywhere nice tonight?"

"I don't think so. You're an expensive date."

"Ah! I only want the pretty things in life. They just happen to be expensive."

We giggled together as my body twisted around to see into him. Those crystal eyes. I got lost in them every time.

"What?" His horns rested against mine. "If you keep looking at me like that, I won't be able to control myself."

"Looking at you how? I'm just looking."

The tip of his nose touched mine. "Then even 'just looking' does it, I suppose." Fingers made it up through my hair and nudged me in close. Our lips touched, electricity surged over my skin.

The air warmed. The void morphed. Quade released me; his nose twitched. "Can't be …" As he turned, the world focused on a red bricked chamber. Hooks hung in neat rows along the edge of the ceiling. Under them a shelf full of trays was covered with rusted tools. In the center of the room an iron chair waited. Leather straps hung from the arm rests, and dangled from the back and leg rests.

Quade shifted behind me. His arms wrapped around my chest tight, my arms curled up at the elbows, my hands rested on his forearms. "Where are we, Quade?"

His breath deepened, moving slow and sharp. "You wanted to know what I did when I worked with your brother. A servant slipped on a pool of blood in the thrown room. The goblet she carried shattered and pricked the king's hand. He kept her alive for as long as her mind would allow." He nudged his head toward the chair.

Strapped in tight, a human woman laid back, stripped naked. A round creature dressed in a white lab coat stood alongside my brother. Bruin's twisted smile grew as he eyed his toy. He raised a gloved hand and pricked her skin with a rusted scalpel. The smell burst into the air like a fresh cut in an orange. My teeth trapped my tongue.

"Doctor," Bruin said in a gentle, soft tone, "what do you think she looks like naked?"

Quade's arms tightened. Each breath became difficult. I glanced up at him, the violet in his eyes streaked bright red. I turned back to the naked woman on the table. The scalpel traced her face. Her mouth opened and screamed — soundless, her voice pinched. Swift movements with the scalpel circled her eyes, blood pooled in her sockets.

"Doctor."

The doctor pulled open her lips. The scalpel in Bruin's hand moved in, out, severing her lip from her gums. Muted screams. Continuing to trace, he split the skin down her arms, fingers, legs, toes in a solid straight line. Once the cut reconnected back at the hairline, my brother passed the tool to the doctor.

Quade's chest stopped. I glanced back at him, the whites of his eyes flooded black. My head snapped back to the woman on the table. My brother's fingers had separated the skin from her forehead. Snaps and rips. My heart pumped. A part of me screamed to look away, but the creature in me couldn't get enough. More. More. My hungry tongue swiped my quivering lips.

The woman's skin peeled from her muscles. Her face twitched. Her naked body vibrated. One final yank and the skin ripped off, leaving bare twitching muscle.

Bruin dragged his claws over her naked abdomen. Her back arched up. The claws lit with a blue light and disappeared into her body. New skin formed where it was severed. Moments later, the woman lay panting on the table as if he hadn't harmed her.

He passed the skin to the doctor. "Make use of this."

"My king is gracious," the doctor bowed.

Bruin then strolled around the table and made eye contact with Quade. He stopped a hair's length from his face. "You enjoyed that, didn't you?" Quade's face remained neutral. "You do great things at my side." My brother dragged his claws down Quade's cheek; blood trailed in their wake. "Come."

My brother, the woman, and the doctor vanished from the room.

Quade's chest rose. His eyes fixated on the empty table. "This is a memory."

My lips graced his cheek. I attempted to turn to him. I reached with my fingers to touch his chin and press his lips to mine. He spun my back into the wall. I gasped as the pressure pushed the air from my lungs. His tongue twisted with mine. Heat filled my face. My robe pooled at my feet as he pulled it off. Swift hands removed my top, lips connected back with mine — my heart skipped a beat. My fingers fumbled to remove his. His teeth clasped around my lip; the pain tingled down my neck. The hairs on my arms rose. His breath rolled down my chest, teeth nibbled at my collar. I could feel his heartbeat against my skin, firm squeeze over my breast. Every bit of him pulled me in. The soft fabric of my pants slid down past my knees. I kicked them to the side. I gripped his back as our tongues intertwined. I hadn't noticed that he had already removed his clothes. Hands gripped my ass, the sharp brick cut my back as he lifted me to his hip. Our eyes locked as he thrusted in, deep moans escaped with our breath.

I buried my head in his neck; my hands dug into his hair. He thrusted harder, faster. The sound of his breath, our skin touching drove my mind wild. Every muscle in my body tensed. Vibrated. I tightened my grip around him, his lips trapped against mine. A pleasured moan breathed out of us. Our lips locked, bodies tightened. Released and slowed. My body limped in his arms.

His lips broke from mine as he glanced over his shoulder. I ignored the whisper and tangled my fingers in his hair. His attention twisted back to me. Once our lips touched, the whisper echoed in the distance, beyond the brick. A growl rumbled from his throat.

My head lifted away from Quade's chest. Lune crouched down beside us. I glanced at Quade. His eyelids squeezed shut.

"I didn't mean to wake you, Nemasa. It's Quade's turn to take watch."

"I will wake him. You can go."

Lune nodded, his eyes shifted between Quade and I before he stood and left.

"Quade?" I whispered.

He took a deep breath in as his crimson and onyx eyes peeled open. I let my fingers caress his cheek. He slid his fingers up the back of my head, inching my head toward his. My thumb stroked his lower lip. A heavy pant from the shadows caused me to glance over. Madness's fangs and eyes shimmered from the light, her dark boney body covered by the shadows.

"What is it?" Quade asked. His fingers turned my head back to him.

I stared at the shadows from the corner of my eye.

"Don't pay attention to her."

She continued her heavy pant. "Yes, continue. Pay no attention to me." I pulled my head away from him. She cackled. "I can give you a place with no interruption." I turned my head to her. "Bring him with you. He can come with us. I'll give you a place for two."

"What?" I breathed.

"Come." She put her hand into the light. "Do what you please with him. No interruptions. No other creatures. Just you and him. Together forever."

"What is she telling you?"

"You told me not to listen."

He breathed a laugh. His hand guided me back to him, my horns back rested on his.

"She's offered me you." I swiped my hand down his cheek.

"You already have me." He dropped his head onto my neck.

"You without anyone else."

"Just us?" His breath rolled down to my chest.

"Yes."

"That's tempting." He let go, and leaned back onto the wall; his hands dropped down to the ground. The onyx in his eyes drained back to white. "Wherever you chose to go, if you want me to, I will follow. What about your human? Would you leave her to the mercy of your brother?"

I bit my lip. As much as I wanted him, I couldn't do that. "No, I wouldn't."

"Then you can wait to give her an answer when you get Hope back. You'd want to get her back to her world, too." He cracked a smile, his amethyst eyes returned in full bloom. "Or you could leave her here for the twins to watch over. I'm sure they'd love that."

"What did you do with Quade? Since when does he care about my human that way?" I shoved his chest.

"It's my watch, then yours. You better get some sleep. You will need all your strength when we get to the castle."

"Oh, yeah, how you going to make me?"

"I could stop dream walking with you. That would give you more rest."

"You wouldn't …" I pressed my lips together tightly.

"Then sleep, Nemasa. It's a few more days to the castle. We ended up backtracking quite a bit when we took that escape route. And when Boss finds out that book is missing, he'll be on our tail."

"But I'm not tired," I argued through a yawn.

"I will wake you if anything exciting happens."

"Promise?"

"Promise."

Chapter Twenty-One

Quade woke me up for my watch. He offered to stay awake with me, but I could tell he was tired. The others laid by the red embers, undisturbed. Nothing stirred in the shadows of the tunnel. I didn't know if I'd be able to stay awake with nothing to do or see.

His arms tighten around my shoulders and chest. He had fallen asleep right after our argument. His droopy eyes and suppressed yawns were all the hints I needed. Plus, I needed him to sleep. I needed them all to sleep.

My fingers gripped the mirror, careful not to activate it. I breathed in deeply. My brother waited on the other side, furious that I had taken my sweet time to come to him. There would be a price to pay. Another deep breath, and the tip on my thumb pressed against the mirror. A cool shiver ran over my body; my eyes fluttered closed and opened to a brightened room.

"You finally came, little sister."

"I said I would. You wanted our meetings to be a secret, so it took longer." My eyes adjusted to the brightness of the room. The

pillars, the marble, all gold. Then my eyes fell on him. Unlike the first time we met, he wore a rich outfit of black outlined with stitch-work of blood red.

"Yes, I did say that." His hair bounced into his eyes as he nodded once. "Now on to business."

"So soon? We haven't seen each other in years." I gave a cocky grin.

"You're in a good mood today." The right side of his mouth turned up and cracked. "I'd love to change that."

"Fine. Though I am supposed to be watching over my friends' safety."

"Robin is taking care of that."

"And what does that cost?"

"You catch on quick, little sister. But right now, we talk about your human. She hasn't been the easiest of humans to keep unharmed. I may have to up your payment." His black-red eyes narrowed.

"Where is she?"

"She is fine … for now." He lifted his left hand, a shadow formed at his fingertips. With a gentle breath he blew. Hope's body formed, suspended in mid-air. Her arms and legs were bound tight by invisible magic.

"Hope," I said louder than I meant. Her lips moved, but no sound came out. I turned to my brother, my face hot. "You said you wouldn't harm her."

"I didn't. It's a neat little trick I found. It's useful. I hate the sound of humans. They give me a headache. Some creatures

enjoy the tormented screams and their useless begging for release."
He shook. "Just thinking about it makes me sick."

"Good to know."

*A firm line formed with his lips. "Now, your payment for being
able to see your human." His feet glided over the marble without
sound. My brother clasped my chin in between his fingers and raised
my gaze to his. His hand glided up my cheek till his palm rested on
my forehead. "That robe didn't come free."*

"I didn't think so." My eyelids grew heavy.

*We entered into another room. Dim candlelight flickered across
my clothes. Red brick formed the walls and ceiling. "Remember this
room?" my brother asked as he stood beside me.*

*I lay where the woman had her skin torn off, my hands and
feet bound to the chair. I wiggled all my limbs with little success.
"Quade's memory?"*

"Yes, a small fee for the robe."

*I tried to read his stone face. The grin he wore filled his
chiselled face up to his eyes, he didn't know what happened after
the memory, or he wouldn't be calm. To know that I had fun with
the price I paid would cause me more harm than good. I chose to
lay silent and still.*

*A shimmer from the corner of my eye made me turn my head
to see his hands. "You watched what I plan to do, although I will
just be working with your face tonight. Little payments for little
looks. Every night something new."*

*His wicked grin grew as the scalpel poked through my skin at
my hair line. I bit my lip as the blood dripped. I held my breath,
eyes closed tight. He stopped. One eye peeked open. His gaze was to*

the door. I turned my eye, tried hard not to move my body in fear of his blade in my skin.

The faceless child stood in the door way, clenching the book.

"Hmm ..." He removed the scalpel. "What are you?" He eyed the book. "Fascinating. How did you get that?"

Her arms tightened around the book, her tiny foot lifted from the gritty floor and touched back down behind her other heel.

He has us trapped in this room, she whispered through my thoughts.

How?

My brother turned around the chair. Each step he took, she took one back, until she pressed against the thick wooden door.

"Now, now, child. No need to move away. What are you?" he asked as he towered over her. The muscles strained at her neck as she tilted her head back. "Speak, child." She remained silent. His hand slammed into the wood above her. "Tell me, or I will make you tell me."

"She doesn't know."

"You knew. Didn't you? Kept this a secret for me." His eye poked out from under his bangs. "What is this child?"

I tugged at my restraints. "I was hoping that you could tell me ..."

"Let me have this." His elbow bent. I couldn't see her past his broad body. I knew he wanted the book.

"What are you offering for payment? That's pricy."

Bruin turned on his heels and tossed the scalpel to the ground. His lips pressed hard and wiggled. The crimson darkened to black.

The warmth of his hand over my face shocked me, but the pain of his fingers as they dug into the wound made me wimpier.

"Your friends will be awake soon. I no longer have time. This will have to do."

Visions of massacre after massacre. Monsters devoured humans, humans devoured humans. Twisted from strangers to people I knew, cared about. All dead around me, just to come back, alive, and get slaughtered again and again. My heart cracked with every scream, every death. When I thought I couldn't take any more, he'd show it to me again and again. My heart shattered over and over.

I stood in a black room with only a candle to light the space. I gasped at each breath while my heart pounded against its cage. My mom, my new mom, the one who still drew breath stood before me. A swift ring of light clasped her neck and vanished. Blood spewed from the light's touch, her face paled, eyes dimmed. My brother appeared from behind her; his fingers brushed her bangs from her eyes. The touch caused her head to drop back, her body and head collapsed to the floor. My heart stopped —

His hand lifted from my face. The golden pillars and marble floor filled the space around us. Hope's wide eyes clung to me; her lips yelled out words I wished I could hear. My knees buckled and slammed into the floor. I gasped for breath as my brother's lip's parted to his eyes and revealed his fangs.

"That worked better than torture."

I swallowed a dry lump. Physical pain, I could handle that. I watched as my friends and family got slaughtered, night after night. Unbearable. My eyes lifted to Hope. For her, I would make it bearable, as long as she was kept safe.

Bruin crouched down and lifted my hand. "Eat this." He placed a red candy in my hand. As his fingers lifted he pinched out a blue thread. "When you wake, this will be with you. Eat it and your friend will be kept unharmed. See you tomorrow, little sister."

The pendant dropped down to my collarbone. I gasped for air, tears stung my eyes, my teeth clasped my lip to keep the cries of my broken heart in. I sat there in silence. Robin watched from somewhere close by. Sati's hair swayed as her head lifted. She dug through the bag beside her and withdrew a small leather pouch that contained food. Her eyes and skin shimmered in the dim light like the moon's light on a lake.

"Sleep well?" I asked with a gentle wave.

She smiled and glided next to me. With graceful movements, she crouched and folded her legs under her. "I did, milady." A stray hair draped over her shoulder as she bowed. "How was watch?"

"Boring."

"There's not much to see or do, is there?" Her fingers untied the string of the bag and opened it. She offered me a piece of the dried meat from inside.

I tightened my hand around the candy. I had forgotten that it was there, too wrapped up in everything I had seen. I took a piece with a faked grin. "Thank you. What do you do?"

"I —" Her lips tightened, then she let out a tiny laugh. "Hope explained to me her life in the human world. She compared it many times to the things we did here. I spent my time wondering what type of human I would be. Hope told me about teachers, police, doctors, and various other types of humans and how they work to assist one another."

"I take it that kind of thing doesn't happen here. I could see you being a teacher."

"A teacher? Why is that, milady?"

"You're patient and knowledgeable. You did well teaching Hope. She can see things I can't, and heal wounds with great skill. You'd make a great teacher." I took a bite of the meat and slipped the candy underneath my tongue. The sweet danced with the salty.

Sati nibbled her piece and thought about life as a human teacher. I sucked on my hidden poison. Little burst of cherries and blackberries tickled my tongue as the ball got smaller. I relaxed my tense shoulders into Quade. His arms cinched tighter.

"He cares for you." She nibbled again with a sweet smile. Then her eyes widened, and her knuckle pressed against her lips to hold in her giggle.

"Talking about me, hmm?" his hands dropped to my waist as his back straightened.

"Only a little," Sati said as she stood. "I will wake the others. We should be off soon."

I swallowed the last little piece of candy and wondered why my brother would give it to me. He had given them to me as a child. There had to be some form of magic, trickery, behind it.

* * *

Three sleeps had passed since the first candy. Each night my brother learned more and more about me and what I feared. Physical pain did little. Psychological torment gave him the results he sought. I watched while family and friends were slaughtered by monsters, by each other, and the worst, by me. Forced my hand to turn on the only ones that cared for me.

I'd let go of the pendant; my eyes would crack open, tears pooled at the edge. The candy lost its sweetness, bitter from the hatred. The gray walls, the black hole we followed — I was sick of it all. I forgot what it was like to feel the heat of the bright sun, the cool breeze, and even the vibrant colors of day. Gray.

The scent of hot stone and the taste of dried meat pushed out the memories of a fresh scent of flowers and the taste of a juicy meal. *Did those things even exist, or was it all just a failed dream that happened to me?* I couldn't remember. Quade's word that those things were real kept my faith strong. Without his support, I would have passed it all off as a dream once had by a younger, more hopeful me.

Sati woke, and offered me a bite to eat after each shift. The thought of another piece of salty meat turned my stomach and stung my tongue with acid.

"You have not eaten in two days, milady. We are approaching the entrance to the Keep. You will need your strength."

I waved her off as my head turned away from her and into Quade's shoulder.

Quade's chest rose and fell while he observed Sati and me. "You know she's right. You should eat."

I pressed my hand down into the stone and pushed myself off of him. "You both know nothing about what I should and shouldn't do." I stepped to the border of the sliver light and shadow, glared into the darkness. Robin and Krista hid somewhere unseen.

"What are you doing?" Quade tried to keep his voice low and calm, but my harsh actions over the past few days had wedged between us. Dream walks had disappeared along with my memories of the Earthly Realm. "We're almost there. I know you want to save her as quickly as possible. If we wear ourselves out, we will be useless against his power. Then we're all screwed."

I turned my gaze to him. My eyebrows bunched together, lips firmly pressed. Hope was fine. He didn't know that; they didn't know that. They knew nothing. The thought of how useless the party had become to me tasted worse than another bite of the disgusting meat they fed me.

"I'm leaving. Don't follow me." I turned again, lifted my foot and crossed over into the shadow. Lune's light created a sphere around us and did not pass over the boundary. Safe Sati thought it was necessary this close to the Keep.

I turned from the sphere I could no longer see and continued down into the darkness. My fingertips glided along the wall to stop me from walking into it. Once out of earshot, I whispered into the black space, "Take me to my brother."

I heard a slither along the ground ahead of me. I kept my pace. "You ssssure?" it hissed.

"Yes."

"You leave the otherssss for fodder?"

The rocks crunched in the darkness behind me. I turned; someone chased after me, the book pulsed through the tattoo. *Quade.* I turned back to the creature who slithered around me.

"I will kill this creature. Then we go. *Ssss.*"

"He comes with us."

"*Ssss.* I kill. Then we go."

"Then I will kill you, and whoever comes after us until one takes Quade and me to my brother. Do you want to die or take me to my brother?"

"Nemasa?" Quade called.

"He's getting closer. He will kill you when he arrives unless I tell him not to."

"Sssssure. I will take you to the king."

"Quade, do not kill the beast that is with me."

His warm hand pressed on to my back. "Why?"

"He's going to take us to my brother. Where's Robin? I expected him, not one of his minions."

"He got held up. *Ssss.*"

"Expected?" Quade's hand squeezed my hip as he pieced together that I had kept things from him.

"Ssssshe didn't tell you? Good. *Ssss.* The king will be pleassssed to hear."

"My brother's pleasures are meaningless to me. I don't care if he's pleased or not. Delay me any longer, and I'll take out my frustrations on you."

"There'sss a sssshort cut to the cassstle that the king has given me. Thisss way." A bright ring formed on the ground. The snake had connected its head and tail to form a ring. One end lifted up from the ground, and as it did, the circumference grew. Wall to wall. Once set in place, the inside of the ring burst, rippled, and formed a watery gateway.

"Let's go." I grabbed Quade's hand, and pulled forward. He stood his ground and jerked me back. "What —"

"I told you I'd follow you wherever you go, and I stand true to that."

"Are you saying you want to stay here?"

"I just want to know, is this really how you want to approach him? He knows you're coming. It could be a trap."

"I know. I just can't stand another night … I have to do it this way." I nuzzled my head into him. "Then you're all mine."

A hungry grin grew and took over his face. He glanced around. "I don't see anyone right now." He gripped the back of my head with his hand and leaned my head close to his.

"I advissse you don't keep the king waiting. *Ssss.*"

I bit my lip, and turned to the gateway. "He's right. We better go."

My hand disappeared into the rippled light. The cool air shivered up to my shoulders. Soon my whole body pressed through, shivers vibrated my skin, my stomach tossed, the grip on Quade's hand held tight.

Chapter Twenty-Two

Golden light glistened off the pillars and marble floor. I released Quade's hand. We stood in the throne room. The pillars expressions gawked, the marble floor lost a bit of its potency. The eery energy of the room caused the hairs on my neck to stand.

"Little sister, you brought me a gift? How Earthly of you," Bruin announced. As he spoke my skin crawled.

"Remember, there aren't gifts, everything has a price."

"Ah, I've taught you well in such a short time. I better watch my step." My brother's body rounded mine, his footfalls unnoticeable. "Have you been liking the treats I've made you." His hand pressed against my forehead, warmed, then slid down to lift my chin. "Ah, yes. Well done, little sister. You followed my instructions and ate every last drop." The corners of his lips turned into his wicked smile. "You're such a good little sister."

I glanced over to Quade; his jaw clenched, shoulders tight. He struggled to restrain the urge to draw his blade.

"You brought something uninvited."

"You lied."

"I lied?"

"You said Robin would meet with me. And you sent a lesser beast. I do pride in the fact Krista didn't wish to collect me." He released my chin and stepped back with narrowed eyes. "Robin was supposed to meet me, and he defied you." I laughed. "Oh, brother, how could you let your warriors treat you with such disrespect?" The veins in his forehead flared. "Did I strike a nerve?"

"You've eaten every candy I ever gave you, and you are still able to defy me."

"Maybe you're not as powerful as you think." A hard sting crossed my face as his hand connected with it. "You hit like a human." I laughed as the slight taste of blood teased my tongue. I turned to Quade as his hand gripped the hilt. "Wait," I ordered. I looked back to my brother, his smile lost to his tempter. His brows bunched and stayed; his wicked eyes glared, fixed to me. The atmosphere thickened with his rage.

"Where's Hope?" I asked. The silence snapped like thin glass.

"You know the payment to see her."

"I want her back."

"Ah, well, there's a payment for that, too, though I doubt you could pay it."

"And what is the price? Keep in mind, if it's too steep, I will kill you and take her back." The child came to mind. *Would he ask for her? Or maybe the knowledge of what she is?*

His right brow twitched. "You were going to kill me either way."

I giggled. "That was the plan, yes. Over time I have changed, modified, and decided what I am going to do with you."

"Oh?" His face relaxed and the smile crept back. "And what would that plan be?"

"A trade."

"What kind of trade?" His head tilted as his arms crossed. His brow and eyes relaxed, amused by the offer.

"I will allow you to keep control over the Sinful Realm. Of course, I will still have final authority. You will have one or two rules to follow, and that seems reasonable. You'd be like a caretaker of the throne. Right now you're doing a damn fine job, so I think that you'd be better to me alive. I'll give you that, for Hope."

Quade remained silent, I could sense his uneasiness. "What do you think, brother?"

"The human is worth more to you than your own realm?"

"I'm not giving you full power. Just letting you continue what you're doing under my authority."

He stood silent. The tension in the air heaved once again. Quade stepped in front of me, his blade pulled from the sheath an inch.

"You insult me, little sister. To think, you would suggest such a foolish request. Understand this, I rule under me. I take orders from no one." He raised his hand. Hope appeared at his side. Her voice pinched and body held in place. "I will teach you who is in charge, and it isn't you, little sister." His body flinched and vanished. His silhouette appeared behind Hope;

his blade pressed to her throat. "Now here is my deal for you. Give me the Nine Tails and I will kill her quickly. Don't and I will make you kill them both."

"The Nine Tails?"

His eyes gleamed with his own pride. "Those candies that you ate will force the Nine Tails from your body. A spell that I conjured myself."

"Why don't you just take the Nine Tails now, if you're so clever?"

The blade cut into Hope's neck. Blood dripped down the blade, that smell … that intoxicating aroma, I took a deep breath in. "I could if I wanted to, my little sweet sister. But this, as you know, is more fun." His crimson irises darkened.

My mouth watered as she thought, *Games, he loves his games.*

"What's it going to be, sister?"

Hope shook her head, careful not to cut herself any more than necessary. Her lips moved as she tried to tell me something important, but I couldn't make out any of it. My eyes were fixed on the blood that dripped down the silver blade.

Quade stepped forward again, wanting to challenge Bruin but held back by my order to wait. He wanted me to set him loose. He'd waited years for this one moment. He went to step —

"Move any closer, and it will be you I kill."

Quade moved back a pace and peeked at me over his shoulder. I wasn't in the right mind-frame to be in control of the situation. I was lost to the temptations of sin, to the lust of blood. He glared back to my brother and took the step.

My brother vanished from behind Hope. A clash of steel woke me from the daze. I twisted to the left and watched my brother's sword meet Quade's between the pillars. Their movements were swift and precise. A hand on my shoulder made my skin jump and spin with a clenched fist. Right before I landed the hit, I was eye-to-eye with Hope.

"Hey," she whispered. "I would have blasted him if he hadn't moved. It took more concentration to keep his magic from affecting me. I couldn't get an attack on him. If I had attacked him when you were not here, I wouldn't have the power to finish him off myself." I couldn't take my eyes from her wound. "Blaze," she gripped both my shoulders and shook me, "focus. You have to help Quade. He can't do this on his own." She shoved me toward the on-going battle.

I turned my head and stepped toward Quade and Bruin. They, too, moved fast. I didn't know how to help. *Where to begin …* I stood like a statue. I was weakened by their skill. My eyes couldn't keep in time with them.

Quade released one hand from his blade, pulled it back to his shoulder. A beam of red light struck my brother in the chest, causing him to take out two pillars before being crushed under the weight of the stone. Quade took the time to gather his breath. I couldn't believe it — he won!

The rocks settled, crumbling into place. My attention drifted back to Hope's sugary sweet scent. The fragments of the pillars burst and chunks of stone sailed through the air. Hope hid behind me as I shielded us from the onslaught.

The deep laugh of my brother howled from within a cloud of dust. "Not bad, little man."

The clash of steel refilled the grand hall. The battle raged on within the cloud of dust. Red light flashed as steel sang. I twitched back and forth, attempting to get in on the action but didn't know where to begin or how to enter. The creature deep inside me clawed at my mind —its cage — as it tried to unleash its furry.

"Help him, Blaze!" Hope hollered. She bolted out in front of me.

The cloud settled, creating a thick layer of gray on the once shiny gold of the room. Each time Bruin parted with Quade, Hope threw in a green orb that exploded on impact. My brother growled in her direction, and countered with an explosive of his own.

Since when have I become this weak? Come on, Blaze! You can do this. I urged myself forward.

Then the moon tattoo on my neck pulsed and everything stilled. My brother's low laugh filled the room, and the sound of liquid splatter over the marble. Hope dropped to her knees, eyes caught in a wide stare.

My eyes struggled to see the truth. Quade released a pain-filled breath. The tattoo burned. Bruin and Quade froze in time. The long, thin blade of my brother's sword plunged through Quade's chest up to the hilt. Blood spilled from Quade's mouth. He turned his head to me right before life left his eyes and his body went limped. Bruin withdrew his needle blade from Quade's body and let it drop to the floor with a lifeless thud.

"Quade!"

The child sobbed as the book evaporated from her hands. Her girlish cry deepened. Rumbled. Growled. In an instant, the golden glow of the room shifted to blood red. My body pulsed, stung, and tightened. I jolted for my brother, my arms swung like a wild animal. The skin on my arms split, red hairs emerged from the cracks. He dodged each attack with ease. My shoulders hunched, till my throbbing hands had to rest on the floor for balance. My fingers cramped and curled and shifted to paws that sent sharp pain up my arms. The room shrunk. I swung my massive paw, a pillar toppled. My brother cursed as he dodged the slow attack. Again and again and again. The marble cracked under the weight of my paw as I pursued him.

Hope appeared in front of me I swiped past her. Her hair lifted around her cheek's impact of my paw, hitting the marble beside her. "Blaze!" she called out. "Blaze! You have to stop. You'll lose yourself. Blaze!" She slapped her hands together, a flash of white light caught my attention. I smashed my paws into the ground at her feet and lowered my snout. A growl rumbled out as she sunk her fingers into the fur on my forearm. "Kill him without letting him take your soul." Her calm voice soothed. "Don't let him take the human soul from you. You're Nemasa, yes, without a doubt that is you. You're also Blaze, the human, from the Earthly Realm. Don't let this creature take that from you." A white light emanated from Hope's body and surged through me, calming my rage.

I caught Bruin's movement in the shadow of the pillar to our left, out of the corner of my eye. In an instant, I shifted back. My hands gripped the hilts of my blades and thwarted his attack by using the pillar itself as a shield. I drew my blades and danced with him, our skills synced. Cuts filled my arms. I'd block left and counter right. The spell Hope cast over me tamed my rage and let me see his attacks with a clear mind. He thrusted his blade forward. With a spin, I dodged and attacked using the momentum of the spin.

Then his elbows lifted, and I saw my opportunity. I let my blade slide up under Bruin's ribs and out the back of his shoulder, his attack stopped by the angle of my sword embedded in him. My other plunged through his stomach, causing him to cough blood.

He pushed his chest down to the hilts. "Well done ... little sister. I will ... still ... get what I want. I win." Blood streamed out from his lips and down his chin.

"Blaze!" Hope called as she ran toward us.

The crimson liquid dripped from wounds and coated my hands. The life in his eyes faded. The corner of his lip curled and a wicked grin grew. He gasped for air, but his lungs refused to fill. Bruin's body pulsed; a red energy emanated around his body engulfed us. A shockwave of pain ripped through my body. The energy brightened, and my eyes slammed shut, unable to withstand the light. The sensation of gravity gave out. The floor collapsed and my blades vanished from my hands. I tried to open my eyes. A force held them closed tight. I tried to breath, but all the oxygen in the world had disappeared. I choked, gasped. Pins and needles prickled my arms, a beep echoed in my head.

Chapter Twenty-Three

My body snapped up from where I laid. I gasped, and choked. White light blinded my eyes. I ripped at the pain in my arm —

"Blaze, stop! Blaze." Hands pressed mine down. I fought them off as my eyes adjusted to the florescent lights. I blinked countless times. I looked at the hands that held me. A thumb rubbed in light movements. "Blaze, it's okay." My eyes followed up the thin arms, up to my mom's red swollen eyes.

I glanced around the room. Dull blues, rows of neat beds. Tubes and wires hung up on the walls. I peeked past my mom. Light blue sky filled the window, a tree swayed as birds danced on the branches. I choked again on the tube shoved down my throat.

"The nurse is coming. I pressed this little button and they will come." She wiggled a white cylinder, at the tip a red button.

I stared at her through wide eyes. Any moment, he would morph the dream; then my eyes found the tree. Bright, beautiful green leaves. *Surely they were never that bright before … he could never capture that.*

"It's okay, dear. You're safe now." Tears flooded from her eyes as the words bubbled out.

I reached up and wiped the stream from her face. It had to be real.

The door to the room swung open, and a tall blond woman rushed into the room. "You buzzed? Blaze! Lay down, honey. I'll alert the doctor."

Mom's hand rested on my shoulder and helped me back down. "Once they take the tube out, I will answer whatever questions you have. I promise."

*Promise...*the vision of the life draining out of Quade's eyes filled my head. I fought back the tears as they pooled at my lids.

"Blaze? Does something hurt?"

Yes, Mom ... everything hurts, I wanted to say.

"It will be okay. I'm here beside you. We will get through this."

The doctor rushed in, the snap of his glove grabbed my attention. "Okay. We will get this over with quick."

With the tubes all removed, my mouth was left sore and dry. My tongue batted around in my mouth, in need of a toothbrush. Pasty and gross. I took a sip of Mom's water, not sure if the doctor would approve.

"Blaze, do you remember what happened?" Mom asked as she held my hand, her thumb rotating in circles. I shook my head. I was sure the answer I had for her was incorrect. "A deer ran out in front of your car while you were on the highway. Your car was destroyed, but I was able to get all your belongings. And best of all, you have no injuries other than a few cuts. The paramedics were shocked. We were all shocked. Anyway ..." Tears tried to spill over. "You have been in a coma for a year. And ... and ..." She bit her tongue. Her free hand pushed the red button.

The nurse came in through the door moments later, her teeth shining in a bright grin.

"Can she go?" My mom sobbed.

The nurse lost her smile; her eyes locked onto mine. "I'll get a chair. Be right back."

"Mom?" My hoarse voice shocked me.

She patted my hand and avoided eye contact. "We should call your father. Oh! And your sister. They will be excited to see you're up. The whole family has been in and out of here. They brought flowers, teddy bears, cards. Amy even snuck in rum for your birthday. A few classmates came in. I brought all your gifts home for you. A boy named Noah was here the most." She raised a brow. "Boyfriend?"

Classmates? You're kidding, I thought.

"No, Mom, I have ..."

An image of Quade sliding off Bruin's blade caused tears to spill down my cheeks. "No, Mom, no boyfriend."

She patted my head. "Oh, sweetheart."

The nurse hurried in with the chair. She and Mom helped me in, both shocked at the muscle strength I had kept over the year. She detached my intravenous bag from a silver pole on the bed and attached it to the wheel chair. Mom put her hands on the chairs handles, eyes attempting to burst at any moment with excitement and cry from a secret sorrow. Her lips bounced between a neutral line and a frown. She wheeled me into the next room. Margaret, Hope's mom, sat hand in hand with Hope. I jolted forward. Mom's hand held me down in the chair.

How'd this happen? What did he do? He told me he won. Is this what he meant? I wondered. I watched and waited. Hope remained still under the thin pale blue sheet that covered her, trapped in his spell.

Acknowledgements

In a world filled with helpful and honest people, I think I've found the best.

Thank you, Kimberly, for being my Dr. Frankenstein. You took my imagination apart and put it together in a way that made it come alive.

To my dearest husband, Mark. If you had not come into my life and found my dusty stories, writing would have remained a hidden dream. Thank you for pushing me towards the pen. I wouldn't have started writing again if it weren't for you.

My family never moved from my side. Thank you to Mom, Dad, and my sister Tayler for encouraging me to reach for the stars, for never forcing me to give up my dreams, and for allowing me to be strange, weird, and geeky. Also to my grandma who read every script no matter how rough. Your endless amount of praise and devotion pushed me through the hardest of times. Grandpa, don't think I forgot about you. If there was something wrong with my computer I always knew I had you to rely on. I couldn't have made it this far without all of you.

A huge thanks to my editor Ann Westlake. There's not enough room to add all the things you have helped me with. I'm relieved to tears that you edited my story. You've picked the script clean, offered your great advice, and answered every question without an hint of frustration in your voice. I can't thank you enough for all the work you have done. I'm lucky to have found you. I'm looking forward to years of working together.

Christine White, your artwork is astounding. Thank you for creating this masterpiece cover for me, and all the great laughs that went along with it. You're a great friend and an amazing artist. I can't wait to see what you will do for Book Two, *Mortal Soul Ascension*.

About the Author

Wicked Soul Ascension is C.B. Dixon's first book published. She grew up with her husband in the small town of Leduc, Alberta Canada. C.B. Dixon is currently working on Book Two of The Soul Ascension Trilogy, *Mortal Soul Ascension*. C.B. plunges into nightmares to bring out heart pumping adventures.

Contact her at:
www.cbdixon.com
cbdixonsbooks@gmail.com
www.facebook.com/authorcbdixon

Made in the USA
Charleston, SC
08 December 2016